Within those stormy, violet eyes was a wilderness that Lilly Tearwater nearly managed to hide.

Lilly started to move, but could not get past Sam on the narrow path. He knew there was no possibility of her pushing past him. Proper etiquette demanded that she keep her distance.

"Sorry." He stepped aside, disconcerted by the conflicting urges that pulsed through him. Battling his need to escape her proximity was the irrational desire to kiss her, to pull her to him and ravage her lips with his mouth, his teeth, his tongue. When Sam realized that his hands were shaking, he turned abruptly away and left her.

What was happening to him? How could he feel such a fierce burst of desire for Lilly, yet be unable to touch her?

Perhaps it was not only the inn that was haunted, but all its fields and acres, too.

* * *

Not Quite a Lady
Harlequin Historical #702—April 2004

Praise for Margo Maguire's latest titles

His Lady Fair
"You'll love this Cinderella story."
—*Rendezvous*

Dryden's Bride
"Exquisitely detailed…an entrancing tale that will
enchant and envelop you as love conquers all."
—*Rendezvous*

Celtic Bride
"Set against the backdrop of a turbulent era,
Margo Maguire's heart-rending and colorful tale of
star-crossed lovers is sure to win readers' hearts.
—*Romantic Times*

MARGO MAGUIRE

Not Quite a Lady

TORONTO • NEW YORK • LONDON
AMSTERDAM • PARIS • SYDNEY • HAMBURG
STOCKHOLM • ATHENS • TOKYO • MILAN • MADRID
PRAGUE • WARSAW • BUDAPEST • AUCKLAND

ISBN 0-373-29302-X

NOT QUITE A LADY

Printed in U.S.A.

Please address questions and book requests to:
Harlequin Reader Service
U.S.: 3010 Walden Ave., P.O. Box 1325, Buffalo, NY 14269
Canadian: P.O. Box 609, Fort Erie, Ont. L2A 5X3

This book is dedicated to my son, Joseph Michael,
a fine young man on his birthday.
Congratulations on your first year away.

Prologue

The home of Jack and Dorothea Temple, London, Spring 1886

"**N**ot bloody likely," Sam Temple grumbled in response to his sister-in-law's remark. He returned to his place at the table, sat down and stretched his long legs out in front of him. "There is not one shred of empirical, scientific evidence that ghosts exist."

He did not like to disagree with his brother's lovely English wife, but the notion of hauntings in country castles or any other building was nonsense. Ridiculous. Certainly not a worthy theory for an intelligent woman like Dorothea to entertain, no matter *who* had sent the letter describing strange doings at Ravenwell Cottage.

"Perhaps not everything can be explained by science," Sam's brother, Jack, said, lighting a cheroot. Since they dined *en famille,* the gentlemen did not leave the table for their brandy. Jack poured a draught for himself and one for Sam, who took a long swallow and gave half his attention to his elder brother. "There may be forces in the world that men will never understand. You have to have faith."

"Supernatural forces?" Sam scoffed. He'd given up on anything but the here-and-now when he and several colleagues had been imprisoned in Sudan, when he'd been tortured and whipped like an animal by the fanatic followers of a religious leader, when he'd been forced to witness the execution of his friend and mentor, Robert Kelton.

He had gone with Kelton and twelve other naturalists on that fated trip to Sudan, each man pursuing studies in his own specialty. For nearly six months, they'd been left alone to collect their data. By the time they'd understood their peril from the Mahdi's uprising, it was impossible to get out. The Mahdi's vicious band of followers reached Khartoum, and Sam's group was doomed.

The only thing that had kept Sam from losing his sanity during his captivity was his ability to focus on his work.

When he'd been desperate to escape his tormentors, he had concentrated so completely on the bees he'd been studying that his mind had separated from the sensations of his body.

Sam swallowed the bitter taste that arose when he thought of the horrors the fanatics had inflicted, and avoided looking at his own torn and ravaged hands when he lifted his glass. At least his fingernails had grown back, such as they were. And he'd regained most of the weight he'd lost when his captors had nearly starved him.

After the British troops had stormed the prison and he'd been released from his cell, Sam had been carried to a hovel outside Khartoum. He'd drifted in and out of consciousness for a long time—he still didn't know if it had been days or weeks. He hadn't known his rescuers, or why they'd taken him in and cared for him.

At some point, he'd been taken out of Sudan in a caravan, lying on a pallet, ailing and feverish. Somehow he'd survived the journey to Cairo, along with several other victims of the Mahdi's bloody uprising.

Sam had been shocked to learn how many months had passed since he and the rest of his party had been ambushed by the Mahdi fanatics. Yet he'd needed three more months to heal and recover his strength before going on to London, where his brother lived with his family…

"Why not?" Jack retorted, jerking Sam's attention from his hideous memories. "Why do you fellows who spend your days in laboratories and classrooms think that everything must be predictable and definable, that science has all the answers?"

"My opinion on the subject has nothing to do with science," Sam said. "It's pure common sense."

"Because the—"

"Because there's a crackpot on every corner who would swindle you for a buck—or should I say, a shilling," he amended, giving Dorothea a nod. "Why should it be different here in England than in any other country?"

Jack just smiled, which infuriated Sam. That was no way to win an argument. One didn't just sit back and smile and take on a superior demeanor to make a point.

"Empirical data is what's needed," he said. "Even the ancient Greeks sought firm evidence to explain the world. Look at the Socratic method. Or at Plato, who states that the visible realm contains ordinary physical objects, and our *perception* of them provides the basis for belief."

"Point taken," Jack said, putting out his cheroot. "But didn't Socrates encourage his students to question the truth of popular opinion? And Plato clearly addressed the difference between *dóxa* and *epistêmê*—opinion and true knowledge."

"But their entire purpose—"

"Mama!"

Sam's argument was interrupted by the arrival of his young nephew, in the arms of his nurse. "Ah, here he is," Dorothea said, appearing glad of the interruption.

The child, little more than a year old, went into his mother's arms with glee, and Jack leaned forward to press his lips upon Joshua's brow. Sam sat back in his chair, unable to make himself reach out and chuck his little nephew under the chin. The thought of touching another made his skin crawl.

Being touched was even worse.

"Have you come to say good-night to Papa and Uncle Samuel?" Dorothea cooed.

"I have the greatest respect for the Greeks," Jack said. "Not to mention Mr. Darwin and his methods. *Your* methods." He turned to face Sam. "But I also believe that there are forces in the world that are not quantifiable."

"Such as?"

Sam noted the subtle glance exchanged by Jack and his wife. It was as though they knew something the rest of the world did not.

"Such as objects…and events…that defy explanation." Jack leaned forward. "Why do you insist that Ravenwell Cottage cannot possibly be haunted? Dorothea's letter is from a very reputable friend—a professor of antiquities at Oxford. Surely Professor Bloomsby is not a crackpot.''

Had anyone else spoken these words, Sam would have laughed in his face. But this was Jack, his older brother—a man who had made some of the most significant archaeological discoveries of the century. Though Jack was an unconventional fellow, there was no doubt that his methods were sound. Sam could not just discount his opinion.

''There is no object or event that cannot be explained,'' Sam maintained. ''If it is examined competently, then logic and the scientific method will prevail.''

Jack picked up the letter from Ravenwell and leveled his gaze at Sam. ''Until you learn otherwise.''

Sam made a rude sound.

''Disprove what Bloomsby says in the letter,'' Jack said, sitting back in his chair.

''Ha!'' Sam barked in reply. ''It's up to Professor Bloomsby to prove his theory.''

''Normally, it would be,'' Jack said. ''But in this case, Sam, I challenge you to demonstrate a *reverse hypothesis,* if you will.''

''Ridiculous.''

''Not at all,'' Jack countered. ''Simply prove that Bloomsby did not see a ghost at Ravenwell Cottage.''

Sam did not appreciate being pushed into a corner. ''I don't have time,'' he said. ''I've got my work, my field studies in York. I can't just change plans in midstride.''

"Why not? You can study honeybees anywhere, can't you?"

"I have reservations at—"

"Cancel them," Jack interrupted. "Disprove Bloomsby's contention."

Sam tossed back his last swallow of brandy. It would be so easy to stay here in Jack's house, swilling liquor and avoiding his professional responsibilities. Why did he bother with his experiments? What would his work ever signify to mankind? Robert Kelton and the others lay in unmarked graves somewhere in Sudan. And Sam had been tortured to the point of utter revulsion at the mere prospect of touching another human being.

To what purpose?

He supposed he had no choice but to pursue a faculty post at the Royal College of Surgeons here in London. Though he no longer had any professional ambitions, his reputation as a well-trained naturalist had fostered connections at the college.

Sam could not rely on Jack's charity forever. Working in a classroom would be dull and monotonous, but he was certain the safety and security of the position would make it worth taking. The recent horrors he'd suffered in Sudan had shown him he was not the adventurer that Jack was. Sam was no daring vanguard of science, capable of packing up and traveling to remote corners of the world to study nature. He was a man destined to a staid and stolid existence within the confines of civilization.

And without the comfort of anyone's touch. Not even the infant in Dorothea's arms. Sam steeled himself to tolerate the occasional handshake, but no more.

He'd already begun his letter to Mr. H. Phipson of the Bombay Natural History Society, declining an invitation and generous stipend to join a scientific expedition in the outer regions of Maharashtra to study wild chinkara and other gazelles. Sam could not face another quest—possibly an ill-fated adventure—on faraway, foreign soil. He'd had enough adventure to last him a lifetime.

"A hundred pounds," Jack said.

"I beg your pardon?"

"A wager." Jack leaned forward and rested his elbows on the table. "One hundred pounds says you cannot disprove Bloomsby's experience at Ravenwell Cottage, no matter how scientific your method."

Chapter One

*Ravenwell Cottage, Cumbria, England,
Midsummer 1886*

Twilight. The time of day when Lilly Tearwater's
illusions worked to greatest effect. While her guests
held their collective breaths and watched speech-
lessly, a filmy human form floated through the air
from the garden gate to the upper story of the inn.
It gave a plaintive cry as it disappeared into one of
the attic windows.

Lilly watched from the garden as the small group
of visitors began to chatter among themselves, in
awe of the spectacle they'd just seen. And she waited
to see what unexpected consequence would come of
her actions.

Something always occurred.

A moment later, a large potted plant fell from the
garden wall and shattered on the cobble walk. Lilly
took a deep breath and felt herself lucky that no
greater disaster had occurred as a result of her hand-

iwork. From experience, she knew that anything could happen, and it was no small worry.

Lilly had never known what to make of her strange abilities, and neither had Maude Barnaby, the childless widow who'd years ago brought her to Ravenwell from Saint Anne's Orphanage in Blackpool. Aunt Maude, as Lilly had come to call her, had forbidden her to use her talent of making things happen with just a determined thought. Maude was certain it could only be the work of the devil, and she would have none of it at Ravenwell.

Yet it did not feel evil to Lilly. It was just…part of her, she supposed, a somewhat embarrassing part, like her distressingly wild, black hair. Or her strange eyes, the color of violets. Lilly guessed she had inherited the talent—like her hair and eyes—from her parents whom she'd never known. Whether they'd been gypsies or itinerant Irish, Lilly would never know.

But Maude had made it quite clear that if anyone ever discovered the power she wielded, Lilly would be ostracized. She'd be shunned and vilified as a sorceress.

"Oh, my heavens!" cried a shrill voice.

Lilly whirled around to see Ada Simpson entering through the gate. The woman carried a small package clutched to her bony chest, and her eyes were locked on the attic window.

"Er…have you never seen Sir Emmett before, Miss Simpson?" Lilly asked, quickly recovering herself. She knew perfectly well that very few of the townspeople had ever seen Sir Emmett and Lady Alice—the two phantoms she'd fabricated from her imagination. Instinct, along with Aunt Maude's prohibition, had caused Lilly to keep the ghostly displays limited. She only used the "apparitions" to ensure that the inn managed to stay in business.

Lilly knew there was a fine balance between overexposure and the unpredictable consequences of using her strange talent. Yet the ghostly visions of the past two years were the only reason there was money to pay off the debts Maude had accrued to keep them from starving. Ravenwell Cottage was too far from the lake to be really popular, though they'd had their regular guests to keep them in business over the years. But only just.

Now Lilly had succeeded almost too well. There was rarely a vacant room at Ravenwell.

Miss Simpson kept her eyes trained on the upper window where the specter had last been seen. Her face was pale, her lips trembled slightly, and Lilly wondered what she was doing at Ravenwell Cottage at this hour. Night fell quickly in the country, and it would be fully dark by the time the woman took the path back to town. Lilly hoped she hadn't come all the way to Ravenwell on foot.

"I—I…"

Lilly watched as the spinster gathered her wits and turned. The woman straightened her spine, pursed her lips and looked down her avian nose at Lilly, making her feel like the needy little orphan who had come to Ravenwell Cottage twelve years before. Miss Simpson cleared her throat. "This afternoon, one of your guests—Mr. Henry Dawson—came down to the shop for my brother's elixir, but we had none."

"Ah…" That explained the package Miss Simpson held so closely. And why the chemist's sister wore her best summer dress on a cool Monday evening. She must have decided to deliver the elixir herself to Mr. Dawson, a decidedly eligible bachelor near Ada's age. There was no other reason why Ada Simpson would darken Ravenwell's door. She and Maude had been rivals since girlhood, the last straw being the day Maude had married Edward Barnaby. Even now, Ada maintained that Maude had stolen him from her.

And Miss Simpson had continued her disdain of Ravenwell Cottage *and* Lilly to this day, three years after Maude's death.

"I believe you'll find Mr. Dawson…umm…" Lilly eyed the group of guests who were still marveling over the apparition, but frowned when she did not see the man in question. "He must be in the sitting room," she said, keeping her tone civil, if not friendly. She had a great deal more to worry about than a budding romance between Miss Simpson and Mr. Dawson. Lilly was behind schedule.

Her neighbor, Tom Fletcher, was doing her the favor of collecting Ravenwell's newest guest from the railroad station in Asbury and driving him up to the inn. And Lilly's longtime friend whom she regarded as a sister, Charlotte Gray, had only now been free to prepare the man's bedroom.

Miss Simpson hurried off to find her prey as Lilly headed for the shed where the garden tools were kept. It would have been much easier to clean up the mess with a blink of her eye, and to make the guest room ready with a mere thought. But the consequences might be severe. Lilly did not want to risk using her magic again.

She swept up the broken pottery, then returned to

the inn, entering through the back. The guests were still milling about the garden, and Lilly did not wish to become caught in any discussion of the ghost. At least, not now. Perhaps she would join them later, once her chores were completed and the new gentleman was settled.

Lilly walked through the kitchen, which was in good order, thanks to Ravenwell's efficient chef and the kitchen maids. She took a lamp and climbed the back staircase in search of Charlotte, who'd come to Ravenwell with her from the orphanage.

Charlotte and Lilly were like sisters in every way but blood. To Lilly's way of thinking, Charlotte was as beautiful as an angel, with hair so blond it was nearly white, her skin as pure as fresh cream. Charlotte's deep green eyes were probably her most striking feature, though all her physical traits in combination were utterly amazing.

Her only shortcoming was her deafness. As far as Lilly knew, Charlotte could hear nothing at all. Not the chirping of the birds, nor the roar of the train when it pulled into the station. At the orphanage, Lilly had taken it upon herself to take care of little Charlotte, who was three years younger. The two had become inseparable, and had even developed a language of their own, using gestures and hand signals.

Lilly's ties to Charlotte had been so strong that she'd refused to leave Saint Anne's Orphanage with Maude Barnaby unless her friend was allowed to come, too.

Reluctantly, Maude had agreed, and to Lilly's knowledge, she had never regretted it. Charlotte had been a sweet-tempered child and a good worker. As long as she was given careful directions, she could accomplish any task.

Many were the times when Lilly had wanted to turn her strange talent to Charlotte's deafness, and mend whatever was wrong with her ears. But Maude had strictly forbidden it. Besides interfering with God's creation, there were always consequences to Lilly's interventions. And to alter Charlotte so drastically…well, Maude would have none of it, and her admonishments still kept Lilly from acting.

A loud crash startled her from her thoughts, and she hurried toward the guest room at the far end of the hall. She discovered Charlotte standing amid shards of broken crockery. The carpet and wood floor were soaked with water.

Charlotte shook her head and made a shrugging motion, indicating that she didn't know how the pitcher had fallen.

Lilly did not have time for this latest disaster, but she could never be harsh with her friend. Whatever had happened had been inadvertent.

"Is the bath done?" Lilly asked. She spoke aloud and gestured toward the room at the end of the hall.

Charlotte shook her head.

Lilly gave Charlotte a signal to go. She didn't want her to watch as she restored the guest room to order in half a second's time. "Finish up in there," she said, "and I'll take care of this mess."

A sudden, sharp wind whipped Sam Temple's hat from his head, and a deafening crack of thunder split the air. He could see no sign of a storm in the vicinity, or even in the distance.

Tom Fletcher stopped the buggy and jumped

down to retrieve the hat, even as the wind continued
its fierce attack. "Sorry," the man shouted over the
gale, eyeing the sky. "I don't know where that could
have come from, although there've been a few
strange happenings ever since the ghosts started visiting at Ravenwell."

Sam managed to refrain from making a derisive
sound, and waited for Tom to climb back into the
buggy and continue on their way. He wished he'd
ridden his own horse to Cumbria. In the months
since his release from the Mahdiyah prison, he was
not a man to sit idly, waiting for departure times.

He had always thought himself a patient man, a
tolerant man. But those months in filthy confinement
had changed him. The hours of pain, of slipping outside his body in order to survive the tortures inflicted
upon him and his colleagues… Sam was no longer
the same young scientist who'd set off to study Af-
rican honeybees near the banks of the Nile River.

Sam needed that job in London. He needed the
calm and staid position that would provide him a
livelihood without putting him at risk. He would find
a quiet little flat near the university and spend his
days in the controlled conditions of a laboratory, and
never venture away from civilization again.

But in order to be assured of the post at the Royal
College, he had to prove his newly postulated theory
about a peculiar bee behavior. Sam's academic cre-
dentials were good, and he'd studied with the best—
Professor Robert Kelton. But the data he'd gathered
in Sudan might not be enough. One final summer in
the country should do it, then he could publish his
studies and present the paper to the board of the
Royal College at year's end.

The hundred pounds he would win from Jack would tide him over until then.

"Not much farther to go," Tom said, appearing unnerved by the strange wind that was still blowing dust and debris into their faces and rattling the trees around them. He was about Sam's age, and just as tall, but more heavily built, with burnished red hair and freckles. "The cottage is just down this lane, past the bend."

Sam's jacket flapped around him, and his hair whipped his neck and face. The dust made him sneeze suddenly, sending a sharp jab of pain through his newly healed ribs.

A moment later, they rounded a curve and Ravenwell Cottage came into view.

"Cottage" was a misnomer. The place looked like a country manor house, with a large front entrance and broad, sweeping wings on each side. As Sam took in the sight, a shard of lightning pierced the night, crashing down from the heavens straight through the roof of the inn.

Fletcher pulled back on the horse's reins and rose to his feet, just as everything became quiet again. The wind stopped as suddenly as it had arisen.

"I'll be damned," he muttered.

Sam felt the same. He was a man who studied nature and all its manifestations, yet he had never seen or heard of such odd weather. Perhaps it was a regional aberration. "This sort of thing happen often?"

Fletcher remained standing for a moment, shaking his head slightly, frowning. "Midsummer is our best season. We'll have the occasional rain, but I've…" He stabbed his fingers through his hair. "I've never seen anything like this. I hope Charlotte—I hope everyone is all right." He sat down again and drove the buggy quickly across the fine gravel of the drive.

"It doesn't appear to have done much damage," Sam said, his gaze taking in all his surroundings. Other than a few branches scattered on the grounds, there did not seem to be anything amiss.

The man did not reply, but continued to the front entrance, where he jumped down and hurried into the inn, leaving Sam to deal with his own luggage.

Sam didn't mind. He had his camera and plates, his microscopes and bottles. He wanted them handled carefully—certainly not in haste. He went around to the back of the buggy and shuffled his things in order to reach the crate with the most delicate instruments. Lifting it gently from the buggy, he turned and carried it through the front door.

The large reception area reminded Sam of a medieval castle's great hall. Here, though, there were wall sconces with gaslights, comfortable sofas and fresh cut flowers in vases. A crowd of people stood together in the center on a large, patterned rug. They were all speaking at once, carrying on in a distinctly atypical manner for the Brits Sam had come to know.

They were puzzled and frightened, yet they seemed…invigorated.

Sam looked for Fletcher, but didn't spot him. Then he glanced around to see if there was anyone on hand to check him in and show him to his room. A large desk, illuminated by two gaslights, stood along the far wall. Sam made his way toward it and set his crate on the floor while the crowd continued to clamor.

No doubt the sudden wind had everyone speculating about the weather, and what would happen next.

Sam was curious, too, but he wanted to get his belongings out of that buggy and into his room before the storm broke. No telling what kind of weather a wind like that would bring. He was just about to ring the small bell on the desk when someone called his name.

"Mr. Temple?" A feminine voice, low and sweet, spoke to him from behind. At the same time, Sam felt her touch, felt her hands sliding over his shoulders as clearly as the wind that had blown off his hat only a few minutes before.

His knees went weak, and he felt his breath whoosh out of him as if he'd been punched. Cold sweat broke out on his forehead and the palms of his hands.

No one touched him. Not after all that had happened in Sudan.

"Mr. Temple?" she repeated. "I'm Miss Tearwater."

Feeling dazed and disoriented, Sam turned slowly and came face-to-face with an exotic gypsy with lustrous black hair. A pair of shell combs were ineffective in holding back the curls that framed her heart-shaped face. Her lips were as red as *Dianthus barbatus,* her skin as pale as *Lilium,* though there was a blush of rose upon her cheeks. Her unusual, deep violet eyes were framed by thick black lashes, her brows drawn into a frown.

"Is…anything wrong?" she asked with that husky voice.

Sam cleared his throat and composed himself. And he realized that there had been no hands caressing his back. "No," he said, rubbing his forehead. "I just… Is there someone who might show me to my room?"

She was not at all what he'd expected the innkeeper to be.

Her eyes flickered away for a second, toward the desk behind him. "Yes, of course. Follow me. Tom will bring your things in a bit."

When her eyes met his, Sam had that odd sensation again, of being touched…caressed. It was suddenly shattered when the lights went out.

"Oh dear!" she said amid the shouts of all those gathered in the main room of the inn. "I must— Will you excuse me?"

Sam felt her move past him in the dark as pandemonium broke out. Someone struck a match and a hush came over the crowd as light appeared once again. And Sam wondered if this was all there was to the so-called haunting of Ravenwell Cottage.

He crossed his arms over his chest and looked around in the near dark while Miss Tearwater went about the room lighting all the lamps and sconces again. Sam had to admit that it was certainly a neat trick. He had no doubt that some mechanism had been rigged to cause all the lamps to be extinguished at once.

And when a man was in the presence of such stunning beauty, Sam guessed he'd be inclined to believe anything she wanted to tell him.

Luckily, he was wise to her ploy and wouldn't be falling for it anytime soon. Her good looks were not going to divert him from his purpose.

Sam picked up his crate just as a portly man in a light linen suit stepped toward the landlady, followed by four other gentlemen. "Miss Tearwater," he said, "a few of us would like to, er, visit the attic. If you don't mind. W-where Sir Emmett, uh, disappeared."

"Feel free to do so, Mr. Payton," Miss Tearwater replied. "But mind the stairs. They're steep. And narrow." She lit the last gaslight and turned to Sam. "This way, then."

Her plain blue gown with its short sleeves and lack of ornamentation set off her feminine form very well. Sam did not doubt that she had deliberately dressed for effect, considering herself a fair distraction from the game.

It had been a long time since Sam's full attention had been drawn by a member of the fair sex. But there was no mistake that Miss Tearwater had his regard now, even though she was a charlatan of the worst sort.

Following her down a narrow hall, Sam welcomed the surge of purely masculine interest—something he thought he'd never feel again. He allowed himself to admire the sway of her hips, the gentle shimmer of her dark hair in the dim light, and knew that this was the extent of the pleasure he would ever enjoy with any woman.

It left him feeling deprived and powerless, but he averted his eyes and continued on course, climbing a staircase to the second floor. Miss Tearwater took him to a room at the far end of the hall, where she opened the door and stepped inside.

"The bath is at the end of the corridor. Towels are here."

A quick glance told Sam that the room was satisfactory. There was plenty of space, as well as a desk in which to keep his journals and ledgers. It would do very well.

Without being too obvious, he kept plenty of distance between them when he stepped into the room. "Quite an uproar here tonight."

She seemed startled by his statement, then had the good grace to appear abashed. "Well," she said, "we don't usually have such strange weather—"

"I meant the lights. Nice trick."

Her hand fluttered at her breast, then fell to her side once again. "Sometimes our ghosts play pranks on us, Mr. Temple," she said, her unusual eyes locking on his. "You must learn to ignore them."

Lilly took a deep breath and looked away. She had expected Mr. Temple to be a stodgy old professor with a bushy beard, a man who would dodder about the inn in a rumpled suit with a book in his hand and a pencil perched upon his ear. Instead, she'd found herself faced with a tall young American, perhaps thirty years old, whose eyes were the color of the summer sky. His hair was dark brown and wavy, with strands of pure white threading through it at his right temple. His features were as rugged as they were handsome, and Lilly refrained from pressing a hand to her heart in awe of the raw energy that pulsed beneath his reserved surface.

He set his crate on the floor and pulled his starched white collar away from his neck. Lilly did not breathe when he stepped over to the window and bent to open it.

"Warm in here," he said.

"I…yes." She realized she was gaping, and quickly busied herself with lighting the lamp at the bedside. "Well," she said brusquely. "If that will be all…?"

She still didn't understand what had happened to all the gas lamps downstairs. There was no reason on earth why they should have gone out—all eight of them at once! The sudden wind was one thing. That was clearly a result of the quick cleanup she'd done in here, with the broken pitcher and spilled water. But the—

"Just one question," Mr. Temple said, straightening up and leveling his light blue eyes at her. His American accent was intriguing, foreign and fascinating to her ear. She could easily make a fool of herself and stand there staring, listening to him for hours, ogling his broad shoulders and narrow waist. "Is there someplace where I can get a bite to eat?"

Lilly blinked and returned to her senses.

No matter how charming a guest's accent or how comely the face and form, Mr. Clive didn't open his kitchen at all hours and go to the trouble of preparing meals for untimely arrivals. Breakfast would be soon enough for Mr. Temple.

"We don't… J-just come down to the kitchen after you've gotten settled," she heard herself say. "I'll have something for you there."

A moment later, she stood outside his room, her brow creased in a frown. She had never invited a guest to the private areas of the inn. No one but the kitchen staff and family—Charlotte and herself, and their neighbor, Tom Fletcher, when he visited—ever went into the kitchen.

Lilly sighed and moved down the hall to the servants' staircase, which led directly to the pantry. She was nothing if not a careful businesswoman. She had trained herself not to give in to whims and fancies, so it was unusual to find herself taking a clean plate from the cupboard and gathering cold meat and cheese for a guest—for a man who believed she was a fraud.

Nice trick indeed.

She certainly didn't need Samuel Temple imputing chicanery, even though it was more often true than not. Her magical ploys hurt no one. In fact, they added a spark of excitement to the lives of those who visited Ravenwell. Mr. Payton, for instance. He and his cohorts were even now scouring the attic in hopes of—

Footsteps interrupted Lilly's thoughts and she sensed Mr. Temple's presence behind her. She felt the shimmer of heat from his body, the smell of his freshly washed skin, the sound of his clothes rustling. A hot flutter of expectation rushed down her spine.

"That looks great," he said in his casual American way. He walked to the opposite side of the worktable and watched while she finished preparing his plate.

No matter how handsome or how intriguing he was, the American was not going to charm her—not after his earlier, insensitive remark. Lilly cut a slice of bread, added a generous dollop of butter and put it on a plate with a slice of beef.

She forced a smile and would have left him to his own devices had not Charlotte come in at just that moment.

Motioning with her hands, the younger woman signaled that she and Tom had carried all of the new guest's belongings to his room. She also added that his boxes were plentiful and heavy.

From the corner of her eye, Lilly noticed Mr. Temple's fascination with Charlotte. Lilly felt vaguely disappointed that he was just like every other man who laid eyes on her friend—completely entranced by her beauty.

It didn't usually bother Lilly, but for some unaccountable reason, she had hoped for something different from Mr. Temple.

"You communicate entirely nonverbally with this young lady?" he asked, his meal apparently forgotten for the moment.

Lilly frowned, puzzled. *He was interested in their language?* "Yes. My sister is deaf."

"Your sister?"

Lilly nodded. "Close friend, actually, but I consider her my sister."

Charlotte's appearance was so angelic, the men who encountered her hardly ever noticed her deafness. Lilly had expected the same from Mr. Temple, but it seemed that their sign language was the first thing he had seen.

Lilly poured a glass of milk and carried it to the table where she and the staff sometimes took their meals. Perhaps Mr. Temple *was* different. Lilly sighed. The kind of thoughts she was thinking were not only improper, they were dangerous to her peace of mind.

"Over here, Mr. Temple."

The man shifted his gaze between her and Charlotte. "The two of you can actually speak using signals?"

Lilly nodded. "Charlotte just told me that you had

a lot of heavy boxes—and that they've been carried to your room.''

''Fascinating.''

''Not so very,'' Lilly said, ignoring the deep cleft that appeared in Mr. Temple's cheek. His appearance might make her heart trip in her chest, but he was a guest—and a skeptical one. ''We've been talking together this way since we were children.''

''My work… I'm studying communication, but of a different kind. A much more primitive sort.'' He sat down but kept his gaze trained on her. ''Is there anyone—a guide—who can show me the best places to find honeybees? A meadow, perhaps? Or a clover field?''

''Honeybees?'' Lilly asked, taken aback by his quick change of subject. ''I'm sure Mr. Fletcher can show you a few places tomorrow.''

''I'd appreciate it.''

''But honeybees are everywhere. There are hives in the meadow down by the lake, and plenty more on the road between the inn and town. We're always careful when we—''

Charlotte tapped the table to get Lilly's attention, then asked about the conversation. Lilly told her about Mr. Temple's interest in honeybees and asked her to see if Tom wouldn't mind taking their guest to the meadow in the morning.

Charlotte pointed to herself, indicating that she would take Mr. Temple.

Lilly snapped her mouth closed. Over her dead body. She would never allow her friend to go off to the countryside with a stranger, especially not Mr. Temple.

She pressed a hand to her breast. There were very few things that Lilly begrudged Charlotte. Time alone with Mr. Temple was one of them.

''Ask Tom when you see him,'' she said.

Chapter Two

Sam dreamed of stinging whips and heavy, cutting chains. He felt flaying lashes tearing off strips of his skin, and the humiliating sound of his own cries of agony.

But through it all, he felt the comforting touch that had so baffled him upon his arrival at Ravenwell. And he imagined it was Lilly Tearwater's hands soothing the pain away.

Which was utter nonsense.

He climbed out of bed and opened the window shades. The morning sun shone brightly, and he saw that a few guests were already eating breakfast, sitting at tables in the garden. It was the perfect sort of day for finding beehives.

Sam washed and shaved, then dressed in casual clothes for his trek across the Cumbrian meadows and fields. All he needed was a cup of coffee, some food to carry along and someone to point him in the direction of the meadow Miss Tearwater had spoken of. He didn't really need a guide.

He packed his rucksack, then headed down toward

the main rooms of the inn, meeting Tom Fletcher on the stairs.

"Good morning to you," Tom said.

Sam gave a nod.

"Good day for hunting up bees," the man remarked, his expression open and friendly. "I'll be away today," he added. "I've just come by to be sure all's well at the inn before I go. I like to keep an eye out for the lasses."

Sam took note of his pointed comments. Nothing would happen here at Ravenwell that Tom didn't hear about.

"Maybe you can give me directions to the lake. I understand there's a meadow down there."

Tom smiled broadly. He set down the bucket he carried. "Come on, then. We'll walk out for a bit and I can show you."

They went through a long hall and out to a wide drive between the inn and a low outbuilding. Tom pointed to the right. "The lake is down that way," he said. "You walk through a small wood, then you'll see the meadow. Full of color this time of year. Lots of clover down there, too."

"Sounds like just the place."

"Sorry I can't come with—"

"Watch out!"

A large canvas basket on wheels came flying down the drive toward the two men. Tom dodged out of the way, and Sam grabbed it before it could fly past them into the flower beds. Charlotte came running behind, her hair loose and her arms flailing.

"Charlotte, what are you doing with the laundry out here?" Fletcher said aloud, although he used his hands and facial expression to communicate the question to her.

The woman replied in her own silent way, and then Sam turned the basket over to her.

"Best be quick, then," Tom said, his gestures making plain what he meant even without the words. "And careful."

She began to push it back in the direction it had come. Tom's eyes didn't return to Sam until she turned the corner and was out of sight.

"I see you share the same method of communication as Miss Tearwater."

He nodded. "I've known Charlotte since she came here as a child. Learned the language right off."

Sam detected a wistful tone in the young man's voice and saw him gaze tenderly in the direction she'd gone. Fletcher's obvious regard for Miss Charlotte made Sam undefinably restive. Unconsciously, he flexed the muscles of his jaw and shifted his knapsack. It was time to go. He was anxious to be away from these people whose lives barely touched his own, and he didn't mind forgoing the coffee he'd been thinking about earlier.

He bid a quick farewell to Fletcher and headed to the path. He followed the trail to a barley field, skirting it until he reached a clearing. From the high ground there he could see a meadow just beyond the wood, and then a lake.

A sudden crash, followed by a heavy thud, made him stop in his tracks. It felt and sounded as if a tree had just fallen. Sam shook his head slightly. He hadn't heard any chopping or sawing, though he could not imagine a tree falling without good cause.

Unless something else had made the noise.

Sam glanced in the direction of the sound and saw Lilly Tearwater coming through the field on a side path, only a few yards away. She stopped short when she noticed him, then continued toward him.

"Mr. Temple," she called, holding one hand over her eyes against the bright sunlight. "You're out early."

"I could say the same about you," he said when they met. Her face was flushed and there was a fine sheen of perspiration on her brow.

"Aye, well, I'm not on holiday, and you are."

"Not entirely," Sam said. "I'll be doing a good deal of field work while I'm here...."

"Ah, yes. The bees."

She was modestly dressed again, but Sam felt a jolt of his pulse at the sight of her delicate neck, of her small ear teased by shiny black curls. His mind was suddenly filled with her scent and the desire to touch the arch of her brow, to press his lips to that tender space between her ear and neck.

He took a step back and brought his eyes into focus again. Where had those images come from?

"...to visit old Mrs. Webster. She's a widow, and gets very... Mr. Temple, is something wrong?"

"No. Nothing." *Everything.* What had just happened to him? "I'll just... This way to the lake?" he asked, even though he knew it was.

Miss Tearwater nodded. "Walk straight toward that big oak and you'll see a path."

He gave a quick nod and started toward the lake. "Er, speaking of oaks," he said, stopping and turning to her, "did you hear a tree fall just now?"

"I, uh...well, yes, I suppose I did." Her gaze shifted to her feet and she bit her lip. It was clear that she wanted to evade him, and Sam was intrigued by her unease. Why should talk of this make her uncomfortable? Was that loud thud somehow related to the chicanery at the inn? Was there a machine of some sort that was used to produce the ghostly apparitions?

"Well, good day to you, Mr. Temple, I'll just be on my—"

"What's the hurry?"

"No particular hurry. Enjoy your bees." She started to move, but could not get past Sam on the narrow path. He knew there was no possibility of her pushing past him. Proper etiquette demanded that she keep her distance.

She looked up at him warily. Within those stormy violet eyes was a wildness that Miss Tearwater nearly managed to hide. Perhaps she was not the proper lady she appeared to be.

"Sorry." He stepped aside, disconcerted by the conflicting urges that pulsed through him. Battling his need to escape her close proximity was the irrational desire to kiss her, to pull her to him and ravage her lips with his mouth, his teeth, his tongue. When he realized that his hands were shaking, he turned abruptly and left her.

What was happening to him? How could he feel such a fierce burst of desire for Miss Tearwater, yet be unable to touch her?

Perhaps it was not only the inn that was haunted, but all its fields and acres, too.

Lilly held her hand over her heart all the way back to the inn, certain that it would beat right through her chest and land somewhere at her feet if she wasn't careful.

Samuel Temple had looked at her as if…

"Everything all right, Lilly?" asked Tom.

"Of course."

"It's just that you're all flushed like," he said.

"No, I'm fine. How's your mother? Are her knees still stiff?"

"Not so bad since she's been using that salve you sent down."

"That's good, then." Lilly would never tell Tom or his mother that the salve was useless—that the ease Mrs. Fletcher felt was due to Lilly's magic. Nor did she reveal the true reason their oldest ewe had borne triplets the day that Mrs. Fletcher's knees had improved.

"I'm driving down to Perry Crag's farm. He's got a few yearlings for sale, and I want to look them over. I won't be back until morning, but you've got young Davy to help you, and Mrs. Bainbridge at the desk…"

"We'll be fine, Tom," Lilly said. "You shouldn't feel as if you must come up and check on us every day."

He pulled a face. "A woman running this business alone, and the inn so full of strangers all the time…"

Lilly laughed. "Tom Fletcher, you'll be having me think you don't believe I can do it."

He started to scold her for saying such a thing, but she slipped away and went around to the back of the inn. She stood in the shade of the garden trellis and took a moment to settle herself after her encounter with Mr. Temple.

Closing her eyes, she smoothed her damp hands

down the front of her gown, as if that could somehow still the thudding of her heart. She could not
recall ever meeting such a potent man, someone who
had the power to make her melt with just a glance.
Something dark and wary lay hidden in the depths
of his blue eyes, and Lilly sensed a vulnerability that
was belied by his considerable size.

"Ah, Miss Tearwater!"

Mr. Payton and his group gathered 'round. They
were dressed for the outdoors—for a day of walking,
or perhaps hiking among the fells. Lilly was aware
that they'd sought her earlier, anxious to discuss the
ghosts they'd seen the previous night and their trek
to the attic.

Perhaps it was just as well to get it done now, and
banish thoughts of Mr. Temple from her mind.

"Good morning to you," she replied. "Did you
sleep well?"

"Hardly," Mrs. Stanhope said. "Not after seeing
that…that—"

"You mean Sir Emmett," Lilly interjected. She
stepped away from the wall and walked through the
gate into her side garden. "Our ghost is quite mild
mannered. You needn't have worried."

"Who is, er, who *was* he?" asked Mr. Payton.

"He was once a visitor to Ravenwell Cottage—
centuries ago, when Ravenwell was a manor house."

"And Lady Alice?"

"The wife of Sir John Bartlett. But she was the
paramour of Sir Emmett." Lilly had practiced well.
She knew the story front to back, and there was no
one in the village who could discredit it. For all anyone knew, Sir Emmett and Lady Alice truly did
haunt Ravenwell Cottage.

Several of the women gasped as they came to the correct, but shocking, conclusion. "Sir John found his wife with her lover."

"And killed them?"

Lilly nodded. "Sir Emmett was taken completely unawares. He was unarmed and…well, Sir John ran him through with his sword."

"A-and Lady Alice?"

"Tossed her out that window," Lilly said with quiet drama. She pointed to the attic window. "There."

"We found nothing up there when we investigated last night," Mr. Payton said.

Lilly shook her head. "They leave no trace," she stated. "Ever."

"This is truly amazing," Mr. Payton exclaimed. "In all my travels, I have never seen such a display! Has anyone ever tried to photograph these pitiful spirits?"

"No!" Lilly exclaimed, more forcefully than she intended. She could just imagine the notoriety that would follow publication of such photographs. Journalists, thrill-seekers, debunkers… The unwelcome fame would make life impossible. "I mean to say," she said more calmly, "those who've tried have never been successful." It wasn't exactly a lie, since no one had tried. And Lilly planned to keep it that way. Word of mouth, stories that her guests told when they returned home—these were enough to ensure a full house and a good living all year long.

"That's a shame," Mr. Payton said. "It would be so fascinating to capture—"

"Where is everyone going today?" Lilly asked,

clasping her hands together. "Down to the lake? It promises to be wonderfully warm."

With the discussion purposely steered from the notion of photographs, the visitors traversed the flagstone walk and left the garden. Lilly sighed and looked over her rosebushes, which bore only the most feeble greenery and a few paltry buds.

She did not know what was wrong with them. She tended them as carefully and lovingly as all the other flowers that flourished in her gardens, yet these poor plants had responded to nothing she'd tried.

And she did not dare use her magic on them. The sudden flourishing of her roses would cause questions that she could not answer, as well as some unplanned disaster. Just this morning, after making improvements to Mrs. Webster's vegetable garden, she'd witnessed a huge maple become uprooted and crash to the ground. All because she'd ripened a few tomatoes and carrots for the poor old widow!

Mr. Temple had been suspicious. He'd heard the tree fall, but what could he actually know about that maple tree? Only that it had fallen. Lilly did not have to worry that he would discover her talent. Trees fell every day, their roots rotted, they were weakened by lightning or some other such thing. There was no reason on earth why he should suspect *her* of causing it.

But she would die of mortification if he or *anyone* ever learned of her aberrant talents.

At the edge of the meadow, not far from the lake, was a dead chestnut tree. It was tall and thick, and its trunk held one of the best *Apis mellifera* colonies Sam had ever seen. Over the past four years, he had studied every aspect of the hive in a number of different locales and had been considered an expert in the field—before his experience in Sudan.

Sam looked up and took a deep breath of pure, free air. He would never again take for granted the sight of the sky and the clouds, of the birds winging across broad, open vistas.

Before his mind could lock on to thoughts of the filthy pit where he and his colleagues had been chained to the walls, Sam turned his attention to the chestnut tree. Its branches were perfectly configured for the platform Sam would build—a perch from which to observe and photograph the bees. The bee project consisted mainly of observing and making notes. He would take photographs and make a number of drawings, of course, and probably track the foragers as they collected pollen. There'd be a few specimens to collect, but Sam doubted that he would need many.

And in the evenings, while the bees slept, he would look for ways to disprove the existence of Ravenwell's ghost.

His fleeting thought that Ravenwell and its lands were haunted had been merely a jest. Sam didn't believe it for a minute. Just because he'd been physically drawn to Lilly Tearwater did not mean there was some enchantment about the place.

She was a compelling woman, beautiful and exotic, and Sam had merely been taken by the pure, feminine sensuousness of her face and form. Just because he could appreciate her did not mean that anything else had changed. As much as he might wish otherwise, he knew what would happen if he actually touched her.

Which he would never do.

He was here for only two reasons. To finish his research and to win one hundred pounds.

Winning the wager would be easy. Somehow, Miss Tearwater, or someone in her employ, was using a clever ploy to make her visitors believe that Ravenwell was haunted.

Sam slipped his rucksack from his shoulders and sat down on the ground near the chestnut tree. Pulling his field glasses from the pack, he surveyed the meadow and saw that he had a clear view down to the lake, a view that would be even better after he'd built a perch up in the branches of the chestnut tree.

There were boats on the water, carrying fishermen mostly, and a few boaters enjoying the morning sunshine. He saw no bathers, though there was a stretch of beach divided by a grouping of large black rocks. The far side looked like an excellent secluded spot for bathing in the raw, as he and his brothers had done in their wild youth.

Growing up in exotic locations all over the globe, Sam and the other Temple boys had been hellions. It wasn't until they'd reached their twenties and entered their chosen professions that any of them had begun to settle down. And now that he was an adult, with a sedate, conventional career ahead of him, Sam would not be diving into any public lake without his clothes.

With that thought, he found Lilly Tearwater once again on his mind.

He looked back and saw her in the distance, walking up the path toward the inn. The magnification of his field glasses gave him a good view of her, dressed in her simple blouse and skirt. She wore no hat, and her hair was wildly curly, though she had managed in some mysterious, feminine way to secure the soft mass on her head, off her shoulders.

He could easily imagine that lustrous hair flowing freely in lush curls across her bare shoulders. It would brush the tips of her breasts when she undressed to swim on the private section of beach…

The unbidden thought shocked but pleased him. It had been a very long time since he'd thought of a woman the way any normal man would. Still, he had no business thinking of Miss Tearwater in such vivid terms. She was merely the proprietress of Ravenwell and the woman he was going to prove guilty of fraud.

Sam rose to his feet and started to walk toward the lake, but turned and detoured toward the farms, heading in the direction from which Miss Tearwater had come. He wondered about the tree that had fallen a while ago, and the strange weather of the previous night. The ground was bone dry. Clearly, there'd been no rain after the wind and lightning.

Nothing seemed normal here. Was it Ravenwell itself? Or something odd about Cumbria and the Lake District?

All the farms that Sam could see were small and neatly divided by hedgerows or squat walls of stone. On the opposite side of the path was a deep grove of mature deciduous trees.

Perhaps that was where the tree had fallen.

Sam continued to walk, waving at a farmer in a distant field, and greeting an elderly woman who worked near her cottage, picking tomatoes.

"Beautiful morning," he said.

"Aye, that it is."

"Quite a garden you have there." Sam didn't know when he'd seen better. Bright red tomatoes were bigger than his hand. Cucumbers, dark green, were long and plump. Cauliflower, string beans, leafy stalks—all were in their prime. And it was only midsummer.

"It always seems heartier after a visit from Lilly," the woman said absently.

"Lilly? Miss Tearwater?"

She looked up at him, and seemed surprised that he was still there. "Aye," she said.

Sam did not know what to make of the woman's statement. Surely she did not mean that Miss Tearwater had some beneficial effect on the vegetables. More likely she meant that her life seemed brighter after a visit from Ravenwell's mistress. Hence, the garden seemed robust to the old woman's eyes.

He looked around, scratching his head. "Did you happen to notice…was a tree nearby cut down this morning?"

"Nay."

"You're sure?"

"O' course, lad," the woman replied. "No one cut it. It just fell."

Chapter Three

Sam headed back to Ravenwell, feeling as if he'd stepped off the train into some strange, fictional Lewis Carroll world. Nothing seemed right.

A sharp pain on the side of his neck punctuated that feeling, and he realized he'd been stung by a honeybee. He rubbed the spot and shifted his rucksack, bracing himself for whatever might happen next. Somehow, he was certain it would not be anything commonplace.

He entered Ravenwell's grounds through a gate at the entry to the back garden. At the outer edges were thick bushes and an abundance of well-tended flowers—*Calluna vulgaris, Digitalis purpurea, Achillea millefollium.* Lilly Tearwater was among them, bent at the waist, tending the beds.

She stood suddenly as if startled to see him. It appeared she'd been so deep in thought she had not heard his approach.

She was still hatless, and her skin again glowed with a fine sheen of perspiration. In consideration of the sun's heat, she'd rolled her sleeves up to her elbows and opened the topmost buttons of her blouse. Sam was treated to a tantalizing hint of what lay beneath, and forgot about the painful sting at his neck.

He was suddenly much more aware of other parts of his anatomy.

Miss Tearwater touched her tongue to her lips and spoke. "Did you find your bees?"

"Bees?" A bead of moisture trickled down her throat and disappeared into the cleavage partially revealed by her open buttons. Sam swallowed. "Bees. Yes. Excellent hive in the meadow."

Miss Tearwater bent to the ground again and picked up the flowers she'd cut. Sam hadn't noticed them until that moment.

"Allow me," he said, taking the bunch from her arms. His hands brushed her warm skin, but he didn't experience the sharp punch of discomfort usually engendered by the lightest touch. He felt a slight quiver of expectation along his spine, but nothing more.

Sam stayed with her as she began to wend her way along the stone path through the flower beds, toward the inn.

He needed to win the wager he'd made with Jack. His money wouldn't hold out for very long. By the time he finished his research at Ravenwell, he would be broke. Which meant that he was going to have to ask Miss Tearwater about the Ravenwell phantoms.

"What exactly do you expect to learn about the bees, Mr. Temple?" she asked, before he had a chance to pose his own question.

He did not let her question deter him, it merely delayed the inevitable. "I have a theory about their dance."

She turned and looked up at him. "Did you say *dance?*"

Sam nodded. "That's what I call it. The movements they make to communicate with other workers in the hive."

Puzzlement flickered in her extraordinary eyes. "I've never heard of such a thing."

"Generations of observers have noticed particular movements in bees returning to the hive. I think these bees are talking to other worker bees."

Miss Tearwater looked skeptical and Sam couldn't blame her. Hardly anyone outside of scientific society understood the theories of Mr. Darwin. But evolution, adaptation, survival of the fittest—these were concepts that seemed to explain a great number of things in nature.

"What on earth do they talk about?"

"Food. At least, I think it's about food."

"And were you watching your bees when you got stung there?" They stopped walking and Miss Tearwater touched her forefinger to the unfortunate place on his neck. "It's quite red and starting to swell, you know."

Sam froze in place and listened to the blood roaring in his ears. Her touch was light and gentle, yet a distinct memory of the torturer's tools, hot on his skin, assailed him.

"Charlotte was stung once," she said as Sam caught his breath. She was so close that he could see every eyelash, and a tiny smudge of dirt beside her ear. "It caused an awful welt."

"It sometimes happens," he said. It was a struggle, forcing himself to stand so still, so close to her. But he would have to spend time with her if he wanted to get the information he needed to win the wager.

"You should tend to that."

She appeared not to have noticed his distress at her proximity, but continued walking toward the inn. "Have you any ice?" he asked. "That's all I need."

She looked askance. "Come with me," she said.

"Right here." Lilly pulled out a chair at the kitchen table for Mr. Temple to sit down. Turning away, she reached into a cupboard for a teacup and heard him place the flowers on Mr. Clive's worktable.

Lilly must have misjudged the time, for Mr. Clive was conspicuously absent. Luncheon was over and the chef was most likely in the kitchen garden, picking the herbs and vegetables he wanted for the evening meal. But she would not let on to Mr. Temple that it made her nervous to be alone with him. He was just a guest, nothing more. It was her responsibility to help him.

"A piece of ice will do," Mr. Temple said. He looked at her as if she planned to treat the sting with a hot poker, which reminded Lilly of some unkind thing Aunt Maude used to say about men and their little injuries. "I'm conditioned to being stung, Miss Tearwater. I barely react."

"I have an excellent remedy," Lilly said, ignoring him. "Sit down. It consists of a few secret ingredients mixed in olive oil. It's a recipe given me by my aunt."

"What ingredients?" Mr. Temple eyed the three small glass jars that she took from a cabinet and carried to the table.

"Now, if I told you, it wouldn't be a secret, would it?"

"Actually, it's all right." He started for the door, but Lilly stepped into his path. "I don't really—"

"You're not afraid that I'll make it worse?" Mixing several drops of camphor into the olive oil, she added a few drops of cedarwood oil and a bit of her precious citronella. Then she dropped in an ingredient as clear as water that had no taste or smell. She didn't know what it was, but Aunt Maude had always placed a great deal of stock in its value.

"No…it's just I, uh…"

"Now then. Sit," she said, noting the way he gritted his teeth as he pulled off his canvas rucksack and sat down. His posture was rigid, his back straight as a rod. "I promise this will be painless."

Mr. Temple turned slightly, settling his bright blue eyes upon her. His hair grew thick and full, and very dark except for those few strands of white just above his ear. Lilly wondered how it would feel if she touched it.

Her movements slowed. She moistened her lips as the languorous haze of afternoon heat drifted through the kitchen.

Mr. Temple wore no jacket, and his shirt was collarless, with rolled-up sleeves, exposing muscular forearms liberally sprinkled with dark hair. His hands were considerably larger than hers, with long, strong fingers clenched in a death grip on his canvas pack. Their gazes locked for a moment and the heat of the day seemed to shimmer between them.

His lips parted and his nostrils flared. When he let out a long, slow breath, Lilly forgot her purpose.

Her heart stopped and her mind ceased to function. At least, that was how it seemed. She shook herself briskly.

"H-have you pulled out the stinger?" she finally asked. He gave a quick shake of his head and Lilly turned her attention to the angry red mark on his neck. "This will only take a minute."

Bending closer to look for the stinger, she used her nail to scrape it from his skin. Then, using one finger, she dabbed a bit of the medicated oil onto the spot. Lilly heard his breath catch when she touched him, and realized how close she stood. *Good Lord!* She should have rebuttoned her blouse.

Abruptly, she stepped away from Mr. Temple. She would look like a foolish adolescent if she started to fumble with her buttons now. Perhaps he hadn't noticed.

Grabbing a towel to wipe Aunt Maude's concoction from her hands, she tried to think of some casual remark to send him on his way. But even had any words come to mind, Lilly knew that her throat would not function.

Without a sound, she walked out of the kitchen, leaving Mr. Temple alone with the cut flowers lying on the large table in the center of the room. In the dim hallway outside, she paused to compose herself. She had work to do. There was no time to dally over such foolishness.

She took a deep breath and walked to a small sitting room that overlooked the rose garden as she fastened her buttons from neck to breast.

"Miss Tearwater." Lilly started at the sound of Mr. Dawson's voice. She had thought the room empty, but the gentleman sat in a wing chair facing the fireplace.

"You startled me, Mr. Dawson," she said. "I didn't realize you were there."

The man folded his newspaper and rose to his full height. He was tall, though not quite as tall as Mr. Temple, and his build was brawny. Mr. Dawson's hair was neatly trimmed, with a liberal sprinkling of silver at the temples. His nose was crooked, as though it might have been broken. Lilly believed his age to be close to fifty. Too young for Ada Simpson, but that was none of her concern. "I understand I missed an event last night," he said.

"An event? Oh, yes. Sir Emmett. You weren't in the garden when he came out?" She had become so accustomed to lying about the ghosts that it came easily.

"Unfortunately, no."

"Miss Simpson was looking for you. Did she find you?"

"Who?" he asked.

"The chemist's sister. From the village," Lilly replied. She went to one of the highly polished tables and picked up a vase of fading blooms.

Mr. Dawson shook his head. "I must have missed her somehow."

"Well, I'm sure she'll find you if it's important." Lilly turned to leave, but Mr. Dawson detained her.

"Miss Tearwater," he said. "There were other events last evening. A sudden wind. The gaslights suddenly extinguished...what do you think happened?"

She had not been out-of-doors to witness the wind, but she'd heard about it from Tom. "Perhaps it was Sir Emmett. Or Lady Alice. I'm sure I don't know, Mr. Dawson."

His scrutiny made Lilly uncomfortable. It was as if he knew there was some other explanation for the ghosts, and was waiting for her to give it.

Lilly almost laughed at herself. No one could possibly know that she had created the ghosts in her imagination and made them exist through her talent. She'd never told Tom what she could do, and Charlotte certainly didn't know.

But Mr. Dawson looked at her as if he suspected something.

"Well. It's a beautiful day today," she said, to change the direction of the conversation. Clutching the vase to her breast, she moved toward the doorway. "Several of the guests have gone hiking. Others are boating."

"Will any of your guest rooms become available in the near future?" he asked.

"I'm not sure, Mr. Dawson. I'd have to check the reservations. Why?"

He did not answer right away, and the appraising look he gave her was disconcerting.

"I have a very good friend in London who would like to join me for my remaining weeks here at Ravenwell."

"I will have to let you know, Mr. Dawson."

Feeling distinctly uncomfortable under his perusal, Lilly left the room and made her way toward the kitchen once again, only to be waylaid by Charlotte. Her friend was distraught and disheveled. Her gown was filthy and her hair in tangles.

"Charlotte? What's wrong?" Lilly asked, dreading the answer. If someone had hurt her, if one of the guests had—

Charlotte's hand signals indicated something was wrong in the barn.

Lilly frowned. What could it be? They only kept one animal—the gelding that pulled the buggy or the wagon when either was needed. Perhaps one of the guests had wandered out there…

"Charlotte," Lilly said, taking hold of her arms to slow her down. "Tell me."

She signaled wildly again, and this time Lilly began to understand. Something was wrong with Duncan, the barn cat that Charlotte had adopted.

"What happened to him?" Lilly asked.

Charlotte indicated that she did not know, but Duncan was terribly ill. She pulled on Lilly's skirt in an urgent attempt to get her to help.

Mr. Temple was gone from the kitchen when they walked through. Lilly set down the vase of old flowers and followed her friend outside. Charlotte broke into a run and Lilly did the same to keep up.

Lilly could hear Duncan's caterwauling the minute she entered the barn. The big, old, stone building seemed hollow, though it housed their horse, as well as the buggy and wagon, and the large gardening equipment that didn't fit in the shed.

She followed the sounds to a far corner, where Charlotte knelt next to the cat, and slid to her knees beside her.

Something was definitely wrong with Duncan. He lay on his side, panting, then growled low in his throat. It did not appear that he'd been hurt in a fight; there was no blood or torn skin. He suddenly wailed.

"Do you need help?"

The voice startled Lilly and she turned to see Mr. Temple standing behind her. She'd been so con-

cerned by Charlotte's anguish and Duncan's distress
that she hadn't heard his approach.

"I saw you two running." He looked uncomfortable, unsure about intruding. "There didn't seem to
be anyone else about…"

"It's Duncan, Charlotte's cat."

"Yes. I hear him."

"Do you know anything about animals—cats—
Mr. Temple?"

He hesitated, and Lilly wondered if he would ever
answer her. He seemed to gird himself somehow,
then crouched down, moving close to the obviously
distressed animal.

Utterly absorbed by Duncan's plight, Charlotte
seemed oblivious to Mr. Temple's strong male presence in the small space. But Lilly was not. Though
they did not touch, she felt the heat of his skin
through her thin summer clothes.

"Let's see now," he said, moving his hands carefully toward the injured animal, to its painfully contracted belly.

And Lilly suddenly realized that the feline they
had assumed to be male was about to give birth!

Charlotte's pleading eyes looked up at Mr. Temple, then at Lilly.

"She wants to know if Duncan will be all right,"
Lilly murmured.

"I think so," he replied, "if she can survive having the wrong name. She's about to deliver a litter
of kittens."

Charlotte turned to Lilly for an explanation, even
as Lilly blushed at his frank words.

She explained the situation to Charlotte, who had
little understanding of such things. Frowning, the

younger woman blinked several times, then looked at her cat.

"Watch now," Mr. Temple said, as if Charlotte could hear. "But don't touch her. She's concentrating."

Lilly did not know whether to shoo Charlotte out of the barn or allow her to stay and watch. It was wholly improper for a lady to watch such an intimate event with a man—a stranger—but the wonder of birth enthralled her.

Sitting back on her heels, Lilly actually felt reassured by the presence of Mr. Temple, who clearly had some knowledge of what was taking place here.

Duncan panted and continued to whimper.

Charlotte was not the only one who had little understanding of such things. Ravenwell had never kept any breeding animals, and Lilly rarely visited any of the farms, besides Tom Fletcher's, so she was also inexperienced. But she'd heard talk, something Charlotte would never do.

The cat's mewling seemed to intensify and Lilly began to worry. There was concern in Charlotte's eyes, too, but that had been there from the start.

"What's happening, Mr. Temple?" Lilly inquired. "Why is she... She seems to be struggling." She didn't know quite what to ask.

"I'm afraid she might need some help," he said.

When the cat gave a loud screech of distress, he moved too quickly for Lilly to feel much embarrassment at his actions. Gently taking hold of the cat's hindquarters, he placed his little finger, firmly but smoothly, into the birth passage, stretching it.

"Easy now, Duncan," he said quietly, moving his

finger just far enough to expand the opening. "Your kittens will be out soon."

Charlotte made several rapid hand motions to Lilly.

"Charlotte wants to know if she can hold the kittens after…?"

"Not right away," he replied. "Let Duncan clean them up and then see how she feels about it."

Though his hands were big, he was gentle with the mother cat, treating her as if she were a prize animal. He spoke kindly to Charlotte, too, even though he knew she could not hear him.

The first kitten came out with a sound that made Lilly smile. Charlotte was clearly in awe as she gazed at the tiny creature. Once it was safely out, and the birth process seemed to be progressing as nature intended, Mr. Temple sat back. He took a handkerchief from his pocket and wiped his hand while the three of them watched Duncan deliver her kittens. An attractive cleft appeared in his cheek as he relaxed and smiled at Charlotte, then at the new kittens.

Charlotte pointed to each kitten as it appeared, counting them. She held up her fingers to show that there were eight in all, then asked another question.

"Charlotte is wondering if Duncan is, er, finished now."

"It looks that way," he replied. "No need to blush, Miss Tearwater. Birth is a perfectly respectable process. Nothing shameful about it."

Charlotte caught Lilly's attention again. "Are there more kittens?" she asked on Charlotte's behalf. "She's pushing again."

"She must deliver the afterbirth—the tissue that

nourishes the babies while they're inside,'' Mr. Temple explained.

Lilly should have felt shocked by his words, but she was more curious than embarrassed. She was certain Aunt Maude would never have allowed the two of them to remain in the barn, witnessing such a coarse event. But watching Mr. Temple, and seeing the pleasure in his eyes as he observed Duncan giving birth, gave Lilly an insight into something she'd never considered before.

That such a natural wonder was anything *but* the dirty, sordid business it was purported to be.

Charlotte clapped her hands together and pointed at the mother cat cleaning her new babies.

''You seem quite experienced in these matters, Mr. Temple,'' Lilly said.

''Hmm?'' One of the kittens struggled to move, and Mr. Temple pushed some straw away so that it could wriggle over to its mother. ''Birth?''

As Charlotte delighted in the sight of the new kittens and Duncan's new motherly attention, Mr. Temple turned to face Lilly in the dusty, filtered light of the barn. ''Yes, I've seen a few new creatures into the world,'' he said, his voice low and intimate. His eyes darkened. ''And witnessed a few ugly deaths, too.''

Chapter Four

Miss Tearwater must have buttoned her bodice in haste.

The sight of her crisp white blouse with its fastenings askew made Sam's blood hum. He'd barely recovered from the first aid she'd given him in the kitchen before instinct made him go rushing into the barn after the two Ravenwell women, certain that some disaster threatened.

Of course, nothing had been amiss. This was England. Civilized, refined England.

But now that the cat had delivered her kittens, Sam felt a familiar tightening in his chest and some difficulty drawing a breath. He had to get out of there. That dim corner of the barn, with all its earthy scents, and Miss Tearwater who knelt beside him, her own scent like the flowers she so lovingly tended…

Hastily, he rose to his feet.

"Will Duncan—"

"She'll be fine now," he stated. Which was more than he could say for himself.

A moment later, he stood outside, bracing one arm

against the stone wall of the barn, taking big, gulping breaths. He was a fool to have come all the way to Cumbria. He wasn't going to be able to prove anything about the ghosts, and it was possible that he could get the appointment to the Royal College without doing any further work on the bee project. His reputation alone would—

"Thank you, Mr. Temple," said Miss Tearwater, coming into the bright sunlight, "for helping with Charlotte's cat. I'm sure I don't know what we'd have done without you."

"Don't mention it," he said with much more poise than he felt. "Duncan probably would have managed even without my interference."

"But if she hadn't, Charlotte would have been devastated and— Mr. Temple, are you all right?"

He pushed away from the wall and brushed his hands together. "Of course."

"Will you let me repay you for your—"

"It's not necessary, Miss Tearwater. Good day." He started walking toward the inn, hoping she wouldn't follow.

But she did. And she took hold of his arm.

Sam recoiled.

"I...I'm sorry," Miss Tearwater said. "I didn't mean to..." She frowned, justifiably puzzled. "Did I hurt you?"

"Of course not," Sam said, turning away. He was not compelled to give an explanation for his aversion to her touch. He wished things were different. God, but he wished he could touch her.

Sam could not remember the last time a woman had tempted him the way Lilly Tearwater did. Just looking at her made his head pound and his hands ache to touch her.

"I'm sorry if I offended you," she said quietly.

"Miss Tearwater." He swallowed. And kept his distance. "You did not offend me. I…" He glanced at the treetops, then across the wide farm fields in the distance. He did not want to alienate her; he needed to get her to trust him. To talk to him about the ghosts. "Do you suppose I could get some lunch up at the inn?"

She blinked her astonishing eyes twice in surprise. She must think him an idiot, unable to hold one thought for more than half a minute. "Of course," she said. "Come with me."

Lilly reined in her joy as she perused the new books that had arrived with the afternoon post. She'd been too busy to look at them sooner, but now that supper was being served, she had a few minutes to skim through *Egyptian Treasures* and *Athens of Antiquity* before she had to make Sir Emmett and Lady Alice appear.

The faraway places of the world fascinated Lilly, especially the ones with ancient histories, like Egypt. She turned the page to view another photographic plate. What she wouldn't give to travel to Cairo and see the pyramids for herself. Or go to Rome to see the Coliseum, Athens and the Parthenon.

She sighed. None of that would ever happen. She'd promised Maude that she'd stay and take care of Charlotte—and Ravenwell.

Even if Lilly managed to earn enough money from Ravenwell to take the kind of trip she longed for, Charlotte would never be able to go. She did not deal well with change, and only managed strangers because she was comfortable and protected in her own environment.

Lilly knew this because of a short trip she'd taken to London with Charlotte and Maude only a year before Maude's death. Charlotte had been horrified by all the traffic and people. She had been terribly nervous and unable to eat or sleep. Clearly, she was not meant to leave their own familiar, pastoral setting, which meant that Lilly had to stay, too.

But Lilly could dream. She satisfied her wanderlust by poring over her books of exotic places.

The books were not inexpensive. Lilly bought the ones that had good quality photographs because they helped her to visualize the foreign settings. Sometimes when she went to bed at night, she lay in the dark, seeing the pictures in her mind. She could almost hear the sounds and smell the sharp aromas of Persia, of South America, of Africa.

She sighed. She was not unhappy at Ravenwell. Lilly often had to remind herself of that, especially in summer, when the inn had guests visiting from all over the world.

But she was not content, either.

Maude had hoped that Lilly and Tom Fletcher would marry one day, but Lilly couldn't think of Tom as anything but a brother. He was a wonderful man who helped her and Charlotte whenever they needed it, but he could never be her husband.

Lilly would never wed. She was tied to Ravenwell—and to Charlotte. And though Charlotte was an agreeable and tractable young woman, Lilly didn't think there was a man alive who would be willing to take on the responsibility of a wife, as well as her impaired "sister." At least, she hadn't met one yet.

But if she had to dream up a man who would love and care for her, he would be someone like Samuel Temple... Tall and handsome, with a patient voice and a kind smile.

He'd been very sweet with Charlotte this afternoon, but when he'd stood with Lilly outside the barn, he'd been distant and surly. She didn't know what she'd done to upset him so. Surely her light touch on his arm hadn't been the cause.

She had been admiring his patience with Charlotte, and feeling grateful for his help, when she'd touched him, imagining him taking her into his arms and...

Better not to take that particular fancy any further. Proper young ladies didn't spend their time imagining brawny chests or masculine chins. They didn't think about kisses or caresses.

Lilly turned the page and focused her attention on the photographs of an Egyptian marketplace. It looked so exotic, so exciting! If only—

"Henry Sanderson hardly ever left his hotel when he researched that book."

Startled, Lilly looked up into Samuel's eyes, then down at the title page of her book. The author was Henry Sanderson.

"You *know* Mr. Sanderson?"

He shook his head. "Not really. We met a few times when I was in Cairo three years ago. Timid fellow. Didn't like to go out into the streets."

"B-but he—"

"Paid a photographer to get all those pictures,"

Mr. Temple said. "And interviewed quite a number of locals for the information he put into the text."

"Oh no!" she cried. "Don't tell me that!"

"All right. Sorry." He was rightly abashed by her reaction. "You have an interest in Egypt?"

Lilly nodded, and Samuel pushed an edge of the book to angle it toward him. "There is a shop right here—" he pointed to the corner of the picture "—where they say Lord Chester's wife met with her paramour every Tuesday afternoon."

Lilly was shocked by the outrageousness of his statement, but intrigued, nonetheless. "Lord Chester?"

"Or so the rumor goes."

"You actually saw… You've been to Cairo?"

He nodded and straightened to his full height. "Many times," he replied. "I'll tell you about it sometime. What about Ravenwell? This is an unusual place."

She turned the page to another photograph and braced herself for a spate of intrusive questions. "Not so very. It was once a manor house, owned by the Barnaby family. It's been an inn for more than fifty years."

"And haunted for all that time?"

"I imagine so," she replied, glancing up to meet his eyes. "I wasn't here for most of it," she said, her voice nearly scorching him.

He was properly abashed, but continued with his questions, anyway. "Did you live here as a child?"

"I did."

"Your name isn't Barnaby."

"You are very observant," she replied. She recognized his tactics. There had been others who had quizzed her unmercifully about the ghosts. Lilly knew that the best way to handle a skeptic was to be direct. "Is there something in particular that you'd like to know about Ravenwell?"

He shook his head. "Just wondering about the place. Seems old."

Lilly was taken off guard. This was not how the questioning usually went. Most only cared about the ghosts. "Y-yes. The manor house was built during the reign of King James. The original family died out and the house eventually came to the Barnabys early in the last century."

"It looks as if you kept a lot of the original artifacts."

"Yes. And now it's my turn to ask—what was it like in Egypt? Did you see the pyramids? What about Thebes and the temples—"

He held up a hand to silence her, but Lilly started to page through her book, looking for the sites she wanted him to describe. "Are the pillars—"

"Much taller than they appear here. And the sun is so hot it would blister your fair skin after only an hour in it."

"That's what I want to know—how it feels, how it smells. Is it wonderful?"

The expression of rapture on Miss Tearwater's face should have been saved for something altogether different. Sam swallowed and forced his mind away from such ungentlemanly thoughts. If she had an interest in Egypt, then he would tell her all about the place.

For a price.

He was going to get her to tell him everything she

knew about the haunting of Ravenwell Cottage. Aware that he'd blundered last night with his flippant remark about the lights, and his earlier reaction to her inadvertent touch, Sam would be careful not to put her on the defensive again. She would be much more likely to slip up if she trusted him.

"I enjoyed Egypt when I was there as a child," he said. More recently, Professor Kelton and the rest of their party had met in Aswân before starting on their trek to Khartoum. "It's a fascinating country."

"What did you see?" Her interest was so intense it was nearly palpable.

Sam shrugged. He supposed his childhood had made him take much of his experiences for granted, but now he wanted nothing more than to forget them—especially the last eight months. "We saw the Philae temples and Abu Simbel before going south into Sudan."

"Sudan? Oh…"

She actually sighed with ecstasy, and Sam's body reacted the way that he'd thought had been lost forever. Her mouth formed a perfect O, and Sam could think of nothing but how it would taste, of how her delicate shoulders would feel under his hands if only—

"Miss Tearwater?"

A man's voice interrupted his thoughts. Sam turned and took note of the short Englishman he'd encountered on his first night, the fellow who'd asked to explore the attic. "Miss Tearwater, I wonder if I might have a word…"

"Certainly, Mr. Payton," she replied, closing her book and sliding it beneath the high desk that separated her from the rest of the room. "I don't believe you've met Mr. Temple."

"How do you do?" Payton said, taking Sam's hand. "Glad to make your acquaintance."

Sam felt his skin go clammy, but he managed to mutter a greeting.

"Miss Tearwater, do you have any idea whether Sir Emmett or Lady Alice will appear again tonight? Or is it more likely they'll be at rest for a few more days?"

"Well..."

She appeared unabashed, considering the question carefully. And as Sam recovered from Payton's handshake, he felt the irreverent urge to applaud her performance.

"It is my experience that they are entirely unpredictable, Mr. Payton. Why, I remember a time when everyone was in the garden, enjoying their coffee or brandy, and Sir Emmett appeared in the parlor, just there." She pointed to the next room. "I was the only one here. But by the time I went to fetch all the guests to come and see him, he was gone."

"Oh! A dashed shame!" Payton growled, while Sam restrained the urge to laugh out loud.

"But Lady Alice actually did appear a while later—up in the attic window."

Sam just bet she had.

A loud shattering of glass sounded somewhere in the inn. The sound came from upstairs, if Sam was not mistaken.

"Oh dear," Miss Tearwater said. "What now?"

"I'd better go out and see to Mrs. Payton," said the little man as he rushed out of the room.

"I wonder where Charlotte could be."

Sam scratched his head. He had seen Charlotte only a few minutes before. "She's in the barn with her cat. Shall we investigate the noise?"

His hostess surprised him by agreeing to his company. "Upstairs, I think."

A few minutes later, they had checked all the empty rooms for a broken window or any other kind of glass. "Shall we try the attic?" Sam asked. He wanted to get up there and see if they'd concealed pulleys or wires.

Miss Tearwater nodded and opened a door. She started to go up the steep staircase, but turned back to Sam. "We'll need a lamp."

"There's one in my room. Come with me," he said, unwilling to let her out of his sight. "You shouldn't go up there in the dark."

He picked up the lamp from his bedside table and they returned to the stairs. Sam took the lead.

"Good gracious!"

Window glass was scattered all over the floor, all the way to the steps. Sam raised the lamp, illuminating the space that was cluttered with typical attic discards. Trunks and furniture, old lamps and framed paintings, a few rolled-up rugs... Any mechanism could be concealed here, and it would take days, perhaps weeks, to discover it.

"I wonder what happened," Sam said. He walked across the glass to the window on the opposite side and looked down into the terrace garden.

A group of people stood together in the twilight, while a hazy light hovered nearby. Sam squinted his eyes and attempted to make out the figure. "What's that?" he asked.

Miss Tearwater came to the window. "It looks like Lady Alice is making an appearance," she said.

Sam shot his gaze toward the tall bushes surrounding the garden. When he located nothing suspicious, he scanned the grounds, but his eyes were inexorably drawn back to the filmy figure. After a few minutes of hovering above the heads of the people gathered below, the foggy form suddenly disappeared, and the guests who had stood *rapt* began to chatter among themselves.

Frowning, Sam turned toward Miss Tearwater. She stood entirely too close for comfort, but he'd been so intent upon finding the device that produced the ghost that he hadn't noticed. He took a step away from the window—and Miss Tearwater—and considered what he'd seen.

It had been the damnedest thing. It had actually been a woman's form floating in the garden. And it hadn't been just a vague shape. It had clearly been a woman with long, dark hair, and Sam had been able to discern her distinctly medieval style of gown. It had even had some color.

Sam wondered how Miss Tearwater had done it.

Perhaps Fletcher was responsible. The man had been conveniently absent all day. He must have returned sometime earlier to set up whatever contraption he used to project gaslight through the smoke, to illuminate it.

Sam had to admit it had been an excellent performance.

But he wondered how the window had broken.

"This should be boarded up." He searched the floor for whatever object must have been thrown through the window, but didn't find anything. It was curious, but certainly not supernatural.

"There's a hammer and nails in the garden shed. And wood planks in the barn, but I don't expect you to take care of this, Mr. Temple. You're my guest—"

"I don't mind." It would give him a good excuse to get down to the garden and catch Fletcher in the act of putting away his projection apparatus.

As Miss Tearwater began to sweep up the broken glass, Sam went downstairs. He picked up an oil lamp, then went out through one of the back doors. The same people who'd watched Fletcher's filmy projection were still out there, chattering excitedly among themselves. Sam shook his head in disbelief at their gullibility and started his search before it became entirely dark.

He began behind a tall hedge, the most likely place to conceal whatever equipment Fletcher had used. Bending low, Sam illuminated the ground, but found nothing suspicious along the entire row. He expanded his search to the surrounding area, and to the small garden shed and behind the garden wall.

But nothing turned up.

Sam knew there had to be a device somewhere. It was just going to take him a bit longer to find it. And the job would be made a lot easier once he had Miss Lilly Tearwater in his confidence.

"Mr. Temple, is it?"

The man's voice startled Sam as he came out of the shed with a hammer in one hand and nails in the other.

"Henry Dawson," the fellow said, holding out one hand.

Sam managed to avoid it, wondering how Dawson happened to know him. They hadn't been introduced, although Sam had seen him in and around the inn at various times throughout the day.

"Quite an exhibition," Dawson said.

"Yes. It was."

"What do you make of it, Temple?"

Sam turned and closed the door to the shed. "Why do you ask?"

"I understand you're a man of science. You, if anyone, would have an objective opinion about this haunting."

"I prefer to have sufficient data before I draw conclusions," Sam replied, taking an instant dislike to Mr. Dawson. Sam was unsure what it was about the man that bothered him. There was an indolence about him that grated, but Sam had known plenty of sluggish people.

From what he had seen of him, Dawson seemed to have hung about the inn all day, when everyone else had gone out—hiking or boating, visiting Asbury. At supper, he'd sat alone in a far corner of the dining room, watching—no, observing—all the activity around him, with flat, emotionless eyes.

Like some of Sam's jailers in Sudan.

To Sam's annoyance, Dawson followed him through the garden and walked with him toward the barn. "Seems odd that every time a ghost appears, there's a crash of some kind. Or a weird spate of weather."

"Frisky ghosts," Sam said. He didn't like the other man's insinuations, even though Sam had made similar ones himself. It was one thing for him to believe Lilly Tearwater guilty of chicanery. But for some inexplicable reason he didn't care for it much when Henry Dawson made the same assumption.

Chapter Five

Lilly held the lamp high to give Mr. Temple enough light to hammer the large plank across the attic window. She didn't know why she was allowing him to do this work—he was a Ravenwell guest. This was something Davy Becker should have handled.

Besides, she sensed that he was observing her closely. He wanted to discover the secret to the haunting, and figured she was the key. Samuel Temple wasn't the first to try.

Lilly would never let anyone know what she was capable of. Mr. Temple would never learn her secret, and he would certainly never guess it.

"Have you been anywhere else, Mr. Temple? Besides Egypt and Sudan?" She asked these questions in order to divert him from his own queries, but also because those places fascinated her.

Mr. Temple finished with one nail and moved to the next. "You name it," he replied. "I've been there."

"Athens?"

"Um-hmm." He had nails in his mouth, so his answer was inarticulate.

Lilly waited until the hammering stopped. "Rome?"

"Plenty of times. And Florence. Venice. Everywhere in Italy."

"Did your work take you there—studying bees?"

"No. My family spent several years in Italy when I was a boy. My father's work kept us there."

That surprised Lilly. "What does he do?"

"He's an archaeologist. Studies ancient civilizations, which makes Italy a choice place for him."

"And you traveled with him?"

His head bobbed once. "All of us—my mother, my brothers and sisters. We made quite a crowd, wherever we went."

Lilly could hardly imagine such a family. She and Charlotte had only had each other—and Maude, of course. But Maude had never been a mother to them. She'd fed and clothed them, and given them directions for work, for school.

Maude had kept them mostly at Ravenwell. She didn't like exposing Charlotte to other children, who mocked her attempts at speech and her misunderstandings. And Maude had worried constantly that Lilly would do something to bring the wrath of the town upon them.

After all those years of being wary and careful, Lilly wasn't going to let down her guard now.

"Tell me about Rome."

"What do you want to know?" He hammered in another nail, giving her a chance to think of the photographs she'd seen in her books and journals, and all the places she'd read about.

"I want to know about the Forum, Palantine Hill, the Pantheon, and Michaelangelo's Sistine Chapel."

"You don't want much, do you?"

"Since I'm not in a position to travel, Mr. Temple," she said, "I'd like to learn all I can about these places."

"Why not take some time off and go?"

Lilly shrugged. "It's just not possible." She'd had one opportunity to leave Ravenwell. But that had been years ago, before Maude's death. Lilly had barely opened the letter from the wealthy Mrs. Blakely, offering her a post as her traveling companion, when Maude had taken ill. Going away had become impossible.

They walked down the stairs together and into the main reception room, where Mr. Payton and the others stood in the center of the room, just as they had the night before.

"It was so close!" Payton exclaimed.

That had been the point of tonight's orchestrated visitation. Lilly had initiated it when she was occupied at the front desk with Mr. Temple, to allay his suspicions that she was the cause of the apparition. And to make sure none of her guests went home with even the slightest shred of doubt. Lilly suspected she would receive a slew of letters requesting rooms in the near future. The price of a new pane of glass was worth the future business she had just attracted.

"You could see the color of her gown—"

"I saw the color of her *eyes!*"

Excited voices continued, but Lilly walked past the group and went to the desk where she'd left her books. Mr. Temple was already there, apparently unimpressed by Lady Alice and uninterested in the group's excitement.

Absently, his long fingers flipped through the

pages of the Sanderson book. "The Ravenwell ghost causes quite a stir."

Lilly shrugged. "I'm accustomed to it by now."

"Does it speak?" he asked. "The ghost, I mean."

"There are two ghosts," Lilly said. His nonchalance irritated her. What would have to happen for Mr. Temple to be impressed? The sight of both ghosts? Maybe five of them? And perhaps they should ruffle his hair or…snap his suspenders.

"Who are they?" He didn't look up from the Egypt book, but kept paging through, stopping to look at one photograph after another.

"Who?" She could play his game.

He looked up at her then. And smiled.

Lilly felt her heart drop to her toes. Perhaps she *wasn't* equipped to play his game. "T-the ghosts?" she stammered.

He waited.

"It was Lady Alice who appeared tonight," she said, once she was in control again. "As the story goes, she was a visitor at Ravenwell. Her husband killed her when he found her with her lover."

"How do you know this?"

"It's just what I've heard over the years. My aunt Maude… Well, she knew the history of the house." Which was the truth. She'd known everything about Ravenwell Cottage, though none of it had included stories about ghosts.

"Where's Fletcher?"

"Tom? At home, I imagine. He takes care of his elderly mother. Or perhaps he hasn't yet returned from Crag's farm."

"Very convenient."

"Are you insinuating that Tom is…that he…"

She slammed her book shut just as he yanked his fingers out of it. She gathered the Egypt book and *Athens of Antiquity* into her arms and turned to him. "You'll forgive me, Mr. Temple, I have work to do."

She left in a huff, angry that she had let his insinuations get the better of her. Mr. Temple's doubt was no different from the few other guests who'd been reluctant to believe in her ghosts. Disbelief was easy to deal with.

It was his cocky attitude that rankled.

Closing herself into the office behind the desk, Lilly hugged her books and took a moment to settle down before going through the door that led to the private apartment she shared with Charlotte. Her friend always sensed disquiet around her, and it upset her.

When Lilly felt reasonably calm, she walked into the sitting room where Charlotte sat beside a window, sewing. Lilly recognized Tom's shirt on her lap, and saw that Charlotte was repairing a tear in the sleeve. She was unaware of Lilly's presence, and Lilly did not want to startle her.

She set down her books and picked up a lamp, causing a change in lighting that made her friend look up. Smiling brilliantly, Charlotte told Lilly about Duncan's kittens, then about the fun she'd had in the kitchen, helping Mr. Clive make pudding.

Lilly was glad Charlotte had had such a grand day. But she wished her friend were capable of understanding the problems she herself faced every day. Ordering supplies, keeping the day maids on task, making the payroll, balancing their income against their debts…

Creating ghosts for the amusement of the guests.

Lilly's keen loneliness struck her hard. She was usually able to keep it contained, but her need to communicate fully with another soul, to speak of her wishes and aspirations, to share her troubles, was nearly overpowering. It welled up inside her and threatened to spill out in a shower of miserable tears.

Charlotte's hands stilled. She tilted her head and looked quizzically at Lilly.

They had never devised any signals for feelings beyond "happy" or "sad." It didn't matter. Lilly doubted that she could actually verbalize the torrent of emotions that rushed through her now. She gave a shrug of her shoulders, smiled wanly and left Charlotte. She set her books on the table in her room, then picked up a shawl and went through the back hall that led to the inn's kitchen.

It was dark, and all was quiet. What Lilly needed was some time away from the inn—just a few minutes to forget about the responsibilities that bound her. She tossed the shawl around her shoulders and slipped out the back door.

Sam blew out a harsh breath and acknowledged that he hadn't handled that encounter very well. It was going to take some time before Lilly Tearwater would be willing to talk to him again, especially about the ghosts.

He supposed it was fortunate he hadn't mentioned Miss Charlotte as a possible trickster, or else the fire in Lilly's violet eyes would certainly have singed him.

There had to be a way to disprove this haunting nonsense. Sam shoved his hands in his pants pockets and left the lobby, passing the group of gullible guests, who were still talking about what they'd seen in the garden.

There was no point in searching the garden again tonight. Sam hadn't been able to find anything in the twilight, and it was fully dark now. But he had no doubt that come morning, he would find what he was looking for. There would be something…maybe even the tracks of something Fletcher had dragged across the lawn.

Where was the mechanism stored? There had to be a device hidden somewhere, and Sam would lay odds that Tom Fletcher was its operator. He seemed to know the place, as well as anyone, so it wouldn't be too difficult for him to arrange the display and make a quick exit afterward.

Stopping in the doorway that led to the garden, Sam leaned against the doorjamb and gazed out at the scene before him. A picturesque stone courtyard was not far from the kitchen, with several tables and chairs tucked into the farthest corner and arranged for eating out-of-doors.

A garden wall, a hedge, flower beds, a bird bath…

And someone sneaking away into the dark.

Even with the moonlight, it was too dark to tell who it was, but Sam wasn't going to let this opportunity pass. If it was Fletcher, he was going to confront him tonight.

The lawn muffled his footsteps when he stepped outside. He made his way carefully to the path that led beyond the garden, branching left and right.

Sam wasn't familiar with the terrain. He'd never considered the possibility that he'd be trying to navigate it in the dark, and had to be attentive at every

step. It wasn't easy to avoid all the roots and under-
brush that tried to trip him up.

Fletcher obviously knew where he was going. Sam
hoped he was carrying his "apparatus," for lack of
a more precise word to describe whatever he used to
make the "ghost" appear. If Sam could catch him
in the act of hiding the thing, that would be all the
proof he needed.

His hundred pounds would be in the bag.

Pleased to have resolved the mystery without having to waste too much time, he continued to follow
the shadowy form through the woods, toward the
meadow and down to the lake beyond. He moved
slowly, which allowed Fletcher to get quite a distance ahead, but even at his unhurried pace, Sam
tripped. Somehow, he managed not to fall, but
landed hard on one foot, jarring his healing ribs.
Cursing silently, he held the injured foot and hopped
on the other until the painful throbbing stopped.

Then he stood still and gave himself a moment to
catch his breath.

Glancing down the path, he saw that the head and
shoulders he followed were much farther away now,
and he could barely see the figure against the slightly
lighter background of the sky. Aware that hurrying
would very likely cause another mishap, Sam picked
his way carefully toward the lake.

When he was only a few yards from the sandy
beach, he stood beside a tree and tried to locate
Fletcher. The sound of a long, loud sigh caught his
attention, and he saw his quarry sitting on a rock
near the water. But it wasn't Fletcher.

It was a woman. Clearly delineated in the moonlight was Lilly Tearwater.

She raised her arms and loosened her hair, letting the inky mass cascade down her back and shoulders. Sam held his breath when she bent down toward the sand. A moment later, she held something away from her body and he wasn't quite sure what— *Her leg!*

She held one sleek limb fully extended, with her toes gracefully pointed, while she peeled down a stocking. Her movements were slow and seductive, enticing, though she had no reason to suspect she was not alone. She lowered her leg, then raised the other, while Sam gaped at her.

Any thoughts of her chicanery fled as wild imaginings streaked through his mind. He pictured himself approaching her, sliding his hands up those smooth legs, standing between them.

He clamped his lips together to keep from groaning aloud.

Her pale skin glowed in the silvery light and her loosened hair curled wildly down her back. When she stood, she hiked up her skirts, exposing her bare legs from the knees down.

Sam gripped the tree and watched her wade into the water, chagrined that the only way he could enjoy a woman was from a distance. She took a few graceful steps, then kicked one foot, splashing water out in front of her. The action was controlled, with a subdued turbulence.

Excitement prickled at Sam's spine. How would she be if she lost her restraint?

His hands clenched tightly. Who was he fooling? Just because his masculine instincts had returned did not mean that he could follow through. Miss Tearwater was a lady.

And there was no room in Sam's life for her.

Had he encountered Lilly Tearwater before the Sudan, he would have joined her in the water, surprised her with his kiss, his caress. He would have sampled the wildness that lay barely concealed in her fiery eyes.

Chapter Six

The following morning, Lilly stood in the attic with her measuring tape in hand, studying the boarded-up window. She didn't know how many panes had shattered, but she thought it had been most of them, and she was going to have to pry off the boards and measure them to order replacements.

She needed to go into Asbury to pick up supplies today, so she might as well see if there was any window glass on hand at Beecher's Store so that Davy could get it repaired as soon as possible.

She picked up the hammer and was about to pull off the plank Mr. Temple had attached the night before when she heard a creak behind her. Assuming it was Davy Becker, she turned toward the sound. "You don't have to—"

But no one was there.

Surely she hadn't imagined the sound. It had been quite clear.

Picking her way across the cluttered attic space, Lilly looked out the opposite window and saw Davy cutting the lawn. Thoroughly puzzled, she stepped over to the narrow staircase and saw no one there.

It must have been her imagination. Shrugging off the incident, she returned to the task of removing the board across the window and took the measurements she needed.

Lilly's part-time assistant, Mrs. Bainbridge, stood at the front desk when she returned with her list in hand. Breakfast was long done and the guests had scattered. Charlotte was in the barn, watching Duncan with her kittens, and Davy still worked on the lawn.

Lilly did not know where Mr. Temple was. Not that it was any of her concern. He was probably down in the meadow, watching his bees…*dance*.

Mrs. Bainbridge came around the desk and handed Lilly another list. "You're nearly out of ink, and while you're in Asbury, you might stop at Mr. Crofton's and order more Ravenwell stationary."

Lilly added Mrs. Bainbridge's list to her own.

"And that comely young American asked for directions into town. You'll likely meet him on the road."

"Mr. Temple?"

Mrs. Bainbridge nodded. "The very one."

Lilly looked down at her clothes. It was the usual attire that she wore for work every day—a serviceable skirt and blouse. Probably too ordinary for town.

She decided that a quick trip to her room for a change of clothes would not be amiss.

Sam crouched beside an old, hollowed-out tree trunk that lay a few yards from the road. A good-size hive had been built in the rotting wood, and he

was able to get a close look at the worker bees as
they returned from their forays into the field.

It was difficult to concentrate on his work after the
sleepless night he'd spent. His bed was comfortable,
the room peaceful, but his memory of Lilly Tearwater's half-clothed romp in the lake had set his
blood on fire.

She certainly hadn't been hiding anything when
she'd stepped into the water.

Giving up on sleep, Sam had climbed out of bed
before dawn, dressed and gone down to the garden
to search the grounds. He'd wanted to get there before anyone had a chance to muddle the evidence of
trickery. But he'd found nothing.

And he hadn't managed to forget about Miss Tearwater.

He tried field work next. Taking the same path
he'd used to follow Lilly Tearwater the night before,
he'd gone to the chestnut tree and observed the bees
for a while. He'd made a few drawings and estimated
the supplies he would need to build a platform in the
branches. From there, he would observe and photograph the hive.

In the meantime, he decided to see if there were
any additional hives to observe during his stay at
Ravenwell. Miss Tearwater had mentioned bees
along the roadside, so he'd spent most of the morning tracking down the hives. There were two of
them, but only one was in a good position for ob-
servation. He had just decided to use the one in the
chestnut tree, as well as the one he was sitting beside, when he heard the approach of a wagon coming
from town.

He stood and walked to the road, reaching it as

Tom Fletcher pulled abreast. "Good morning to you," he said.

Sam greeted the man in turn.

"Everything all right at Ravenwell?"

"As far as I know," Sam replied. "I've been gone since daybreak."

"Give you a ride back?"

"No, thanks. I'm not quite finished here." Besides, he planned to walk to Asbury and see if he could order the supplies he would need.

"Ah, your bees."

Sam nodded and gestured toward a large sheep in the back of the wagon. "I thought sheep farmers let their sheep wander to graze."

Fletcher grinned. "This fellow will, too, once I get him home. I drove down to Coniston yesterday to buy him. He's a good healthy ram. The ewes have been asking for some new blood." He chuckled at his own jest.

"Yesterday?"

"Aye. So I'm anxious to be home. Left my aging mother alone for the night."

"I'm sure she's all right." Sam was baffled. If not Fletcher, who had been the one to stage last night's ghostly performance? It hadn't been Lilly Tearwater—at least, not last night. Perhaps it was someone else at Ravenwell—the young fellow cutting the lawn?—who was culpable.

"I'll be off, then," said Tom. "I'll probably see you at the inn later."

"Sure."

Fletcher drove off and Sam shrugged. His absence the previous night was just another part of the puzzle. Someone had been responsible for putting on the show. Sam just hadn't figured out who yet, or how. But he'd eliminated the primary suspect. Maybe he shouldn't have discounted Miss Charlotte as a possibility. Just because she was deaf didn't mean she couldn't understand the principles of the game, or that she wasn't capable of carrying it out.

Or perhaps it *was* Lilly. And maybe she'd gotten rid of whatever mechanism she'd used when she'd walked to the lake last night.

Sam forced his thoughts from his intriguing landlady and returned to the place where he'd left his knapsack. He swung his pack onto his back and started down the road to Asbury. By the time he'd walked about a mile, he heard the sound of a horse and wagon coming up behind him. He stepped off the road and saw that it was Lilly Tearwater at the reins.

Miss Tearwater was the key to understanding what was going on at Ravenwell. And to get her to talk, Sam was going to have to get into her good graces.

Her interest in foreign cultures would likely start her talking to him again. It had been impossible for him to miss her curiosity about Egypt and Greece, and there was plenty that he could tell her. Things that no book would ever describe.

Even without Tom's forewarning, Lilly would have recognized Samuel Temple at a distance. His tall frame, those broad shoulders and narrow hips, that long, athletic stride…no other man in the district looked like him.

She was still flummoxed by his insinuation that Tom was responsible for the haunting of Ravenwell. Lilly supposed that as a man of science, Mr. Temple would naturally have a skeptical attitude. Still, she did not appreciate the implication that she, or anyone else at Ravenwell, was a fraud. She was an honest woman at heart, even though she might be an oddity. She did not care to consider what he would think if he knew the truth about Ravenwell's ghosts.

He turned as she drew closer, and took off his hat in a friendly greeting.

She pulled alongside him. "You're on the Asbury road, Mr. Temple."

He nodded. "Lucky for me, since that's where I'm headed."

His bright blue eyes gazed into hers. Lilly shifted in her seat, refusing to be captivated by his good looks or anything he might say. "Nice day for a walk," she said, dismissing him as she released the brake on the wagon.

In one quick move, he vaulted onto the seat beside her. "But even better for a ride."

Irritably, Lilly snapped the reins and continued on toward Asbury. Mr. Temple kept his distance, but she could smell the outdoors on him, and the soap he'd used. His scent filtered through her senses, settling somewhere in the back of her mind.

What did he think of her? He did not seem to mind riding with her, although he'd situated himself far enough away that they would not inadvertently touch.

Lilly wondered what he would say if he learned of her talents—that she was an aberration of nature, surely. Possibly that she was an instrument of evil.

She bit her lip. "Is there something in particular in Asbury that you want to see?"

"I assume there's a decent mercantile…"

"Of course."

"And I need to get some lumber."

She looked over at him. "You're planning on building something?"

He nodded. "In the meadow. There's an old chestnut tree with an excellent hive. I've got to build a platform high enough and big enough to support me and my photography equipment."

"I have wood. Didn't you see it in the barn?"

"Those boards are too small. I'll need bigger planks."

"Did you study bees while you were in Sudan?"

He nodded.

"What was it like?" she asked. "The people?"

He stretched his legs to the side and settled in for the ride, quickly steering the discussion away from Sudan. Instead, he began to speak of one of his childhood adventures on a Greek island.

"My brother Cullen and I decided to stow away on a local fishing boat. I was about ten years old."

"Good heavens! Don't those boats go far out to sea? For days or weeks at a time?"

He nodded, grinning as she imagined the young boy would have done, coming up with such a plan. "That was the point. We sneaked out of the house in the middle of the night and ran down to the docks. We climbed onto the first ship we found, which turned out to be captained by a Frenchman, a friend of my father."

"Did he discover you?"

"Not right away," Mr. Temple said. "They put out to sea before dawn, but it wasn't until noon that they found us."

"What happened?"

"Well, sometime while we lay hidden together under a bolt of sailcloth, Cullen got the idea that we were pirates—that we could commandeer the ship and sail to Tahiti or some such place. We found some wooden stakes to use as weapons…"

"No!" An amused laugh escaped her.

"But Monsieur Etienne spiked our plans."

"What did he do?"

"He scared the tar out of us."

Lilly looked ahead and saw Asbury nestled at the base of the hills. She slowed the horse, loath to arrive in town before he'd finished his story. He hadn't embellished it at all, but Lilly could easily picture the two handsome young boys huddled together on the fishing boat. Or wielding their make-believe swords.

"Etienne D'Aubigne apprehended us as if we were actual pirates. He shackled and blindfolded us."

Lilly's heart jumped into her throat. Those poor little boys!

"Then he threatened to toss us overboard."

She turned to him, mouth gaping, appalled.

"He didn't," Samuel said with a grin.

She snapped her mouth shut.

"But Cullen and I did hard time for a month after that escapade. My father had us sifting sand at his dig site for thirty days." He pointed to the church spire at the far east end of town. "What's the name of that church?"

"Saint Jerome's. Reverend Graham is the vicar."

"Has it been there long?"

"What do you mean?"

"The church. When was it built?"

Lilly shrugged. "It's ancient. I'm not sure when it was constructed, but it's older than Ravenwell."

"Good. Then it will have records of your Sir Emmett and Lady Alice."

Every one of Lilly's senses came to full alert. "No...their bodies were taken away for burial. Their funerals did not take place in Asbury."

"The magistrate, then? Surely someone investigated? A reeve? Who would have been the authority then?"

She shrugged. "If there were any records, they were destroyed when most of the town burned in 1749."

He muttered something that Lilly could not make out.

"Here we are," she said. "The Asbury Mercantile. Will you want a ride back?"

"If I do, I'll look for you."

It would have been good form to hit the ground first, then help her down, but Miss Tearwater didn't give him a chance. Which was fortunate. He wouldn't have been able to lift her out of the wagon, anyway.

It had been sheer hell to sit so close to her and be unable to touch her. Especially now that he knew what was concealed under her skirts.

Sam dismounted and followed her into the stuffy mercantile. When Miss Tearwater spoke to the shopkeeper, her voice, low and appealing, cascaded through him. Desire hit him like a punch. A year ago, he wouldn't have stood gaping at her like a lustful adolescent. He'd have stopped the wagon before they reached town, and pulled her onto his lap. Then he'd have tasted those full, sweet lips of hers.

Thoroughly disgusted with himself, he stormed out of the shop. He wanted Lilly Tearwater with a fiery need that he would never be able to satisfy, not if his aversion to touch persisted.

He walked only a few steps before a truly frightening thought struck him. What if he was never, *ever* again able to make love to a woman?

That hadn't really bothered him until he'd come to Ravenwell. Just thinking about Lilly Tearwater and her soft, smooth skin made him ache for her touch.

But that would never happen. He'd never made a habit of seducing respectable women, and now he wasn't capable of seducing *any* woman.

Chapter Seven

It was a long walk back to Ravenwell.

Sam didn't mind it—he liked being able to exercise after his long confinement in the pit. He had a new appreciation for his freedom, and he needed to become accustomed again to using his muscles.

It had been nearly a year since he'd been freed. His body still became sore with overuse, and he was dealing with the prospect of spending the rest of his life without the pleasure of another's touch.

Kicking a small rock out of his way, Sam muttered a quiet curse. He took another look at the hive he'd chosen near the Asbury Road, then walked on to the inn, where tea was being served. He wondered if he could get Miss Tearwater to join him at his table, and perhaps talk frankly about the ghosts—not the rehearsed patter that she told everyone else. He'd recounted his adventure with Cullen on the Isle of Aegina. Perhaps she would be amenable to trading stories.

Surely the inn hadn't only recently become haunted. If Miss Tearwater had lived here since childhood, she must have some early memories of the ghosts. He wondered what she would say if he asked her.

Sam walked through the garden gate and encountered Miss Charlotte, who gestured excitedly, clearly indicating that he should follow her to the barn. She was not distressed, so Sam was certain there was nothing wrong with Duncan or the kittens. He glanced toward the inn, where he assumed Lilly would be circulating among her guests, then followed Charlotte, curious.

It was quite late in the afternoon, so the light in the barn was poor, but a lamp illuminated the far corner where the cat and her litter were nesting. There were odd, scraping sounds coming from the loft above, although it was clear that Charlotte was unaware of them. Sam had gotten no more than halfway to the far corner when a small wooden crate fell out of the loft with a crash, then Lilly Tearwater slipped halfway down a ladder.

She let out a small squeal and struggled to get a grip on the ladder to keep herself from falling, but landed in a heap on the floor. Sam stopped abruptly.

She appeared uninjured. Her hair tumbled wildly around her shoulders, while her skirts fluttered in disarray around her knees. One long tear split her dark stocking, from her calf to a hidden place beneath her skirts.

Sam's breath caught in his throat when Lilly lifted her skirts to check on the damage. She twisted her body slightly and groaned.

When she looked up and saw him, she pulled her hem down, drew up her knees and held them close to her chest. At the same time, she touched one hand to her head and realized that her hair had come un-pinned.

She probably thought she looked awful, but Sam had rarely seen such a fetching sight. Lilly Tearwater was beautiful.

And Sam had no idea if he'd have been able to prevent her from falling if he'd reached her in time. Would he have reached out to her? Would instinct have prevailed over his aversion to touch?

"Mr. Temple! I—I didn't see you!"

"Are you all right?"

She started to move one hand to her hip, but reconsidered. "Yes. Fine. Perhaps my pride is a bit bruised, but I'm sure that's all."

Charlotte helped Lilly to her feet. Mortified to have made such a spectacle of herself, Lilly felt the heat of a blush darkening her cheeks. She started to brush dust and straw from her skirt, then realized she was only calling further attention to her mishap. She looked up to face Mr. Temple.

His hands were clenched into fists at his sides, and his face was as pale as her own was flushed.

"Truly, I'm all right, Mr. Temple," she said, to allay his obvious distress over her accident. "Was, er, was there something that you needed out here?"

He looked away for a moment, and when he turned back to her, he seemed more at ease. "Your sister intercepted me in the garden. I think she wanted to show me the kittens."

"Ah, yes. She told me earlier that we should invite you in to see the babies, since you'd had such a hand in the birth."

Mr. Temple came no closer, but his eyes slid down

Lilly's body, creating a coil of tension that made it
difficult for her to breathe. Perhaps if he touched her,
her heart would start beating again.

"Your skirt is torn."

Momentarily dazed, Lilly glanced down. "So it
is," she said, hardly recognizing her own voice.

Charlotte clapped her hands.

Lilly swallowed. "She wants you to come and see
Duncan's kittens."

Mr. Temple said nothing, but followed Charlotte
to the far corner, where Duncan had made her nest.
Lilly picked up the crate she'd dropped and assessed
its condition while she settled her nerves. The
wooden box was only slightly damaged. Lilly could
repair it easily with a hammer and a couple of nails.

What she could not easily do was understand Mr.
Temple's reaction to her fall. It had been a minor
mishap, certainly nothing to seriously trouble them.
But Mr. Temple had reacted as if…well, as if she'd
nearly lost life or limb.

Lilly carried the crate to an old worktable, took a
hammer from the shelf above it and thought about
Mr. Temple's puzzling reaction to her fall.

He was a tall, strongly built man, with hands that
had obviously done a good deal of manual labor. His
arms were thick with muscle, his back broad. He
walked and spoke with masculine confidence, having
traveled the world since his early youth. Obviously,
Mr. Temple was not a man to fear anything…

Except the possibility that she'd injured herself.

That was a notion that intrigued Lilly, even as it
made her bones melt. He seemed to care what happened to her.

She closed her eyes and imagined how it would

feel to caress his powerful shoulders, to touch her
lips to his sun-kissed skin. She flushed hotly at her
risqué thoughts as the barn door flew open and a
savage, unnatural wind blasted through.

Good Lord! It wasn't just a passing thought. *Lilly
had made it real!*

Charlotte ran past to shut the door against the
wind as Lilly turned to look at Mr. Temple. He appeared shocked, his eyes hot and fixed on hers. Lilly
swallowed hard. That look… It took her breath
away.

She whirled away from his gaze. What would he
think? That the improper caresses he'd felt had been
his imagination? Lilly could only hope that that
would be the case, and that he would fail to notice
the strange gust of wind.

"Miss Tearwater."

His voice, directly behind her, startled her. Bra-
zenly pretending she hadn't heard him, Lilly started
to hammer a nail into the plank that had broken off
the crate.

He moved to her side. "Miss Tearwater."

"What?"

She would surely die if Mr. Temple had any inkling that she had actually thought about touching
him in such an intimate fashion.

"I have the strangest…" He shook his head and
looked toward the door. "This weather—it's not at
all what I expected in midsummer. Do you often
have bursts of gale winds?"

The same wind and a few odd thunderbolts had
occurred on the evening of Mr. Temple's arrival, but
that had been the result of the cleanup Lilly had
done. Certainly it hadn't had anything to do with…

Lilly bit her lip. When she'd first seen Mr. Temple, she'd experienced an overpowering desire to run her hands across his strong shoulders. She'd wanted to slip her fingers up his nape and into his hair.

And then the gaslights had gone out.

"I...we..." She couldn't choke out the words. Her magic had never just *slipped out.* Before now, Lilly had always been in complete control of it.

Samuel's eyes narrowed and Lilly turned away from their scrutiny. She attempted to speak naturally, without tripping over her words. "We...sometimes have odd weather in midsummer. This is England, Mr. Temple. It might rain at any time."

"I wasn't talking about rain."

With forced nonchalance, Lilly shrugged and finished hammering the nail into the crate. When it was intact again, she carried it to Duncan's corner, where Charlotte again knelt, avidly watching the kittens.

Lilly put the crate on the floor and signaled to Charlotte that she could place Duncan and the kittens in it now. Then Lilly would be free to go back to the inn, to the privacy of her rooms, where she could think through this odd turn of events.

"Mama Duncan probably won't allow it," Mr. Temple said, breaking into her thoughts.

Lilly stole a glance at him. He stood, tall and forbidding, with his hands on his hips, watching her.

"She's already got her nest. She won't be ready to move her litter for a while."

"But I told Charlotte she could move Duncan into our apartment."

"Not yet."

Lilly felt his eyes on her back, brooding and questioning. But there were no explanations to be made.

Mr. Temple would have no choice but to attribute all those strange sensations to his imagination. Obviously, no one had actually touched him.

Although Lilly wished she could.

It was a thoroughly improper thought, but ever since she'd dealt with his bee sting, that desire had hovered there, just under the surface—the yearning to feel the heat of his skin, the dark rasp of his whiskers, the soft texture of his hair.

Lilly told Charlotte they would have to wait until Duncan was ready to move her kittens. Charlotte turned to Mr. Temple and, in her own way, asked how long. Mr. Temple held up seven fingers, as if he'd been communicating with her all his life. "One week," he said.

Charlotte's shoulders slumped at his answer, while Lilly stood gaping at their exchange.

"What?" Somehow, Sam managed to stay calm, even though conflicting emotions warred within him.

"It's just that…well, only Tom and I… No one takes the time to figure out how to talk with Charlotte."

"It's not that complicated," he said, distracted.

Could it have been his desire, plain and simple, that had caused him to feel Lilly Tearwater's hands all over his body? Surely that had not been the case the first time it had happened, because he hadn't even met her then.

But what about now? Was his mind somehow tricking him into feeling this woman's touch, since the physical reality could never take place?

Sam wanted to touch her, too. He wanted to take her down to the beach where he'd seen her lift her skirts to wade in the water, wanted to lay her down on the sand.

Arousal flooded through all his senses. Sam didn't know what was worse—the physical need or the impossibility of ever satisfying it again. Of never knowing true heart-stopping intimacy with a woman.

With no small discomfort, he walked out of the barn and down the path to the chestnut tree. The cure for what ailed him was simple—he would occupy his mind with work until all thoughts of Lilly Tearwater had faded.

When he reached the tree, he climbed to a branch above the hive, then lowered himself to the bough where he would build his platform. He tried to concentrate on the activity of the hive, but couldn't erase Lilly and the fascinating sensations from his thoughts.

What was it about this place? It couldn't be haunted, yet he'd found no evidence of trickery. Lilly had not physically touched him, but every nerve in his body tingled with the sensation of her soft hands caressing him.

Sam entertained the possibility that he was losing his mind. Certainly his body was not the same since Sudan. Why should his sanity have been spared?

He dropped to the ground and followed the narrow path to the beach. He still wanted Lilly Tearwater with a disturbing ferocity. He wanted her under him, clutching him, moaning his name when he pleasured her.

He walked across the sand to a private cove, then kicked off his shoes. He tore off his shirt, then dropped his suspenders and trousers, anxious to douse his sensual fixation in the lake. When he was naked, he ran into the water, making a shallow dive, then swam until the muscles in his arms screamed for respite. But even then he kept on stroking, until exhaustion extinguished the fire that drove him.

Sam didn't know how long it took before his lust finally died, but his muscles felt loose as jelly when he stepped out of the water. Standing in the brilliant orange light of the sunset, he used his shirt to dry himself, then pulled on his trousers.

There had to be a way to find some peace.

The most likely course would be to give up on his ridiculous wager with Jack. He should return to London and write up his Sudan research as he remembered it, then present it to the Royal College. Once he had his own flat and the post at the college, he could settle into a routine.

Sam was so immersed in his thoughts, he did not hear the startled gasp behind him. But the words that followed were uttered in little more than a whisper. "Dear heavens, what happened to your back?"

Chapter Eight

Lilly was horrified by the angry red scars that criss-crossed Samuel Temple's back, and even more appalled that she'd exposed her shock aloud.

Keeping his back to her, he jerked on his shirt, covering the recent wounds. ''I paid the price for being in the wrong place at the wrong time.''

She closed the distance between them and would have put her hand on his arm if he hadn't shrugged away from her. He grimaced slightly before bending over to pick up his shoes and stockings.

''It must have been terrible!'' she exclaimed.

Shaking the sand out of his shoes, he walked to the flat rock Lilly always used to remove her own shoes, and sat down. ''Yeah. Terrible,'' he muttered.

''Is that why you always withdraw from me? You'd rather not be touched?''

In silence, he pulled on his stockings, then his shoes.

''You hated it when I put the ointment on your bee sting.'' She remembered how he'd squirmed. And the way he always moved out of range whenever anyone got too close.

She couldn't blame him. After seeing those wounds, Lilly imagined how his skin would crawl if anyone came near. She understood that he wouldn't want to talk about it, either.

"All of the guests are in the garden waiting for an apparition," she said.

"Do you think the ghosts will give a performance tonight?" He seemed relieved at the change of subject.

"I don't know. Our ghosts are unpredictable." The lie was becoming tedious. Lilly wished she could pack up her things and go as far from Ravenwell as her money would take her. She would travel on trains and ships. She would ride a camel in Egypt and a gondola in Venice.

If only she were not so tied to the inn.

"Your vicar doesn't know what to make of the ghosts."

"Reverend Graham?"

It was nearly dark now, but Lilly was able to see Samuel's head bob once. She took a seat on the rock next to him, but not too close. "He wouldn't. I don't think he's ever seen them."

"No. At least, that's what he said," Sam remarked. "And he told me there were no records dating prior to 1749."

"You and Reverend Graham must have had quite a visit." Lilly was annoyed that he'd felt the need to check up on her, but the idea that the vicar had discussed Lilly's ghosts made her distinctly uncomfortable. A little bit of harmless deceit for business was one thing, but to mislead a man of the cloth…

"His son asked about you."

This didn't surprise Lilly. "How is Alan?" The

younger Reverend Graham had performed services the previous Sunday, and he'd told her that he expected to take over his father's parish now that the vicar was nearing retirement.

"Pompous."

Lilly laughed. Yes, that was Alan Graham. Handsome, tall and as blond as a Viking raider, Alan had always made her uncomfortable with his righteous zeal. She was sure he was going to be a fire-and-brimstone pastor.

"Reverend Graham said he plans to come out to the inn some evening to see if he can catch sight of the ghosts."

That thought gave Lilly pause. "With Alan?"

"Alan was particularly interested."

"So are you," she remarked.

"Of course. Is there a man of science in all the world who wouldn't like to prove the existence of ghosts?"

"But you want to *disprove* it."

"It's all a matter of perspective."

Lilly bit her lip. That was easy for him to say. Sir Emmett and Lady Alice were the only means Lilly had found to make Ravenwell even halfway prosperous. If Mr. Temple spread the word that the ghosts were a sham, business would suffer. She wouldn't be able to pay off Maude's loans, and she and Charlotte would never be able to crawl out of debt.

"What would convince you that Sir Emmett and Lady Alice are real?"

"What difference does that make, since it's not something you can control?"

"I just wondered." She picked up a handful of

sand and let it drift through her fingers. "What is the kind of evidence that would convince a man of science?" While they talked, Lilly sensed an easing of the tension that had shimmered from Samuel only moments before.

The peaceful setting was responsible. She often came to the beach alone—when she was happy, or when her troubles seemed overwhelming. She'd never shared this place—her own perch near the water—with another. But sitting here, chatting with Samuel, seemed the most natural thing. She even considered telling him the truth about the ghosts.

But quickly thought better of it. *No one* could ever learn of her talent. As Maude had warned, Lilly would be considered an oddity at best, a Satan-worshipper at worst. She did not relish the prospect of being labeled a witch.

"I imagine business has been quite good since the Ravenwell ghosts started making appearances."

Lilly studied his profile against the darkening sky. He seemed relaxed, yet she knew that if she ventured any closer, he would stand abruptly and withdraw. "People come to see them," she said quietly.

They sat together as lovers might do, but there was an unbreachable space that separated them. Attraction shimmered between them, yet the slightest touch—much less a kiss—was forbidden to them.

Lilly would caress his hair, would thread her fingers through the glossy thickness, if he only would allow it. She would touch her lips to his—

"Look at that!" Samuel stood as a sudden burst of shooting stars rained over the lake.

Lilly winced. Once again, her desire had inadvertently translated into physical form. Samuel brushed a hand over his mouth and looked down at her, then up at the sky.

At least the shooting stars hadn't caused any damage she would have to repair.

It was the damnedest thing. Sam could have sworn that Lilly had touched his lips, but that was impossible. She hadn't moved any closer to him.

But the sensation had been exquisite. He was as aroused as if she'd pulled open his shirt and run her tongue over his nipples. He had smelled her scent and felt the soft texture of her lips, just as the shooting stars lit up the sky. The tiny lights were every bit as stunning as the sensations he'd felt only a second before.

"That was…" Lilly's voice sounded strained, as if she'd felt the same sensations. She cleared her throat and changed her tone. "Well. I've never seen such an…unusual display."

Neither had Sam. Not in the desert sky, or over the open sea. He'd certainly never experienced anything like Lilly's touch—or whatever had happened between them. He was beginning to believe there *was* something strange about Ravenwell. He turned to take hold of Lilly's shoulders, to force her to explain all these unsettling events that he'd recently witnessed. He desperately wanted to haul her into his arms and feel her feminine curves against his body, to bury himself deeply inside her to ease this intense craving.

But he could not. A horrible dread filled his chest when he thought of touching her, and his hands trembled. He took a few deep breaths and balled his hands into fists, even as he craved her touch.

He wanted her as badly as he needed to escape her.

The turmoil in his head made it feel as if it would explode. He raked his fingers through his hair and across his scalp as if that would somehow contain the chaos going on inside. He stood abruptly. "I'm going back."

When she got up to follow him, he felt another burst of alarm. He didn't want her to come along. He needed time to settle his nerves, to try to figure out what was happening between them, what was going on at Ravenwell.

"Miss Tearwater," he said suddenly, turning to face her. She was so lovely in the moonlight. Every muscle in his body clenched with the desire to take her in his arms and carry her to some private bower where he could make love to her until dawn.

She looked up at him expectantly, and Sam turned away.

"The scars you saw…" He clasped his hands behind his back, then forced out his next words. "They barely scratch the surface of what was done to me when I was imprisoned in Sudan."

Sam detested having to admit to such weakness. Any one of his brothers would have survived the same imprisonment and tortures without this bizarre consequence—this crippling revulsion to being touched. "I cannot…Miss Tearwater…" He turned to face her again. "You are so beautiful, so capable. Any man would be flattered to receive your notice. But I…"

A slight frown marred her brow, but Sam took a deep breath. "As much as I would like to touch you—'' he swallowed ''—to steal a kiss, it is beyond me.''

Though it was ungentlemanly, and perhaps cowardly, Sam left Lilly standing on the sand and made his way along the path that led to Ravenwell's garden. Though it was a beautiful night, none of the guests were outside when he entered through the gate. Supper was long past, and the inn's guests were probably waiting for ghosts to appear somewhere inside.

All those people should have been outdoors, looking at the sky when it had been filled with shooting stars. That was the true magic. Sam felt restless and shaky, his muscles tired from his swim. He still didn't understand what had come over him at the beach, how he could possibly have felt Lilly's touch.

But it left him wanting.

He lit a cheroot and took a seat at one of the tables on the stone terrace to settle down before retiring. The sight of those shooting stars had been one of the most amazing things he'd ever seen—hundreds of pinpoints of light cascading across the sky.

And just as he began to wonder what the astronomers would say about it, Lilly came through the gate. Walking with purpose, she went to the service door that led into the kitchen, and disappeared.

Sam inhaled deeply of his cheroot, then tossed it away in disgust. He could hardly believe that his life had come to this—sitting alone in the dark, letting a beautiful woman slip away.

He leaned his elbows on his knees and propped his chin on his hands. Safe and dull. That's what he had to look forward to.

Prior to his experience in Sudan, Sam had lived

for the next challenge, the next adventure. He knew that life in London was going to be a deadly bore, but the thought of another adventure in an exotic locale made his palms sweat and his heart pound. Sam knew he would never again be able to endure the jostling crowds of Persia or Africa, or the physical contact of another human being. The mere thought of leaving England's civilized shores made him queasy.

He had no choice but to seek the post in London. Any further consideration was pointless, and the sooner he accepted that fact, the better.

Tomorrow he would build his platform in the chestnut tree and get on with the study he'd started in Sudan. He estimated he needed at least six weeks to reproduce the work he'd lost there. After that, another two months to write the article that would footnote the work of the other naturalists who had gone before, and then his own conclusions. By year's end, the appointment to the Royal College would be his.

The idea didn't particularly please him, but he wouldn't dwell on it. He wasn't going to be able to—

Someone slipped quietly into the garden and stopped near the building, directly across from Sam. It was a man, judging by his height, but Sam could not see him well enough to recognize him. The fellow looked to the left and right, then crept stealthily to the door that Lilly Tearwater had entered only a few minutes before.

Sam wondered if this was the culprit who was putting on Ravenwell's frequent haunting performances. It was unlikely that Fletcher was involved, but

Sam was sure someone around here must be doing it.

When the fellow slipped inside and closed the door quietly, Sam got up and followed him. He stepped through the doorway and looked within, but there was no light. He could barely see the shadows of the tables and chairs that he knew were there. Nothing moved.

Sam remembered that there was a large pantry in the wall to the right, and a stairway to the root cellar directly opposite him. Perhaps the man had already left the room, or was hiding in the pantry. He was probably preparing for another ghostly display.

A whisper of sound at Sam's left made him turn.

But he saw nothing. After his months in dark confinement, his night vision should have been better. Instead, the absolute darkness of the room—so similar to the pit where he'd been held in Sudan—nearly paralyzed him.

Sam suddenly realized he needed to make his way into the light before panic seized him. He took one step forward, and then another.

And then he felt it—someone in the room with him, circling around him, behind him. He was without a weapon, just as he'd been in the dark pit. Except that in the pit, his attackers had brought candles.

The back of Sam's neck prickled with awareness of the enemy. His skin became chilled and clammy, and his breath caught in his throat. Dropping to a crouch, he prepared for the attack, though he knew there was nothing he could do when they pinned his arms and started slashing.

But his jailers were strangely quiet this time. He

could only hear the faint whisper of breath, the slight rasp of cloth.

Sam blinked sweat from his eyes. He had to strike first—had to show them that he was unafraid and would resist whatever torture they had planned. He lashed out with his fist, but his target somehow managed to dodge the blow.

Sam spoke in Arabic, his voice a quiet threat. "I'm right here," he whispered in the language of his captors. "Come and get me."

A fist slammed into his shoulder, knocking him off balance. He returned the punch, his knuckles connecting with flesh and bone, but his enemy remained silent.

"Bastard!" Sam growled, moving aside.

Metal crashed to the floor, then something hard hit Sam on the side of his forehead. It stunned him long enough for his jailer to run out and escape. A wave of dizziness hit Sam when he tried to stand.

He braced himself, but fell against a table, losing consciousness when he hit the floor.

Chapter Nine

A loud crash brought Lilly into the kitchen. With the aid of a lamp, she saw Samuel lying on the floor, bleeding from a gash in his head. On the floor beside him lay two of the pans that Mr. Clive kept hanging on a rack near the stove.

Samuel must have hit his head on them in the dark.

Lilly set the lamp on the table and got a clean cloth from a drawer, then pumped cold water onto it. She returned to Samuel, carefully pressed the cloth to the wound, aware that he would never allow her to lavish such attention on him if he were conscious.

The cut was deep and would require stitching…

Unless she did something about it before he regained consciousness.

She told herself that it was perfectly sensible to repair the damage before he came 'round. No one else knew of his mishap, and if the unforeseen consequence of mending his wound was as benign as those shooting stars, then there was no need to worry.

Half a second later, Samuel was coming to, rubbing his head, sitting up. Lilly knelt beside him, but kept her hands to herself.

"What happened?"

"You must have bumped your head on one of Mr. Clive's pots." She pointed to the rack above the worktable.

Lilly hardly noticed his dubious expression as she wondered whether anything had shattered, burst or crumbled somewhere in the inn. Perhaps there'd been a bolt of lightning or another shower of shooting stars. She hadn't heard any untoward noises, but there must have been *some* consequence resulting from her meddling.

"Are you all right?"

He moved his hand from his forehead and looked at it as if he expected to see blood. "I was sure I…" He glanced at the heavy skillet that lay on the floor beside him, then up at the rack over the worktable.

Lilly didn't like his frown or the questions she saw in his eyes. Suddenly realizing that the damp cloth she held was still bloody, she tossed it into the dry sink before he could take note of it.

"Were you looking for a bite to eat?" she asked, to divert his attention. It was a reasonable question, since he seemed to miss meals fairly often. The only other reason he might have had for coming into the kitchen—checking for evidence of chicanery—was extremely unflattering to her, though she could not deny that his instincts were good.

"No. I…" He frowned again. "I had a smoke out on the terrace. Decided to come in through here when I was done."

He was prevaricating. Lilly was sure of it, but resisted assuming the worst.

She was also very careful with her thoughts, afraid that one of them would inadvertently take shape the way it had done a little while ago at the lake. She blushed at the thought of it.

"Next time, perhaps you should light a lamp."

Rising to his feet, he made a low sound in his throat. Lilly changed the subject. Better to divert his attention from his mishap with talk.

"I forgot to mention… The lumber you purchased in Asbury is still in the wagon in the barn. There was no point in having Davy unload it, since you'll want to cart it somewhere tomorrow."

In the light of her small lamp, his eyes seemed dark, suspicious. "I'll only need the horse and wagon for an hour or so." He still sounded dazed.

"It's no matter. I'll have Davy hitch the horse so you'll be able to go right after breakfast." She attempted normalcy in her tone in hope that he would be distracted from the strangeness of the evening's events. "Perhaps you should go to your room and lie down, Mr. Temple. It's late, and you're looking rather pale."

He seemed to study her. "I guess I will." They stood together. "What the hell?"

Every cupboard door stood open, casting long, ominous shadows to the ceiling. Lilly felt fortunate that the consequence of healing Mr. Temple's wound hadn't been any worse.

"Oh, uh… I suppose it was Sir Emmett or Lady Alice. They sometimes make mischief. Well, good night."

His posture made it clear that he didn't believe a

word she said. She did not venture to look into his
eyes, but handed him the lamp and left abruptly. She
went to the reception desk and let herself into
the office, then to her apartment, where Charlotte
worked in their small kitchen, ironing blouses, oblivious to Lilly's comings and goings.

Lilly stood with her back to the door, willing her
heart to slow. She sighed and watched her friend.
There were times when Lilly wished her own life
were as simple and uncomplicated as Charlotte's.
She longed to be content to stay at Ravenwell.

Charlotte loved the place. She took great satisfaction in all the little details of their life at the inn,
while Lilly yearned to be free of it, to travel to the
faraway places she would only ever visit in her
books.

Sam studied his reflection in the mirror over his
washstand. He would swear that his assailant had
sliced open a piece of skin on his forehead, yet there
was no sign of any gash—not even a scratch. He
was starting to believe he was losing whatever tenuous grasp he had on his sanity.

Sam gripped the washstand with both hands and
lowered his head. He should just forget about the
bee project and the wager and return to London. He
was accomplishing nothing here besides turning his
life upside down. Shooting stars, phantom caresses
and ghosts. He *was* losing his mind.

After spending another restless night in his Ravenwell bed, Sam took another look at his forehead.
He must have been mistaken about the blow that had
knocked him cold. That's what had distorted everything. There was no other logical explanation.

Though logic had played little part in all that had happened in the past year.

A life within the safety of London's boundaries was never going to appeal to Sam. He hadn't forgotten the thrill of his past adventures; he just couldn't imagine facing them again—not when he could barely abide the touch of a beautiful woman. Not when he spent nights in a cold sweat, afraid of hidden shadows that might hold him down and do their worst.

He sat at the desk in his room and took out the letter he'd begun to Mr. Phipson in Bombay. Sitting with his pen in hand, he considered how to word his refusal of the invitation.

He hadn't been to India in ages—not since at least six or eight years before, when he'd joined his parents and siblings for a month together in Karnataka. They had stayed near his father's excavation site near the Hoysala Temple, then traveled to various parts of the province, visiting a number of ancient wonders. At the time, Sam had thought of several different projects he might have pursued in India, and he'd looked forward to returning some day.

He was about to pass up a very good opportunity to do so.

He ran one hand over his face and sighed. This was not a good time to write to Mr. Phipson. He needed to do it after a good night's sleep, when his mind was clear. Folding the letter, he slipped it into the battered leather portfolio that had traveled the world with him. It was one of the few possessions that had been recovered from his jail near Khartoum.

Half an hour later, he was driving the Ravenwell wagon down the path toward the chestnut tree. He had borrowed tools from Davy Becker, the young man employed to do odd jobs for Lilly. Sam had already taken measurements and drawn a detailed plan of the platform. He was sure it would take no more than a few hours to build it.

He had gotten as far as the place where the path split when he encountered Miss Charlotte, carrying a large basket of ripe vegetables toward the inn. She greeted him with a wave and signaled a question. *Where was he going?*

Before Sam could figure out how to answer her, she had placed her basket inside the wagon and was climbing up. Sam didn't mind her company, but he'd gotten the distinct impression that Lilly would not want Charlotte to go off with him.

Unfortunately, when he tried to convey his doubts about her coming with him, she did not appear to understand.

Sam drove the wagon toward the water and turned off the path near the chestnut tree. When he stopped, he began to unload the supplies he'd bought in Asbury. Charlotte helped. His ability to communicate with her was improving significantly.

Interpreting the questions she asked in her own way, Sam took out the drawings he'd made of the platform and showed them to her. Then he pointed to the hive in the tree, which was a good three yards above the ground.

Charlotte's eyes widened when she realized what he planned to do.

Sam enjoyed this part of the project. He could immerse himself in the task, emptying his mind so that his memories did not intrude. He could put Lilly Tearwater from his mind and set aside the intense desire he felt whenever she was near. Working with his hands took his full attention.

Sam slung a coil of thick rope over his head and arm like a bandolier, then climbed the tree. He straddled the thick branch that lay nearly perpendicular to the hive, while he devised a pulley to haul up the lumber he would use.

When he climbed down, he came face-to-face with an angry Lilly Tearwater. Charlotte was not in sight.

"Mr. Temple," she said. She wore a simple blouse and skirt, attire that should not have been alluring in the least. She pressed one hand to her breast as her violet eyes flashed hotly. "I don't allow Charlotte to cavort with strangers."

"Cavort?"

"Associate, keep company, consort. She is compromised by her deafness." Then she sighed and let her hands drop to her sides. "I'm sorry," she said simply as her anger faded. Or perhaps Sam had been mistaken and it had not been anger that he'd seen. "I worry… I sent her down to Mrs. Webster's farm for fresh produce. She was gone for an awfully long time."

Lilly had beautiful hands, delicate and expressive when she spoke. It was no wonder he'd imagined their touch, time and time again. What normal man would not?

She glanced up at the tree and Sam couldn't help but admire the elegant lines of her throat, her delicate ears…

He swallowed. "Are you sure you don't mind all this?"

"Of course not."

"I'm going to hang a rope ladder here." He

pointed out the broad branch across from the hive where he would construct his platform. "The tree is dead, but I won't do much more damage to it."

She nodded, and Sam remembered that he would have to get her talking if he was going to learn anything about the Ravenwell phantoms.

"You'll watch the bees from there?"

He nodded. "I'll be taking photographs, too. That's why I have to build the platform."

"What will you do if it rains? Won't your camera be ruined?"

He took out the drawing that he'd shown Charlotte. "I plan to hang a canvas canopy above it."

She pulled her lower lip through her teeth as she studied the drawing, and Sam suppressed a shiver of arousal. The attraction he felt was pointless. Even if he could overcome his trauma and touch her, it would be entirely improper.

"You said that the bees dance?"

"It's as good a word as any to describe the movements the workers make when they return to the hive."

"I've never noticed it."

"You probably don't spend a lot of time watching hive activity."

She laughed. "You're right about that."

"It's my theory that, over the centuries, the foragers evolved to develop a method of communication with bees in the hive."

"About food."

She remembered, and Sam was inordinately pleased. "The workers make specific movements when they return to the hive. I was in the process of documenting those movements while I was in Sudan. I plan to finish the project here."

Sam wasn't going to give her a long lecture on Mr. Darwin's theories. He just wanted to get her comfortably conversant with him, so that she would eventually open up.

He wanted no more intimate moments such as those in the barn or beside the lake. Just enough information to lead him to an explanation of the ghosts and to the hundred pounds that Jack would owe him.

"Does your work have anything to do with Mr. Darwin's theories?" she asked.

Sam nearly dropped the planks he held. "You know about evolution and adaptation?"

"Some," Lilly replied. "I don't understand why Reverend Graham believes Mr. Darwin's theory is antithetical to creation."

"It isn't."

"I didn't think so, either. Believing in Darwin's evolution theory doesn't necessarily negate the notion of a creator, or of creation."

Sam gaped at her. Then he snapped his mouth shut and carried the lumber to the base of the tree. He couldn't have been more surprised if the Ravenwell ghost had appeared then and there, sitting on a branch of the chestnut tree, dangling its legs high above them.

Lilly would have to have lived in a cave to miss hearing of Charles Darwin and his radical theories. Mr. Graham had expressed his outrage from the pulpit on more than one occasion. Even Alan, a much younger man, had expressed displeasure with Darwin's work.

"Did you ever meet Mr. Darwin?" she asked Samuel.

"No. But my mentor was one of his students. He was killed in Sudan."

The tone and cadence of his speech changed, and Lilly heard anger and frustration in his voice.

"What happened?" she asked quietly.

He did not answer right away, and Lilly wondered if perhaps she should not have asked. She had no doubt that it was a painful subject...

"He was tortured to death. Before my eyes."

Lilly felt her knees go weak, but she placed one hand on the wagon for support. "Why was he killed?"

Her voice was a quiet addition to the peaceful afternoon. The birds chirped, squirrels chattered...but the two of them spoke of a brutal killing. A horrible murder.

Samuel looked at her starkly. "He was killed for no reason. There was a rebellion going on in the southern regions. When we were first taken, we believed we were hostages."

"But you were not?"

He shook his head and turned away. "Our captors cared nothing about the Mahdi or his demand for reforms. We were hapless victims of power-mad fanatics."

"You'll never go back, will you?"

He turned away and unloaded the rest of his supplies. "Subject myself to the whims of madmen again? No."

There was silence between them as Samuel tied

two of his planks to the rope, then climbed to the branch where he would build. Pulling in the rope, he raised the lumber to his level. Lilly had work of her own to do, but it was fascinating to watch him. Surely Tom Fletcher had never moved with such agility. Alan Graham did not have such broad shoulders and muscular thighs.

She blushed at the impropriety of her thoughts, especially after all that Sam had just said. He'd watched his friend be brutally murdered.

Lilly could not imagine such a dreadful thing, and she would not question him any further. She already knew more than he'd intended to tell her.

His hair was moist from his exertion, shoved away from his forehead by his fingers. There was no trace of the gash he'd suffered the night before, and since he didn't mention it, Lilly said nothing, either.

She could help him. He was miserable with his grief and his terrible fears. Lilly could use her talents to ease them...

She looked away in dismay. Helping Samuel would be as impossible as healing Charlotte's deafness. As Maude had said so many times, "Some things are meant to be."

The consequences of easing the memories of his time in Sudan could be devastating.

Chapter Ten

"Tell me about your ghosts, Miss Tearwater." He climbed up to the high branch, then braced himself against the tree trunk to pull up the lumber. "How many are there altogether?"

"Two." Thoughts of consequences disappeared as the muscles of his forearms flexed and bunched with his effort.

"Would you toss me that hammer and the bag of nails?"

She did so and he caught them deftly. He lowered himself to straddle the branch. "And these ghosts are male and female?" he asked, almost absently.

"Correct. Sir Emmett and L-Lady Alice." He was obviously warm. Perspiration had soaked a V in the back of his shirt from his shoulders to his waist.

"How do you know their names? Do they talk?"

Lilly had never been asked this question. She looked away for a moment to think through her reply. If she told him that they did speak, he would want details. If she said they did not, he would ask how she knew who they were.

"Lady Alice has spoken on occasion."

"Ah."

When he balanced one board in place and started hammering, Lilly wondered if he believed her. It was difficult to conclude anything from that simple "ah."

"She…once said that she'd been murdered." It was a bold-faced lie, but Lilly told it even though it made her uncomfortable. But perhaps this much information would thwart any further questions.

"And the knight? You were able to surmise his fate, too?"

Lilly gave a hesitant nod under his curious gaze.

He hammered the second board in place, then climbed down from the tree. After tying two more boards to the rope, he started to unfasten the buttons of his shirt. Lilly blushed to the roots of her hair at the sight of his muscular chest, with its light coating of coarse hair.

"Now would probably be a good time for you to head back to the inn," he said, pulling his shirttails out from his belt. "Unless you don't mind watching me work without a shirt."

Lilly would not have minded watching him work shirtless, but she knew that such a thing was entirely inappropriate for a lady. So she left him and returned to the inn, where she encountered Ada Simpson in the reception area. Mrs. Bainbridge was not in sight.

Miss Simpson stood at the desk, trying to communicate with Charlotte. By the time Lilly reached them, Miss Simpson's color was high and she was tapping her foot. Clearly, what little patience the woman possessed was gone.

"Oh, thank goodness you're here," Miss Simpson said when she saw Lilly. She held the same small package she'd brought with her the other night, and Lilly concluded that the woman hadn't yet managed to meet with Mr. Dawson. "Finally, someone who—"

"Is something the matter?"

"I just can't get this...this *person* to understand that I am looking for Mr. Dawson."

Lilly managed to control her anger at the way the woman spoke of Charlotte, and turned to the desk to jot a quick note. Giving it to Charlotte, she asked her to take it to Mr. Dawson's room and wait for a reply. Then she spoke to the chemist's sister.

"Miss Simpson. Charlotte is merely deaf. There is nothing wrong with her mind." Lilly tried to keep the irritation she felt out of her voice, but found it difficult. Many of the people of Asbury treated Charlotte as if she were an imbecile, rather than just deaf.

The woman was oblivious to the rebuke. With her backbone straight as a stick, she walked to one of the windows and stood gazing through the glass while she waited. Lilly considered stripping the spinster of *her* ability to hear, but decided that a bit of petty revenge was not worth the risk.

Unwilling to leave Miss Simpson to her own devices until Mrs. Bainbridge returned, Lilly sorted through the correspondence neatly stacked on the desk. She could keep every room in the inn filled every month of the year, though there was the occasional cancellation. Usually, it was not difficult to fill those rooms on relatively short notice, which was the primary benefit that Sir Emmett and Lady Alice brought to Ravenwell.

When Charlotte returned to the desk with Mr. Dawson behind her, Lilly paid no attention to the exchange between him and Miss Simpson, but considered the logistics of her day. Several of the guest rooms had been vacated that morning, and new guests would be arriving on the afternoon train. She would have to send Davy Becker down to Asbury to collect them.

"Here you are, Miss Tearwater," said Mrs. Bainbridge. She carried a stack of mail in one hand and an open letter in another. She came 'round the reception desk and eyed Miss Simpson and Mr. Dawson, who spoke quietly together near the door. "Now, there's a question."

Lilly smiled. "I'm afraid the answer might be too embarrassing to consider."

Mrs. Bainbridge laughed. "I would not be so sure," she said. "I've seen Mr. Dawson making calf eyes at you, m'dear."

"Don't be silly. He's..." But Lilly saw that he was hardly paying attention to Miss Simpson, who had threaded her arm through his as she spoke animatedly. "I—I'm sure you're mistaken."

Lilly shook her head and took the letters, retreating to the small office beyond the desk. She sat at her worktable and set out a large ledger, with her calendar beside it. She had a system for dealing with correspondence related to room reservations, as well as a method for scheduling the ghostly apparitions.

The ghosts could not appear too often or Lilly would constantly be cleaning up or repairing some minor disaster around the inn. Or trying to explain a strange disturbance in the weather.

She studied the list of current guests and saw that two of them did not have check marks beside their names, which indicated that they had not yet witnessed the ghosts. These two would leave the inn on Saturday, which gave Lilly only two nights to provide what they had come to Ravenwell to see.

With several new visitors arriving today, Lilly decided to wait one more night. That would allow anticipation to build among the new arrivals.

She took an hour to deal with all her correspondence, then checked on the maids who were working on the vacated guest rooms. The urge to shirk her duty had never been stronger.

Circling 'round to the back of the inn, she came upon Mr. Dawson and Miss Simpson sitting at one of the tables on the terrace, sipping tea. They seemed an unlikely pair, but Mr. Dawson was much more suited to a woman of Miss Simpson's age than her own. Anyway, Lilly had seen plenty of unusual couples during her years at Ravenwell.

Her favorites were the newlyweds. Though she couldn't understand anyone wanting to remain in tiresome England for their wedding trip, Lilly took pains to make their stay at Ravenwell special. Beautiful flowers, private morning tea service in the bedroom, romantic suppers on the terrace, rose petals on the bed linens every evening in summer...

She sighed. A simple room in Rome was what Lilly dreamed of as an ideal honeymoon. She would want to look out of her window and see the Piazza del Campidoglio—or some other equally spectacular sight. She wanted to hear something other than English spoken around her, to eat unfamiliar dishes and smell the foreign scents in the markets.

Lilly's thoughts wandered to Samuel Temple. She wondered about all the places he'd been, what other marvelous sights he'd seen. He was a puzzling man—so strong and virile at one moment, then human and vulnerable the next.

Lilly hurried across the lawn later that afternoon, wearing an apron and carrying a stack of clean, folded tablecloths from the laundry. She checked her mental list of things that still had to be done before tea as an open buggy pulled into the front drive. Asbury's mayor alighted and called to her. "Miss Tearwater!"

Lilly could not imagine what would prompt a visit from Mr. Hinkley, and would have preferred a moment to repair her hair and put away her apron before facing the mayor. But Mr. Hinkley gave her no opportunity.

Fortunately, the man seemed to understand honest work and would not think the worst of her.

"Good to see you, my dear," he said. Hinkley was a prosperous banker in Asbury. He was a portly man, no taller than Lilly. His wealth was evident in his attire, in the gold tooth that gleamed in the sunlight when he smiled at her, and in the large ruby ring that adorned the little finger of his right hand. "If I might have a word, Miss Tearwater?"

She nodded. "Of course. Shall we go inside?"

Lilly wondered what he wanted of her. Hinkley's bank held Ravenwell's mortgage and Maude's other outstanding loans, but Lilly had never been behind in the payments—at least, not since Sir Emmett and Lady Alice had appeared.

Lilly led the man into the sun parlor and sat down across from him. "I have a few ideas for your business that I would like to discuss with you," he stated.

"Oh?"

"Yes. Ways to improve upon your existing operation here." Restrained enthusiasm was reflected in the banker's eyes, in his posture.

Lilly had no interest in changing anything at Ravenwell, but she leaned forward as if she hung on every word he spoke.

"Of course, you are aware that the inn brings a great deal of business—wonderful prosperity—to Asbury," he said. "Several new shops have opened in the past two years, and there are plans for even more. Attendance at church is unsurpassed. The more business you bring to Ravenwell, the better we like it in Asbury."

"What do you propose, Mr. Hinkley?"

The banker leaned forward and placed his hands upon his knees. "Expansion."

He said it as though it were a revelation, an unprecedented vision of the future.

But Lilly had already thought of it. When the inn had started to make money, she had considered adding another wing, making enough rooms to host a hundred guests, maybe more.

But then sanity had returned. Ravenwell was well-suited to her needs. She and Charlotte lived very comfortably here, without having to hire more workers than she could manage.

"The Royal Cumbria Bank of Asbury is prepared to offer you the capital necessary to build—"

"Mr. Hinkley, I don't think—"

"Before you answer—" he held up one hand, palm out, to stop her "—I want you to consider one more thing—a coach line that would run from Asbury to Ravenwell. It would cover the journey here from the railroad station, freeing you from the task of having to send young Becker into town to collect your guests. Think of it. Hundreds of new visitors to our district every week.''

Lilly drew her lower lip between her teeth and studied Mr. Hinkley before responding. ''Your ideas…'' she finally said. ''Well, thank you for coming to discuss them. I'll consider everything you suggested, Mr. Hinkley.'' She rose from her chair. ''Thank you so much for coming.''

''Don't wait too long to think it over. We're well into the building season and it will take time to draw up plans.''

''You're very right. Well—''

''Plans for what?'' Samuel Temple asked.

''Mr. Temple, isn't it?'' Hinkley turned toward Samuel and extended his hand. ''We met yesterday in Asbury.''

Samuel looked at it as if it were a poisonous snake, poised to strike. His face paled and Lilly saw his throat move as he swallowed thickly. Without thinking, she dropped her linens at her feet.

''Oh, how clumsy!'' She bent down to retrieve her tablecloths, but Samuel and Mr. Hinkley also moved to help.

Somehow, Mr. Temple ended up with all the table linens piled in his arms. ''I guess I'll just take these…where?''

''Heavens, no! I'll just…'' She turned to the mayor. ''I'll consider your proposal very carefully, Mr. Hinkley. Now, if you'll excuse me…''

She reached to gather the linens from Samuel, but he moved aside. ''I've got them. Just tell me where they go.''

"Miss Tearwater," Hinkley said. "Bear in mind that the Royal Cumbria Bank will back you, whatever improvements you decide upon."

"Thank you again, Mr. Hinkley."

She turned in the direction of the inn's dining room and Samuel followed, causing a prickle of awareness to cascade down her spine. Did he realize that she'd intervened intentionally to keep him from being compelled to shake the mayor's hand? Now that it was done, Lilly felt embarrassed by her presumptuousness. She should have left him to deal with Mr. Hinkley just as he'd done with Mr. Payton the day before. Except that she'd seen his distress then, and wanted to prevent a repetition of it.

They entered the dining room and Samuel lay the linens on a long mahogany sideboard. "Thank you. I appreciate your assistance," she murmured.

He made no move to leave, but leaned against the sideboard, pinning a questioning gaze on her, but Lilly spoke first.

"Did you finish building your platform?"

He shook his head. "Not yet."

She was close enough to smell sunshine on him, and the pine needles that were stuck to his trousers. Lilly felt self-conscious under his perusal and slid an unruly bit of hair behind her ear. A heated awareness flashed in his eyes and her heart fluttered. If she moved one step closer, he would be near enough to touch, to kiss…

Lilly had never felt such a compelling attraction before. She'd never desired a man's touch, or his kiss, the way she yearned for Samuel's.

Even if he felt the same, Lilly would never allow such liberties. She'd been raised as a proper young lady.

"A favor, Miss Tearwater?" His voice sounded deeper, hoarser than before.

She swallowed and licked her lips. "Of course."

Their eyes met. Samuel leaned toward her, his lips slightly parted. Lilly felt his breath on her skin, saw the sheen of perspiration appear on his brow. A harsh breath escaped him. "I missed lunch. You wouldn't mind having a word with the kitchen staff for me?"

It wasn't what Sam had intended to say, but his request was entirely more appropriate. And possible.

She blinked those long, dark lashes, masking the expression in her eyes for an instant. "Why, y-yes, Mr. Temple. I can have the kitch— No, Mr. Clive will have started preparations for tea." She hesitated for a moment, then turned toward the door. "Come with me."

He walked beside her to the reception area, where the friendly, gray-haired Mrs. Bainbridge stood behind the reception desk, poring over maps and talking with a young couple who were about to go walking among the fells.

"This way, Mr. Temple," Lilly said, leading him around the desk into an office. It was clearly her office, with framed prints on the walls—pictures of Egyptian pyramids, the ruins of the Roman Coliseum and the Greek Parthenon.

A door at the far end of the office led to a private apartment.

"Charlotte and I have our own kitchen here," she said. "Rather than interfere in Mr. Clive's domain, we sometimes prepare our own meals."

Sam realized he had made some progress with her if she was willing to take him into her private rooms.

"I can make a small meal for you here, if you don't mind something simple."

"I appreciate it."

He enjoyed watching her. Every movement was done with purpose and confidence. Lilly Tearwater was a woman who knew what needed to be done, and she did it without thinking about appearances, or what anyone might say. Who else would have deliberately dropped her table linens to prevent him having to take Hinkley's hand?

Sam followed her into a small, sunny room with a table and two chairs. A compact stove was fitted into one corner between neat rows of cupboards, and there was a sink and water pump under the window.

Lilly put on an apron and stoked the fire under the kettle. Sam couldn't help but notice the way the band of the apron spanned her waist and the bib hugged her breasts.

Deliberately, he turned to look out the window, although he took no notice of the view outside. If he had found himself alone with a beautiful woman like Lilly Tearwater a year ago, he wouldn't have confined himself to just looking, merely appreciating her beauty.

By this point in their acquaintance, Sam would have gently moved her against the cupboard and placed one hand on either side of her. He'd have dipped his head, tasted the pulse point at the base of her throat with his tongue. Her feminine scent would have permeated his senses, her warm breath feathered over his forehead and hair. A slight shifting of his legs would bring his body in contact with hers, and she would recognize the intensity of his hunger for her. Her own quickening arousal would be unmistakable when she moved against him with a sigh…

Sam gripped the windowsill. Gritting his teeth, he put all his effort into restraining his lustful imagination. Such fantasies had no place in his life anymore.

He took a deep breath and turned toward her. "You ever see any ghosts in here?"

The almost imperceptible slowing of her movements nearly escaped Sam's notice. But not quite. She was on her guard. "Usually they're out in the garden."

"Usually" wasn't a good answer. But Sam didn't want to antagonize her. He wanted to get information from her.

"Even in winter?"

"It's likely, although no one spends much time out there when the weather is inclement."

He started to relax. Like her first reply, this answer was quick and clever without saying anything. "So they show up indoors then?"

She took out a knife and a block of cheese and began to cut. "They appear inside and out, all through the year, although I cannot vouch for any apparition that is not witnessed."

She filled his plate and handed it to him. "You saw Lady Alice and the broken attic window she caused. I don't understand why you're so skeptical."

"It must be my training," he said, taking a seat at her table. "A scientist learns to question most everything."

Lilly turned to the stove and busied herself pouring tea. Then she deliberately changed the subject. "You should keep better track of the time when you're working, Mr. Temple, so that you don't miss any more meals. Or I can have the kitchen staff prepare something for you to take with you on your forays."

"I'll bear that in mind." Sam decided not to push the discussion of ghosts, or she might withdraw from the conversation entirely. Better to pursue it another time. He started to eat. "You didn't seem very enthusiastic about the mayor's proposal."

"He wants me to expand Ravenwell."

"Isn't that a good idea? More space would mean more paying customers."

"Yes, but I'm satisfied with the size of the inn. It's no more than Charlotte and I can handle, and besides…" She shrugged and placed two cups of tea on the table.

"Besides?"

"It's nothing."

Her blush indicated it was anything *but* nothing, though it embarrassed her.

"There's no reason why you should have to enlarge the place. You're the owner—it's your decision."

She took off her apron and sat down across from him, curving her hands around her cup as she gazed absently into it. "True."

Her reasons for keeping Ravenwell unchanged had nothing to do with him. Expansion made perfect sense, but it would also mean a lot more work for Lilly. And there was a particular character to the place… It was small, intimate and friendly. Lilly spoke to each of her guests personally. She recommended sights to see, activities to pursue. That might well change if she added another wing.

A pensive crease appeared on her brow and her tongue darted out to moisten her lips. They were full and soft, ripe for a kiss.

Her eyes rose to settle on his hands, then up his chest to his neck. A moment later, her gaze reached his mouth. She had to know that he would not make any advances, and it wasn't only because of propriety. *He could not,* damn it, no matter how desperately his body craved her touch, her taste. But her breath quickened and her eyes darkened with arousal in spite of what she knew about him.

Chapter Eleven

A lock of Samuel's hair fell over his forehead and Lilly reached out and pushed it back without touching him. Instantly, a china teacup fell from the cupboard and smashed on the stove, but they hardly noticed. Samuel's eyes drifted closed while Lilly touched his neck and stroked his shoulders. She wished she could do more. She wanted to run her hands across his chest, and touch her lips to his...

The thoughts and desires that filled her mind were outrageous, of course. And pointless. But that did not stop her from using her power to touch his lips, to stroke his neck and his chest, to caress the muscles of his thighs.

When his dazed eyes drifted up to meet hers across the table, Lilly realized how far she'd gone. Shocked by what she'd done, she stood so abruptly that her chair nearly tipped over. She caught it before it could fall, righted it and scooted to the stove. "I—I must have left that cup on the edge of the shelf."

She started to brush the broken pieces of china into a dustpan, but Samuel came up behind her. He moved close, but maintained a distinct distance be-

tween them. "Lilly..." His voice was strained. "I
don't... Somehow, when I'm with you..." She
heard the harsh rasp of his sigh and turned toward
him. His face was a picture of pain and regret. "You
are so very beautiful. If only I..."

Her heart pounded with expectancy, but she did
not doubt the severity of his inner wounds. Whatever
lay between them would be left unexplored, buried.

"Lilly, if I were capable of touching you, making
love to you, nothing would stop me. And I'd be free
again. Free of the nightmare that keeps me shackled
here in the security of civilized society."

He shook his head, then turned and left her. He
walked out of her kitchen, out of the apartment.

Standing alone, she realized her own breathing
was ragged, her hands shaking. And she finally understood that if he ever managed to overcome his
fears and touch her, he would leave her.

By early evening, the platform was complete. Sam
built it as if it were a seaworthy raft. Smooth planks
made up the base and strong beams reinforced it
from underneath. He nailed the entire contraption to
a wedge of stout branches that supported it securely
at a height directly across from the hive.

He immersed himself in the work, managing to
escape being stung by the bees, and avoiding
thoughts of what had transpired in Lilly Tearwater's
kitchen. It was just so much nonsense, spawned by
his damaged mind, although he realized that what
he'd told her had been true. If he could overcome
his aversion to touch, the other terrors would abate.
And he would be free.

Standing on the solid platform, Sam reached up

and secured the canvas tarpaulin over his work area, making sure that it was entirely protected in case of rain. His camera and plates were too valuable to leave at the mercy of the elements. So were his notes and drawings.

All of his work in Sudan had been lost. He'd had to replace his camera and tripod, and he was still trying to reconstruct the notes that had been destroyed. It was a massive amount of labor, considering that he had to replace months of experiments and observations.

Satisfied that he'd built a satisfactory perch from which to observe the bees, Sam used the extra lumber to construct a box where he could keep his camera equipment and his notebooks when he returned to the inn every night. It was not practical to haul everything back and forth every day.

It was nearly dark when he returned to the inn. He took the wagon to the barn and arranged to borrow it one last time in the morning, then went to his room to clean up and change clothes. By the time he returned to the dining room, supper was already being served.

But at least he'd made it in time. He wasn't going to impose on Lilly for a private meal again.

The dining area was a pleasant room with tables covered in white cloths and fancy china ware. The sideboard where Sam had placed Lilly's tablecloths was now laden with covered dishes and crystal decanters. Sam particularly liked the windows that overlooked the side garden, although it had become too dark to fully appreciate the flower beds.

Lilly stood at the opposite end of the dining room, near the kitchen, making friendly conversation with the guests at the farthest table. The deep violet of her gown was rich and lush, and Sam knew that its color would match her eyes.

Serving girls moved among the tables, setting down platters of food, serving coffee. Since his arrival at the inn, Sam had met many of the visitors— all people who had flocked to Ravenwell to catch a glimpse of the ghosts.

He took a seat near one of the windows and caught sight of Miss Charlotte, walking toward Lilly. A moment later, the two stepped out of the dining room together.

Sam ordered his meal and tried not to think of Lilly in her elegant gown, with its neckline that left her delicate collarbones exposed. He closed his mind to the way he'd imagined it would feel if she actually ran her fingers through his hair, or touched his mouth with her lips, the way he'd imagined that afternoon. Far better to consider what might be planned for the Ravenwell ghosts this evening, and what part Lilly and Miss Charlotte would play in the farce.

With a pleasant smile on her face, Charlotte returned to the dining room and walked toward the kitchen. When her eyes alighted on Sam, she changed course to head in his direction.

Interpreting a few of her hand signals, Sam realized she wanted to sit down and join him. He invited her to do so, although he didn't know how well he would be able to communicate with her.

He sat back in his chair and stretched out his legs as he waited for her to indicate what she wanted of him, wondering if his suspicion about her involvement with the apparitions was valid.

Charlotte wasted no time, but sat down across from him and started to gesture with her hands.

"The bees?" he asked, interpreting her signs.

She nodded, then pointed to her eyes.

"You saw...?" he guessed. "You—"

Charlotte tapped the table lightly, then moved both hands as if they were sliding up a wide column. At the top of the column she flattened one hand, palm down, and moved it sideways.

Sam frowned. He could not fathom what she meant.

Lilly saw Samuel's puzzled expression and knew she had to rescue him. She gave him credit for not squirming uneasily as Charlotte tried to talk to him, and watched him struggle to understand. Crossing the dining room, Lilly sat down in a chair next to Charlotte. "Good evening."

He gave her a curt nod, but kept his attention on Charlotte. If he was uncomfortable after their parting in Lilly's kitchen, he did not show any sign of it.

"The chestnut tree," he said, finally understanding her gesture. "Where the hive is. My platform."

Lilly took pleasure in watching him work out the puzzle that was Charlotte's form of conversation. He didn't ask for Lilly's help, and his manner did not belittle Charlotte. He was genuinely interested in understanding her. Lilly knew only one other man who'd ever bothered to learn to communicate with Charlotte—their friend Tom Fletcher, who had become as close to them as a brother.

"Climb?" Sam asked. "You want to know how I climb up there?"

He took an old envelope from his pocket, and a

pencil, and drew a quick sketch of the tree. Then he added a rope ladder and showed the paper to Charlotte.

"You're getting good at this," Lilly said.

"Nothing to it," he replied, and returned his attention to the deaf woman. She asked whether he would allow her to climb the ladder and see the platform he'd built. She told him that she would love to see Ravenwell Cottage and all the fields and the lake from up high, but Lilly doubted Samuel would understand all that, although he could not have missed her basic question.

Samuel turned to Lilly. "You'll have to answer this one."

She was saved from saying anything immediately by the arrival of Samuel's meal. Surely Charlotte would be safe with him. Lilly herself had been alone with him several times—instances when he might have taken liberties, but had not. He *could* not.

"What do you say, Miss Tearwater?" he asked. "Will you and Charlotte visit me in my bower?"

Charlotte had been snubbed and ridiculed most of her life. She meant nothing to Samuel Temple, yet his respectful attitude was remarkable.

And Lilly felt herself fall a little bit in love with him for his kindness to her friend.

"Yes, of course," she said. "Charlotte and I would be delighted to join you."

Clearly pleased with Lilly's reaction to the question, Charlotte left the table and disappeared into the kitchen, where Mr. Clive would have a task for her.

"She gets along very well despite her deafness," Samuel said.

"We manage, at least, up here at Ravenwell."

''But…not in town.''

Lilly gave a slight shake of her head. ''She stays away from Asbury, except for church. Charlotte needs looking after because she's young and vulnerable. And she is so beautiful that there have been a few…incidents…involving young men who…''

She bit her lip, too embarrassed to speak of it.

Samuel nodded once, clearly understanding her intimation. ''You two are very close.''

''We are,'' she said. ''Maude Barnaby brought us here from an orphanage in Blackpool—to keep her company, and to work.''

''Strange that she would choose Charlotte, given her deafness.''

Lilly felt her cheeks heat with color at the memory of the way she'd insisted that Maude take Charlotte. She looked away guiltily.

''You were responsible for that, weren't you? For insisting that Charlotte come along?''

She shrugged. ''Charlotte was so small. And she didn't understand anything. I got it into my head that I wasn't going to leave Saint Anne's without Charlotte. But I don't think Maude ever regretted bringing Charlotte here.''

It was lovely to sit and talk so freely with Samuel. They'd begun a perfectly enjoyable discussion that afternoon about Mr. Hinkley's suggestion that she enlarge the inn, but she'd ruined it with her impulsive phantom touches.

Lilly was ashamed of herself. She had seen the scars resulting from Samuel's injuries. She could not imagine the anguish he'd suffered in Sudan. His abrupt departure from her rooms that afternoon was a clear indication that he'd been upset, and rightly so. She should not have used her magic to make him feel her touch, when he was clearly uncomfortable with the very thought of human contact.

Lilly had to keep tighter control. She couldn't let her attraction to him dictate her behavior. From now on, Samuel was merely a guest. There would be no more encounters at the lake, no late lunches in her private quarters.

"No doubt you're right. Tell me…will the Ravenwell ghosts appear tonight?"

Lilly shook her head, aware that they were playing a sort of game. Something like the tug-of-war she and Charlotte and Tom had played as children. "It's possible. Anything's possible."

She eased back into her chair, preferring to stay where she was, but ready to leave if he was going to interrogate her about the ghosts.

"So there's no pattern to their appearances?"

She shook her head in reply. "It happens fairly frequently—several times every week."

"There are two, right?" he asked. "Do they both appear?"

"Do you mean each time?"

He nodded.

"No. Occasionally, Lady Alice or Sir Emmett will be seen alone, pining for their beloved."

Samuel made a derisive sound. "Save your soliloquy for someone who believes in the illusion."

"You mean you don't believe in such a love, Mr. Temple?" Lilly asked, pretending to misunderstand his skepticism. "One that transcends all barriers…including death?"

His eyes, icy blue, met hers for several heartbeats.

Then he slowly shook his head. "When it happens, I'm sure it's rare."

Lilly did not want to believe that. She might have become a practical businesswoman, but she wanted to believe that the kind of bond she'd created between Lady Alice and Sir Emmett was real. It irritated her that Samuel Temple would not concede that fact. "I suppose that love isn't scientific enough for you?"

He propped his fingertips together and gazed at her. "I've been all over the world, Miss Tearwater, and seen all kinds of people, in many different cultures. Trust me when I say it happens rarely."

His cynicism triggered a perverse reaction from Lilly.

The gaslights in the dining room flickered, then Lady Alice and Sir Emmett came to life at the table beside them. The two ghosts seemed to float just above the surface of the table, and Lilly made certain that every feature, every detail of their clothing was clearly visible.

With one thought, Lilly directed the actions of her ghosts. Completely absorbed in one another, they appeared to pay no attention to their surroundings, just as Lilly imagined two lovers would do. Sir Emmett took Lady Alice in his arms and kissed her. Colorful light shimmered around them as Lady Alice's hands slid up Sir Emmett's back, pulling him closer. He intensified the kiss, then trailed his mouth down her neck, kissing her throat and the bare skin above her bodice.

"*Christ!*" Samuel Temple's voice was a harsh whisper.

Lilly suddenly remembered that the dining room

was full of guests when Mr. Payton and several others came closer to watch in wonder as the two ghosts played out Lilly's whimsy.

"They don't notice us, do they?" Mr. Payton exclaimed. "So very…enamored, are they not?"

Samuel left his table and joined the others. He watched Lady Alice and Sir Emmett for a short time, then peered up at the ceiling and to each of the walls in turn. Then he circled the table, holding one arm up, as if waving to someone at the far end of the room. Apparently dissatisfied with that maneuver, he looked under the table.

Lilly kept the two entwined until she was certain Samuel was convinced they were real. She would not allow him to continue believing she was a fraud, nor would she let him think there was no such thing as everlasting love.

Love was something no one could predict or define. It was the least scientific wonder in the universe.

The roar of thunder and crash of lightning nearby did not distract any of Ravenwell's guests who stood spellbound in the dining room. Even Sam felt astonished and more than slightly aroused by the spectacle.

These were not shadowy figures appearing in the moonlight. They were not wisps of smoke. The couple was clearly visible in the bright light of the room. There were no images being projected—at least, none that Sam could detect. There was nothing under the table or above it—no method of suspending the figures in thin air.

The possibility that the ghosts were real crossed

Sam's mind for the first time since he'd heard about them. Perhaps Ravenwell truly *was* haunted.

Rain pelted the windows of the inn while the ghosts made love to each other, their actions becoming more intimate with each move of their bodies. The erotic tableau was shocking, but even more astonishing was Lady Alice's appearance. She looked exactly like Lilly Tearwater.

And Sir Emmett was a duplicate of Sam.

Chapter Twelve

The experience was like watching from afar while he made love to Lilly, yet his breathing quickened and his muscles tensed as he watched. Her kisses and caresses shot through every nerve of his body, right to the center of his being.

He pressed her soft curves close to his hard length, fitting them together in a sensual haze while nipping at her lips with his teeth. His arousal met her softness, drawing him closer and closer to the brink of paradise.

And suddenly the ghosts vanished.

Sam's glance whipped across the table toward Lilly, but she instantly rose to her feet. "The rain…" Her voice was unsure. Shaky. "I-It's coming down so hard, there might be leaks…"

Sam hardly noticed the clamor of voices around him. He should pursue her. He should find a quiet, private place where they could undress each other slowly—taste and touch and stroke every aroused inch of their bodies. He saw Lilly's eyes, and knew she hadn't been indifferent to the stirring display.

But he took several deep breaths and sank into a

chair, while those who had witnessed the "apparition" discussed it in shocked and bewildered tones. There was no point in going after her, of catching up to her. He was incapable of taking her in his arms, of showing her the depth of his desire for her.

Several minutes passed while Sam composed himself. When he felt steady enough to walk, he left the dining room and walked down the hall to the reception area. It was ridiculous to have become so inflamed by what must have been photographs. Somehow they'd managed to make the pictures seem to move.

Standing at the window near the front door, Sam watched the rain and considered the methods that might have been used to cast his and Lilly's images into the space above the dining table. There were many new scientific advances outside his own field—the telephone, the phonograph, incandescent lights—and though they were not widely used, Sam was sure that an enterprising individual could figure a way to make use of these inventions.

Lilly Tearwater must have hired someone to do this.

Sam had an old friend who worked for Mr. Edison at Menlo Park, and they'd talked many times about the innovative work going on there. Perhaps Mr. Edison's laboratory had developed a method that could make photographs seem to move, and a way to display the image in the atmosphere. Sam would make a point of writing to his friend in New Jersey tonight.

The rain suddenly ceased.

One minute it was brutally pounding the inn, and the next, it was over.

Tom Fletcher burst in from outside and called for

Lilly. Rain dripped off him, forming a puddle on the floor, before he noticed Sam and walked over to him. "Have you seen Charlotte? Or Lilly?"

"No—"

"What in hell happened here? The lightning alone was spectacular, but the rain…"

"What about the rain?"

"It only fell here—at Ravenwell. Every place else in the district is dry, at least, as far as I can tell. Was anyone hurt in the storm?"

Sam felt his forehead crease. He shook his head. Fletcher had to be mistaken. "Not that I've heard. How can you be sure the storm only occurred here?"

"Well, it wasn't raining down at our place. When I saw that lightning strike so close to the inn, I— Charlotte!"

Charlotte walked past Sam and smiled up at Tom, oblivious to his distress. He took her shoulders in his beefy hands. "Are you all right?"

Sam saw that she was puzzled until Tom let her go and made a sign with one hand. Then she nodded and signaled something back to him.

"*Why?* You want to know why?"

Tom drew her outside, where Sam couldn't watch or hear the rest of their conversation. It was just as well, because he planned to investigate what Fletcher had said. He couldn't believe the man had it right— that the storm had occurred only at Ravenwell. That was preposterous.

But when Lilly came into the room, carrying a bucket and a handful of tools, Sam was distracted from his purpose.

"Have you seen D-Davy Becker?" she asked. Her color deepened and she avoided Sam's gaze.

She was clearly unnerved. Was it because the scene in the dining room had so clearly represented them? Or was she worried that he'd discovered how it was done, now that he'd had a closer look?

He hadn't, but he had no intention of admitting it to her.

"No, I haven't," he answered. Unwilling to let her off too easily, he nodded toward the tools she carried. "Do you need some help?"

The question flustered her, but she finally replied. "We've got a b-bit of water coming in through the kitchen roof. Davy can fix it—I just have to find him."

"I don't mind doing it," Sam said. He took the bucket and hammer from Lilly. "Show me where."

He wanted to see her squirm.

Sam followed Lilly into the kitchen, where an older gentleman with a balding pate frantically placed cooking pans on the floor and on various surfaces in order to collect the rainwater that dripped through the ceiling.

"Miss Tearwater!"

"I'm doing what I can, Mr. Clive," she replied. "Have you seen Davy?"

His mustache twitched. "Look at my beautiful Bavarois! Ruined!"

"I'm terribly—"

"I wouldn't worry about it," Sam said. He didn't care for the way the chef badgered Lilly, as if she were personally responsible for ruining the fancy pastry. "I doubt anyone will be looking for dessert tonight."

Not after that scene in the dining room.

He went outside to assess the damage.

*   *   *

The kitchen was a one-story addition to the building, so the roof was not dangerously high. Samuel took the lantern from Lilly's hand and illuminated his climb up the ladder. "It's charred," he called down. "Lightning must have hit here. It should be covered until it can be properly patched."

Lilly could tell that it was bad by the amount of rain pouring into the kitchen. She considered repairing it with one thought, but the lightning had been caused by her magic, and she didn't want to risk another disagreeable consequence. Who knew what would be ruined next time?

Lilly could hardly believe she'd let her irritation with Samuel goad her into such an impulsive display. She'd let her deepest desire manifest itself for all to see. She was mortified.

"Is there any canvas in the barn?"

"What?"

"Canvas. Have you got any canvas in the barn?"

Lilly bit her lip and watched him climb down. His backside was streaked with rainwater and she closed her eyes against the memory of how it had felt under her hands as she'd pulled him against her. The vision had been as real to her as if she'd actually touched him.

"I—I'm not sure," she finally replied. His kisses and caresses had felt just as she'd imagined them, and her bones had fairly melted. "Davy will know. Or Tom."

"At least it's not raining anymore."

"True." She had to get hold of herself. It wasn't as if she'd *really* touched his— "I'll go and find Davy!"

She left Sam with the lantern and ladder, and fled.

Meeting no one in the reception area, she skirted the dining room and went up to the attic to see if Davy was there, checking for more leaks. He wasn't, but at least all was dry up there. And quiet.

Lilly lowered herself onto an overturned box and rested her head in one hand. There was no reason to be embarrassed. Samuel would never know that she was responsible for that performance tonight. And once he left Ravenwell, she would never see him again.

His disbelief had grated on her, and because of that, she had made a fool of herself. Putting her own face and Samuel's on the ghosts… Everyone must have noticed. Even Samuel.

She wondered if the sensations that had coursed through her during the spectacle had affected him, as well. Judging by the expression in his eyes when he'd finally looked over at her, he'd been equally aroused.

Once again, she'd let her talent shift out of her control. And the "ghosts" had behaved shamefully—exactly the way she would wish to do if she were not a proper young Englishwoman.

Sam awoke in a cold sweat.

It was well before dawn, but he knew that further sleep would elude him, at least for tonight. The dreams haunted him—hands holding him down, poking with sharp sticks, pulling and tearing… Sam's fingertips throbbed with the memory of his nails being pulled out while his comrades had been forced to watch. And for what reason?

To strip the westerners of their manhood as their

captors slowly killed them? If that was it, the Mahdi's men had succeeded very well. Sam was the only one of his party to survive—if anyone could say that the life he had now was worth living.

He had to get outside, into the fresh, clean air.

Desperate to get out of the confines of his dark room, he threw on some clothes and slipped out, making his way quietly through the dark halls. No one else was astir.

A few moments later, he let himself out the door leading to the back garden and stood still, taking in a deep lungful of flower-scented air. Only then was he able to stop shaking.

Morning stars filled the sky and the sight of them eased his heart. There had been a time when he thought he'd never see the sky again, never hear English spoken, never again touch a beautiful woman.

He supposed he ought to be grateful for the first two, but he'd become greedy in the days since his arrival at Ravenwell. He wanted Lilly Tearwater. And he didn't care if she was a fraud.

In the predawn light, Sam picked his way through the garden and arrived on the path that led through the meadow to the lake. He could have carried some of his equipment and left it at the chestnut tree, but he wanted to walk unfettered, as if he had all the freedom in the world.

Sam was beginning to suspect that his brother had made the ghost wager for more than one purpose. Jack had probably assumed that once Sam left London, he'd be forced to overcome the terrors that plagued him. It was likely that his brother had wanted to push him beyond his secure, comfortable environment.

But Jack hadn't been in the Sudan. He didn't understand the monumental effort it took for Sam to climb out of his bed every morning and face the day, knowing that he was the only one of his group who'd survived.

Jack couldn't understand that the aroma of certain spices, the smell of unwashed bodies…any number of things could trigger Sam's most horrific memories. Just those few moments in Ravenwell's dark kitchen had somehow transported him to the pit. He'd actually believed that his captors had come for him.

He didn't know what was worse—feeling such an intense attraction to Lilly and being unable to do anything about it, or facing the rest of his professional life working within the dull confines of a university office or classroom.

Alone.

Sam wasn't bred to live a tame existence in the civilized cities of the world. Since childhood, his life had been one exotic experience after another, exploring new and distant sites all over the world. There was a time when Sam believed he'd find a woman like his sister-in-law, someone who loved adventure and would be willing to give up a comfortable life to travel with him, wherever his research took him.

But if he couldn't stand the thought of climbing onto an elephant's back, if the crowded streets of Calcutta made his blood run cold, if the slightest whiff of camel dung nauseated him, then how could he ever resume the life he'd known and loved for all of his thirty-one years?

He let out a slow, deep breath, then sat down on

the sandy beach and cherished the sight of the wide expanse of sky above him. He had a feeling that if he could overcome his aversion to being touched, then he would be able to master the other dark fears that tormented him. The rest of his life would fall into place.

The earliest whisper of dawn crept across the tops of the trees, and Sam heard the first chirps of the birds as they awakened. It was a peaceful setting, something he would never again take for granted.

There was no point to putting off writing his letter to Mr. Phipson. Until Sam could do more than just *watch* himself make love to Lilly Tearwater, he was powerless to go out into the world.

Chapter Thirteen

Dressed for travel in a modest, dove-gray suit, Mrs. Stanhope stood at the reception desk, glowering at Lilly. Her husband stood slightly behind her, his expression slightly embarrassed.

"Are you certain you wish to leave, Mrs. Stanhope? Our ghosts do not usually—"

"We will remain at Ravenwell not one second longer, Miss Tearwater. Last night's display was… was—" The woman covered her nose and mouth with a delicately embroidered handkerchief. "Such lewdness…"

"My wife understands that you are not to blame for the behavior of ghosts, Miss Tearwater," Mr. Stanhope said. "But…"

The man continued to apologize for their abrupt departure, while Lilly felt ashamed all over again. She could not blame the Stanhopes for leaving, but they'd reserved their room for two weeks. Lilly needed the income from that room, but she did not feel justified in holding the Stanhopes to their agreement.

She hoped none of the other guests were so offended that they would also decide to go. She could not expect to find anyone who would take the room on such short notice, even if she had a list of patrons interested in visiting. Lilly knew of no one who could just leave home to go on holiday at a moment's notice.

Mr. Stanhope settled their bill and walked out with his wife, just as Mrs. Bainbridge joined Lilly at the desk. "I've set Davy to patching the kitchen roof," she said. "I can't get over it. A storm, just here. We had nothing down in Asbury. Not a bit of rain. And the lightning—why, it glowed orange. Never seen anything like it."

Lilly shrugged as if it puzzled her, too.

"The Stanhopes are leaving?"

Lilly nodded.

"The ghostly antics, I suppose." Mrs. Bainbridge pursed her lips. "I heard a few stories... Is it true?"

"Is what true?"

"What they say happened in the dining room last night? Sir Emmett and Lady Alice...er..."

Lilly bit her lower lip. "Unfortunately, yes."

"Well..." Mrs. Bainbridge sighed. "There's nothing for it. We'll just have an empty room for the next two weeks."

"Ladies," Mr. Dawson said, folding his newspaper and tucking it under his arm. He'd been sitting in a comfortable chair near the windows and could not have missed Mr. and Mrs. Stanhope's abrupt departure. It seemed to Lilly that over the past few days, Mr. Dawson had been in her sight every time she'd looked up.

She supposed that wasn't so odd, considering that Ravenwell was not a huge place, and Lilly rarely ventured far from it. But she hoped Mr. Dawson was not becoming infatuated with her as Mrs. Bainbridge had suggested. Besides the fact that he was much too old for her, the frank interest she saw in his eyes made her distinctly uneasy. She did not feel the same attraction.

"May I help you, Mr. Dawson?" asked Mrs. Bainbridge.

"I could not help but overhear that you have a sudden vacancy."

Lilly suddenly recalled Mr. Dawson's earlier request for a room for his friend. She had forgotten about it, since the inn had been fully booked for months and cancellations did not occur very often.

"I'm certain my London friend would be willing to let the room, even without forewarning."

Lilly did not hesitate to answer. "If you'll give me the gentleman's address, I'll wire him this morning."

"Allow me, Miss Tearwater," Mr. Dawson said. "I was planning to go down to Asbury this morning, myself. I'll be happy to let Mr. Hamlet—my friend—know that you have a room for him."

"That was convenient," Mrs. Bainbridge said when Mr. Dawson had gone. "If Mr. Hamlet arrives tomorrow, you'll only be out the price of one night's lodging. And whatever meals the Stanhopes might have taken."

Lilly tapped one finger against her lips and wondered if it wasn't a bit too convenient. A moment later, she discounted her misgivings. Mr. Dawson might make her uncomfortable, but he certainly had not convinced the Stanhopes to vacate their room.

It had been Lilly's own rash conduct the night before that had done it.

There would be no apparitions tonight. Lilly had made that decision immediately after last night's disaster, and she reiterated it to herself once again. Mr. Payton and all the other Ravenwell guests had enough to marvel over for weeks. And those who were scheduled to leave today already had plenty to talk about when they returned to their homes.

By late afternoon, Lilly's new guests had arrived and were settled, tea was being served in the garden, and she had an hour to herself, before Mrs. Bainbridge left to go home.

Lilly collected her newest books on Egypt and Athens and left the inn, heading for the beach. As she took to the path, she had no intention of even glancing in the direction of the woods where she assumed Samuel was working in his chestnut tree. It seemed impossible to control her impulses when he was near. And Lilly did not know how she could face him after all that had transpired the previous night.

She didn't know what had been worse, the indecent spectacle in the dining room, or running away from him later, as if she been guilty of...

Well, she *was* guilty, she supposed. But there was no reason for Samuel ever to discover that fact. And she would certainly never admit that Lady Alice's actions in the dining room mirrored Lilly's deepest longings.

She wanted to lie in a lover's arms, to feel loved and cherished...to know that she was all-important to him. And the love that Lilly returned would know no bounds.

That kind of intimacy wasn't likely to be found at Ravenwell or in Asbury. The men at the inn were primarily husbands, traveling with their wives. Samuel Temple and Mr. Dawson were the exceptions. As for the men in Asbury, everyone in the district knew that Lilly was responsible for Charlotte, and most of them believed Charlotte was a simpleton.

The only Asbury man who'd shown any serious interest in Lilly was Alan Graham, the vicar's son, and he had been away at university so long that Lilly doubted he remembered anything about Charlotte. Even so, he was pompous and much too enamored of his own appeal. Lilly could not imagine herself entertaining tender feelings toward him.

Especially not since meeting Samuel Temple.

Lilly stopped in her tracks and hugged her books to her breast. Her attraction to Samuel had been instantaneous, even though he'd come dangerously close to accusing her of fraud. She could hardly fault him for that, since it was true.

She knew her longing for his touch was irrational. She was a respectable woman. A lady. She could not indulge in a love affair with a stranger, even though her heart longed for such intimacy with Samuel Temple.

Lilly cringed when she thought of his scars. She had seen the damage done to his hands, and could only imagine the horrors he'd endured, the things he'd seen. Her throat burned when she thought of it, and Lilly could not blame him for his revulsion to being touched. It was surprising that he could function at all.

If only he would allow small amounts of contact, she might be able to help him become accustomed to touch again. It seemed only logical that with a gradual exposure to her touch, his memory of the horrors associated with his imprisonment would recede.

But he would never allow it. Lilly had to face the fact that every time she'd forced the *illusion* of her touch upon him, it had only upset him.

Discouraged, she resumed her trek down the path, but was intercepted by Charlotte, who motioned for her to follow. They were so close to the chestnut tree that Lilly knew that's where they were headed, and she tried to ignore Charlotte's request. But her friend was insistent, so Lilly prepared herself for an encounter with Samuel.

He stood at the base of the tree, beside a thick rope ladder that hung from one of the branches above. "Miss Tearwater," he said, as if there was no awkwardness between them.

Lilly felt relieved.

"Hold this, will you?"

He handed her a small box that contained a row of glass jars, and left her standing by the tree, balancing the box on top of her books, while he went to Charlotte. Handing her a sketchpad, he used hand gestures to communicate with her, after which Charlotte nodded and walked off into the meadow, among the wildflowers.

"What is she doing?" Lilly asked.

"Tracking a worker bee."

Lilly handed the box back to him. "You learned to talk with Charlotte so quickly."

"We manage," he said, turning to climb the rope

ladder. "She's bright and she's interested. She asks about everything."

Lilly sighed at the sight of his backside, and remembered how it had actually felt during those few moments last night when she had experienced all that Lady Alice had felt: the taut muscles flexing under her hands, the heat of his skin as he held her close. And Lilly thought of her own response, a quickening of her blood and a deep heat that had permeated to her core.

"You never said anything about last night's apparition," he called down to her.

Lilly choked and nearly dropped her books.

"Are you all right?"

She squeaked out an affirmative sound.

"Did anything about last night's apparition strike you as being different from the usual...antics of the ghosts?"

Lilly dodged a honeybee that flew down from the hive, and avoided looking up at Samuel, who sat high on the wooden platform, his long legs dangling over the edge.

She was so embarrassed.

"Am I the only one who thought Lady Alice bore a striking resemblance to you, Lilly?"

Her gaze shot up to the branch where he sat. "I'm sure you're mistaken, Mr. Temple. How could—"

"That's exactly what I would like to know. And I'll figure it out before I leave Ravenwell."

At least, Sam hoped he'd figure it out.

"Aren't you afraid of being stung?" Lilly asked. He was somewhat surprised that she didn't just bolt when he said he was going to determine what was going on at Ravenwell. Perhaps the distance he'd put between them reduced her unease, although he'd done it for purely selfish reasons. The farther away he stayed, the better.

"I'm not exactly fond of bee stings, but I don't react much to them anymore." He'd used an age-old method to neutralize his reaction to the bees' venom when he'd first started working with them. The series of stings he'd received in a controlled fashion had rendered him nearly immune to the bees' venom. The sting he'd received on his first afternoon at Ravenwell would have gotten no worse without treatment.

Sam wore special gloves and coveralls when he had direct contact with the hive, but that part of his research was weeks away. And he didn't want to talk about bees now.

"Your ghosts... It seemed as if their appearance lasted longer than usual last night."

"I can't say that I noticed the time."

"Trust me," he said, remembering the taste of her lips and the way her hands had caressed him. "The episode persisted."

"I'll take your word for it. Now, I'll just lea—"

"Last night's storm was strange, too, wouldn't you say?" he asked, to keep her from running away from him again.

"Yes, it was. It certainly was unusual," she replied, making a show of being interested in the crates that were stacked nearby. She wore a serviceable blue blouse, tucked neatly into a black skirt. Miss Tearwater did not appear to be encased in thick petticoats, so Sam was treated to a natural view when she bent to open the lid of one box.

He imagined undressing her, layer by layer, touching her smooth skin as he exposed her. Caressing her throat, teasing her breasts with his thumbs, spanning her waist before he moved lower.

He jabbed his fingers through his hair and looked away. "Have you ever been away from Ravenwell, Miss Tearwater?"

"Once, a few years ago." She opened the box that contained his microscope.

"Where did you go?"

"To London. Maude took us, but Charlotte despised it."

"Why?" he asked, beginning to feel more controlled again.

"There were too many people who couldn't understand her. She was very..." Miss Tearwater looked up at him. "It was very frightening for her. I'm quite sure Charlotte will never leave Ravenwell again."

"And what about you?"

She turned away and peered into another crate. Sam had noticed the books she carried, and remembered her fascination with foreign places. He'd wager another hundred pounds that her dearest wish was to travel to some of them.

But she had told him she could not leave Ravenwell.

"I promised Maude that I would take care of Charlotte. Which means I must stay and keep Ravenwell profitable. In any event, I'm reconsidering Mr. Hinkley's suggestion. Perhaps it *would* be best if I built another guest wing. And started up a coach line between here and the railroad."

"I thought you didn't like that idea."

"I may have been hasty. What are these?"

She held up the can and bellows he used when he wanted to smoke out a nest. The way Lilly and he communicated was not unlike the bees' dance, he mused. They took steps forward, then circled. They intimated without stating outright what they wanted to know.

"I'll show you some time." He glanced up at the clear blue sky. "I have traveled far and wide and have never witnessed such strange weather as you have here at Ravenwell."

Not that Lilly had any control over it, but it was one of the many oddities he'd encountered since his arrival here. Were the ghosts a part of some climactic aberration, rather than a hoax or some supernatural phenomenon?

Sam had to admit that the two phantoms had seemed spectacularly real last night. And he could no longer deny that he'd physically *sensed* Lilly during the apparition in the dining room. He'd felt none of the agony of physical touch, only the pleasure.

. "I am at a loss," she said, breaking into Sam's thoughts. "I can no more explain the weather than I can the ghosts."

There. She'd put into words the connection he'd just made. Only he didn't know what conclusions to draw.

She picked up his field glasses and looked through the lenses toward the meadow. "There's Charlotte! It's as if I could reach out and touch her!"

Charlotte might appear close, but Sam was getting no nearer to understanding Ravenwell.

Perhaps the question of ghosts was a larger riddle than either he or Jack had anticipated.

Still, he was going to write to his old friend at
Menlo Park and see if there'd been any develop-
ments in electromagnetics that would make any of
these mysterious events possible. What other explanation could there be? Lilly Tearwater had not
slipped up once in her story, and Sam had found no
one capable of carrying out an illusion of the mag-
nitude he'd seen here.

Sam still had his suspicions about whoever had
bashed in his head, but even that incident might have
been exaggerated somehow. He didn't like to think
it was his own mental instability that caused him to
believe he'd been gouged, but the alternative wasn't
much better.

"Charlotte is quite good at following the bees'
course. Not many people are able to concentrate so
well."

Earlier, he had trapped one bee and dropped a dot
of bright blue paint on its back in order to keep track
of it. "When the bee returns to the hive, we'll retrace
the pattern of the dance she makes and see how it
correlates to her course in the meadow."

Lilly looked up at him. "You said 'she.' How do
you know it's female?"

Sam grinned. "All of the workers are female. The
drones are exclusively male. And they have only one
function." Since it was wholly inappropriate to discuss such matters with a lady, Sam let it drop, but
he knew the moment she caught his meaning. Lilly
flushed slightly and turned away to look at Charlotte
through the field glasses again.

Another woman would have climbed right up and
slapped his face. It pleased Sam that Lilly was not a
prudish female.

''You mentioned the bees' dance before.''

Sam had planned to keep his distance from Lilly, but found himself climbing down the ladder to join her on the ground.

It was to continue their peculiar dance, he supposed, circling around one another without touching, intensely aware of each other. He would have been attracted to her in any location, but something about Ravenwell made every encounter with her seem more intimate than the last.

The mere anticipation of her illusive touch aroused him beyond anything he'd shared with a *real* lover.

He let his eyes drift closed and waited for the sensation of Lilly's touch to come over him, just as he'd felt it last night when Sir Emmett had taken Lady Alice in his arms.

He knew that Lilly had felt it, too. She'd bolted from the dining room the instant he'd caught her eyes…

The fresh summer breeze ruffled his pant legs and cooled his skin. The scent of wildflowers and sunshine drifted through his senses.

Sam crossed his arms while he waited, silently bidding the illusion to commence. His breath caught while he anticipated the sensation of Lilly's hands on his shoulders, caressing his chest, sliding down to his waist. Last night he was certain that he'd felt her hands on his thighs, moving fluidly toward his most sensitive parts.

He shuddered and wiped the palms of his hands on his trousers, and waited for sensations that never came.

Chapter Fourteen

Lilly kept her thoughts under tight rein as Samuel stood unmoving behind her. She was not going to repeat her past mistakes with him, even though she had spent an inordinate amount of time last night dreaming of how it would feel to lie in his arms.

With a mere thought, she could sequester them somewhere, and repeat Sir Emmett and Lady Alice's performance of the night before, but without the guise of the ghosts. It would be just the two of them, Samuel and Lilly, experiencing every intimacy—without actually touching.

It was tempting, but wrong, even without considering whatever untoward effect her magic would have. The inn might burn down this time, for all she knew.

If ever she touched Samuel, it would be with his consent, a mutually agreeable event that would not make his heart quake or his skin go pale.

She really ought to leave now. Take her books and head down to the beach as she'd planned, and forget about Samuel Temple and her imagined interlude with him.

"Lilly…"

Her breath caught at the sound of his voice, and she turned slowly toward him. His hands dropped to his sides, clenching into tight fists. Small beads of perspiration broke out on his forehead.

Lilly felt his gaze on her mouth.

She moistened her lips and waited expectantly. Only a few steps would bring him within touching distance. He could come to her and brush his lips against hers—softly, just the barest whisper of a touch—and see that no harm befell him.

He took a step toward her, while Lilly stood perfectly still and reminded herself that she could be patient. No matter how desperately she wanted to throw herself into his arms, she was capable of waiting for him to come to her.

Vague thoughts of impropriety crossed her mind, but she disregarded them as he came even closer. He raised one hand and barely brushed the few wisps of hair that had come loose from her combs.

"You are so beautiful," he whispered as his eyes closed.

Lilly held her breath and savored the light touch. Something snapped nearby, but she scarcely heard the sound. She leaned slightly toward Samuel and waited for his mouth to descend upon hers. Her heart thudded heavily in her breast and her own eyes drifted closed.

"Miss Tearwater!"

They both jumped at the sound of her name. Lilly took a shuddering breath, then looked to her left.

Mr. Dawson approached them through the trees. "I'm glad I found you. I say, Temple, you've got quite a contraption here," he added.

Lilly sensed Samuel's withdrawal. As Mr. Dawson stepped up to the rope ladder that hung from the thick branch of the chestnut tree and admired its ingenuity, Samuel tied a box of equipment to the pulley and hoisted it to the platform.

"Very good, Temple," Mr. Dawson said, then turned to Lilly. "Mrs. Bainbridge said you were going to the beach. Shall I escort you, Miss Tearwater?"

Lilly did not wish to encourage Mr. Dawson's attentions. But she saw no way out of it.

"Here is Charlotte," Sam said to Lilly. Then he turned to the pissant Englishman who thought he was going to take Lilly away. "Feel free to head down to the beach, Dawson. Miss Tearwater and Miss Gray are assisting me at present."

A surge of purely male possessiveness shot through Sam when Henry Dawson took Lilly's elbow and approached Charlotte. Sam felt like tying *him* to the pulley, hoisting him up to a high branch and leaving him there.

Frustration flooded through him. *He'd actually touched Lilly!* But before he'd been able to do anything more than make the most fleeting contact with a shimmering lock of her hair, Dawson had intruded on the moment. He'd spoiled it.

Charlotte approached, keeping her eye on the bee as it flew toward the chestnut tree. Lilly slipped out of Dawson's grasp and moved away to stand beside Sam.

"What will you do when the bee returns?" she asked.

"Watch how it behaves when it flies up to the hive."

"Will it dance?"

"I'm betting on it."

Lilly stood far enough away that there would be no accidental contact between them. Sam wasn't sure he should be grateful for that space.

Charlotte came closer, pointing to the bee, with its leg baskets full of pollen. Sam picked up the field glasses and watched it land on the hive. He observed the dance—a simple circle, since the chosen bee had not traveled far or wide to fill her pollen sacs.

Sam gave Charlotte the field glasses and showed her how to use them. When she'd focused on the hive, she whipped the glasses away from her eyes and gave him a shocked look.

Sam laughed. He actually laughed aloud.

It had been months since he'd felt such humor, the kind that reached all the way down to his bones and Sam relished the good, wholesome sense of it. When Charlotte put the glasses to her eyes again, she kept them there, turning toward the meadow, then toward Ravenwell. Each new sight was met with Charlotte's version of excitement—not speech, but a quick intake of breath.

Lilly enjoyed her friend's excitement, joining in Sam's laughter. She started to reach for him, but lowered her hand just before touching him. "Neither of us has ever looked through such glasses before," she said.

Sam wished there was no barrier between them. He wanted to take her up to his bower and hold her in his arms while she looked across Ravenwell's acres, and laugh with her when she delighted in the sight of a bird's nest, or a squirrel skittering high up in a tree with its kits.

Perhaps it was possible. *He had touched her hair!* A sliver of hope wedged itself into his heart.

"Have you always studied bees?" Dawson asked. "Are you considered an expert on the species?"

"No, I'm not an entomologist," he replied, throwing in a word that he was sure Dawson wouldn't recognize, "but a naturalist."

"Like Mr. Darwin?"

He nodded.

"Can't say as I know much about the man. Miss Tearwater," he said, dismissing Sam. "Shall we adjourn to the beach?"

She took the field glasses from Charlotte and raised them to her eyes. "Thank you, no, Mr. Dawson. I believe I'll stay here a while." Lowering the glasses, she looked at him. "But don't let me keep you. You won't want to miss the afternoon at the beach. It's lovely this time of day."

Dawson bristled, even though Lilly had kept her tone friendly. But both men understood what had just transpired. Lilly had sent him about his business while she remained here with Sam.

"Is that your camera?" Lilly asked Samuel.

He turned to look up at the equipment he'd arranged on his platform high up in the tree. "You want to see it?"

She nodded. "I've only seen a camera once before, in London. Maude and Charlotte and I had our photograph taken in a studio."

He seemed pleased by her interest. "Do you think you can manage the rope ladder?"

Lilly felt her face heat. "If you'll just turn away for a moment, Mr. Temple," she replied with a laugh, "I'm sure I'll manage. But it might be an indelicate sight."

He did as she asked, and Lilly climbed up to the platform without much difficulty. The structure felt solid, but she kept her balance by hanging on to a branch as she walked to where the camera sat on its tripod.

A moment later, Samuel was beside her. He handed her the field glasses. "Look through them now," he said. "But sit down first. The view might be disorienting."

Lilly lowered herself to the floor. "You can see for miles! There's Charlotte."

Her friend was on her way down the path toward Mrs. Webster's farm. And Mr. Dawson had disappeared into the woods.

"If you could leave Ravenwell, where would you go?" Samuel asked.

Lilly took the binoculars from her eyes. "I don't know. Do I have to choose only one destination?"

"List them in order of preference."

"Rome. That would be first. I'd want to see everything—every statue, all the catacombs."

"And after Rome?"

Lilly picked up the glasses again and watched Charlotte while she considered. "A Moroccan bazaar? The Egyptian pyramids? Perhaps, but…" She lowered the glasses. "I think India would be next."

"Why India?"

Lilly sighed and looked up at Samuel, happy to speak of her favorite topic. "I suppose I've heard more about India than any other place. A number of

our guests have either visited or lived there. I want
to see a Bengal tiger and men riding elephants. I'd
love to taste *masala gosht,* lemon rice and *kali elai-
chi.*"

"You've heard of *masala gosht?*"

She nodded. "From one of our visitors last year.
He'd served as a sergeant major near Delhi for most
of his career."

"I imagine he kept you entertained with his tales
of India for many an hour."

They talked about the things she had learned from
Sergeant Dillard, and Samuel started to assemble his
camera. Lilly watched through the field glasses as
boats on the lake floated lazily into view. A few
fishermen napped with their hats pulled over their
eyes. Two boats with young men at the oars raced
each other to the far side.

And another boat contained a pair of lovers,
touching and leaning toward each other to share a
few kisses. Their small craft began to rock precari-
ously when the man left his seat to stretch out beside
his sweetheart, and the lovemaking intensified.

"Did he tell you about the Red Fort in Agra? Or
the Taj Mahal?"

"Hmm?" She barely heard him when the man in
the boat slid his hand up his companion's skirt.
"Y-yes...I would want to see them. And the Pink
City," she added absently.

The woman in the boat responded eagerly, giving
him free access, while her own hands explored his
body.

Lilly knew she should lower the binoculars, but
she could not. She felt frozen in place, unable to look
away from the sight of their bared flesh, their brazen

caresses. Her heart pounded and her legs felt as rubbery as if she'd swum all the way to the island halfway across the lake.

The woman opened the buttons of her companion's trousers and slipped her hand inside. When he threw his head back, Lilly saw his throat move jerkily and she dropped the field glasses to the floor.

"Oh! I'm so sorry! I'll just—"

"They're all right." He picked up the field glasses and set them beside the camera.

Lilly felt as though her blood was on fire. She saw the same kind of intense heat burning in Samuel's eyes when he looked at her, but he made no move to come closer. The muscles of his body seemed tense and the expression on his face was one of confusion and agitation.

But he could not come to her.

"I should get back to the inn," she said, hoping he would say something to stop her. Just a word would keep her there in his bower.

But it never came.

Lilly spent an hour at the beach, looking over her books. But her mind continually wandered to the sight of the lovers in the boat. An odd pressure deep within her body grew, making her restless. She turned the pages of her book, but saw nothing but the woman's hand, pleasuring her man.

All at once she stood, dropping her precious books in the sand at her feet. It was ridiculous to dwell on such a sight. She should have turned away as soon as she'd realized what the man and woman were about.

But she had not, and Lilly did not think the image would ever leave her.

Gathering up her books, she left the beach and walked up the path toward Ravenwell, meeting Charlotte on the way. They found Mrs. Bainbridge on the terrace in the garden, arranging the tables for tea. Lilly felt remiss in staying away so long, but she could not regret the time she'd spent with Samuel at the chestnut tree.

He'd been so kind and patient with Charlotte. That in itself endeared him to her. And the possessive way he'd dismissed Mr. Dawson had been wonderful. Lilly sighed. Not that it had been the correct thing to do, but she'd never before been the recipient of such unexpected masculine attention. It was as if Samuel actually cared for her.

Lilly could not help imagining herself sharing with him the kind of intimacies she'd seen on the lake. He had actually touched her this afternoon, leading her to believe that in time, more might be possible.

She and Charlotte left Mrs. Bainbridge to finish her work on the terrace while they went to their private rooms to change into fresh clothes after their afternoon of leisure.

Lilly walked into her bedroom and began to undress. She felt very strange—invigorated, but languid. Fascinated, but puzzled. She removed her blouse and skirt and tossed them on the bed, then stood at her mirror and took the combs out of her hair. Perhaps she should have given Samuel more time to come to her. She was a fool to have run away from—

Charlotte clapped twice to get her attention.

"What is it?" Lilly asked.

Charlotte took her hand and pulled her into the sitting room. Pointing to the open window there, she lifted her shoulders to ask if Lilly had left it agape.

Lilly frowned. She did not remember leaving it open and indicated as much to Charlotte.

Lilly indicated she was fairly certain she hadn't opened the window. "You're sure *you* didn't leave it that way?" she asked.

Charlotte shook her head, indicating that she'd felt too cool that morning to have opened it.

Standing in the sitting room, wearing only her corset and petticoats, Lilly felt a chill in contrast to the heat that had inflamed her most of the afternoon. She pulled down the sash and locked it, then hugged herself, rubbing her hands up her arms to warm them.

"I must have opened it." She pointed to herself. Though she didn't actually remember it, there could be no other explanation.

Unless someone else had come into their private rooms.

Lilly glanced around to see if anything had been disturbed, or seemed out of place. Charlotte's sewing basket lay on the hearth where she'd last seen it. None of the furniture had been altered, and the pictures and lamps appeared to be untouched.

Then a terrible thought struck her. Quickly, she turned and went back into her bedroom. Her comb and hairbrush seemed to be in the exact position that she left them every day. Hairpins. Candle. The framed tintype of herself, standing with Charlotte and Maude. Her best shoes, neatly arranged against the wall. Everything was in its place.

But when Charlotte touched her shoulder, Lilly

spun around, her heart pounding for no good reason. Nothing was amiss. She told herself that no one had invaded their private rooms while they were out.

She or Charlotte had simply forgotten about opening the window.

"Nothing's wrong," she replied to Charlotte's quizzical expression. "I must have left the window open and forgotten about it when I left this morning." And no wonder. She'd been so preoccupied with thoughts of Samuel.

Charlotte went to her own room, and Lilly dressed. She pinned her hair into a careful chignon, then watched Charlotte go to the kitchen, where she would be given chores by Mr. Clive. Lilly was in the process of lighting the gas lamps when she heard horses and a buggy drive up. Likely it was Mr. Hinkley again, here to press his proposal.

The front door opened, and when Saint Jerome's pastor stepped in, with his son behind him, Lilly could not have been more surprised. "Why, Reverend Graham," she said. "How lovely to see you."

The pastor hadn't been up to Ravenwell in three years, not since the day Maude died.

"I would have brought Mrs. Graham, but after I heard what transpired here last night…"

Lilly did not know what to say. *If only she had thought before putting on that display!*

She took a deep breath, then swallowed. "W-what brings you to Ravenwell?"

"Need you ask, Miss Tearwater?" Alan replied for his father. His voice was stern, his expression harsh.

"Well, yes, I—"

"We've come to see if the tales are true."

"Tales?" A heavy sense of dread settled in the

pit of Lilly's stomach. It did not help, knowing that Reverend Graham would never learn that Lilly herself was responsible for last night's lewd apparition.

Heaven help her if he did!

"You should close Ravenwell," Alan said.

"Close Ravenwell?" She was beginning to feel like a parrot, repeating every word they said, turning her head to and fro to follow the two clerics.

"Miss Tearwater," said the elder Reverend Graham. "We've come to stay the evening and bear witness to the antics of these ghosts of yours. After we've seen them—"

"It's unlikely they will appear tonight, Reverend," she interjected, Alan's remark still ringing in her ears. "You are welcome to stay; of course, and have supper with us. But the ghosts rarely show themselves on two consecutive nights."

"We shall see," Alan said. "And when we do, rest assured that I will do what must be done."

"I'm not certain I understand."

"Exorcism, my dear girl. I will exorcise them from this place."

Lilly clamped her mouth closed. She needn't reply to Alan's ludicrous remark. He was not a likely candidate ever to witness a ghostly exhibit at Ravenwell.

"We would be pleased to stay for supper, Miss Tearwater," Reverend Graham said, "if it's no trouble."

Lilly glanced toward the dining room. She already planned to feed more than fifty guests. How could two more be any trouble?

Sam's good spirits turned foul when he saw Lilly sitting beside the pastor's tall, good-looking son. Her posture was stiff and formal, not at all the way she'd been with him that afternoon.

He wondered if she'd have stayed with him longer had she not sighted the couple making love in the boat on the lake.

Sam smiled. Clearly, it had distressed her, but not in the way some women would have been disturbed.

Lilly was different from the ladies in Sam's past. No timid country lass, she wanted to know about everything he did, hear about all the places he'd traveled. Her desire to leave Ravenwell was palpable, but she was trapped by her promise to care for Charlotte.

If only...

Sam couldn't begin to think about taking Lilly away.

"Mr. Temple," she said as he walked toward his usual table, "won't you join us?"

There was a hint of desperation in her voice that Sam could not ignore. Either something was amiss, or she simply did not care for the company of the two ministers. He greeted the men and sat down.

The younger of the two was the more stern, although his father didn't appear to be in high spirits, either.

"I supposed you saw the Ravenwell phantoms last night, Temple?" Alan Graham asked.

Sam nodded. "I did."

"And would you say that the display was indecent?"

It was clear that Lilly felt herself under attack. And Samuel could do no less than ride to her rescue. His scientific background would stand him in good stead.

"The question is not so much indecency as whether the manifestation is a variation of some pre-existing form. Is it a variation in bodily structure, or of mental capacity that follows some natural law of which we are wholly unfamiliar? Or are these organisms malformations of a species heretofore undiscovered?"

Sam knew he had them when their eyes glazed over. But he did not relent. He continued speaking of organisms and peculiar anomalies of species until the meal was served and Lilly excused herself to visit with her other guests.

Her subtle smile betrayed the shared intimacy of his joke. She left the table and Sam watched her move through the dining room, graceful, warm, hospitable...

And so arousing that he barely heard Mr. Graham's reaction to his scientific diatribe—something about staying to watch for the ghosts to appear tonight. But all Sam could think of was Lilly and the smile that she bestowed upon every guest she encountered.

"Such an indelicate spectacle is utterly unacceptable in this parish, Mr. Temple," Graham the younger said. "It will not be tolerated."

"And how do you propose to stop it?" Sam asked. "If these apparitions are actually ghostly visions, then it follows that they are beyond your control."

"What do you mean, *if?*"

The last thing Sam wanted was to get in the middle of this, but he wasn't about to let these men rattle Lilly. Or interfere with the way she ran her inn. To Sam's way of thinking, the ghosts were none of their business. "It's just scientist talk. We question every-thing."

"Which may not necessarily be the most wise course, young man," said Graham the elder.

"Yes, well, I'd like to know how you intend to discipline Ravenwell's ghosts. Will you stand up to them and demand that they desist? Perhaps prayer... Will enough prayers stop them?"

"My dear Mr. Temple," Alan Graham said, "never underestimate the power of prayer."

The man had obviously never been strapped down while the skin of his shoulders was viciously flayed or hot embers were dropped onto his belly. He'd never prayed his heart out to a deaf God while being forced to watch his closest friend bleed to death slowly from unspeakable wounds, his cries fading as his life flowed out of him.

"Sunday services will begin at nine o'clock sharp tomorrow, Mr. Temple," the elder Graham said. "Perhaps it would do your soul good to join us?"

"I don't see how it would."

Chapter Fifteen

Lilly felt uneasy the next morning. Besides being unable to dispel the sense that someone had prowled through her private rooms, she had the troubling sensation that she was being watched—and that someone knew she had made Lady Alice and Sir Emmett appear and wanted to catch her at it. It was ridiculous, of course, but her nervousness persisted.

Ravenwell's more hearty guests walked to town for Sunday service. For the rest, Lilly always arranged for carriages to convey them to and from Asbury. She and Charlotte drove themselves every Sunday, except this morning. Samuel had offered.

His offer seemed to surprise him, but Lilly appreciated it, since the feeling of being watched had not abated with her morning activities.

He left them at Saint Jerome's with the promise to return at the end of the service. Lilly did not try to persuade him to join them. She'd gotten the distinct impression the night before that there was no love lost between Samuel and the two reverends.

Lilly and Charlotte walked to their usual pew near the front of the nave, and she was vaguely surprised to see Mr. Dawson already in church, sitting beside Miss Simpson and her brother. Tom Fletcher's mother murmured a quiet greeting as Lilly slid into the seat beside her, and they stood almost immediately for the opening hymn.

Alan Graham performed the service, but it was a struggle for Lilly to be attentive. Ever since Samuel's arrival at Ravenwell, events had careened out of her control. She'd lost confidence in the powers she'd taken for granted all her life. That had never happened before.

She was going to refrain from any use of her gift for the next few days. Most of Ravenwell's current guests had seen Sir Emmett and Lady Alice, and the others would have to wait…at least until she was certain she could produce a manifestation that would be inoffensive to everyone.

Reverend Graham's sermon did not help Lilly's peace of mind. He decried the sins of the flesh, admonishing every member of the congregation to eschew their earthly desires, to cast off all such weaknesses.

Lilly heard the words guiltily. Not only were sins of the flesh on her mind, but deceitfulness and envy, as well. Everything about her life was untrue—except, perhaps, her love for Charlotte.

She bent her head and prayed for the fortitude necessary to be content with her lot. Life at Ravenwell was a good sight better than what many other young women her age enjoyed. She ought to be grateful for it.

When services were over, the Reverends Graham met the congregation out on the lawn, exchanging warm greetings. They spoke with Miss Simpson and

Mr. Dawson at length, while Lilly looked around for Samuel.

"Will you and Charlotte come have your dinner with Tom and me?" Mrs. Fletcher asked.

"I really shouldn't, Mrs. Fletcher," Lilly replied. "But Charlotte is free."

Tom's mother shook her head. "A bit of advice, Lilly Tearwater," she said. She'd been more of a mother to Lilly and Charlotte when they were children than Maude Barnaby had ever been. The two girls had spent many a spare hour with Mrs. Fletcher and Tom at their farm, learning about normal household chores and helping to tend the sheep. "You need to find some time to yourself, lass, or you'll take sick."

Lilly laughed. "I'm as healthy as that new ram Tom brought home."

"I'm not saying you're unhealthy, only that too much work will turn you into a shriveled turnip. A bit of time for yourself would not be amiss."

They walked toward the Fletchers' wagon. "And who will take charge of Ravenwell while I'm enjoying all that leisure?" Lilly asked.

"I didn't say you must leave," Mrs. Fletcher retorted. "Only take a day now and then to do nothing but sit on the beach, walk the fells, fish in the lake. Or sit on the beach doing nothing but looking at your books of faraway places."

Charlotte and Tom walked ahead, and Tom laughed at something Charlotte said with her hands.

"It was a raw disappointment for you when Maude fell ill and you couldn't take that post as Mrs. Blakeley's companion. I know how you wanted to travel with her," the older woman murmured.

"Well, there'll be no traveling for me now, in any event." Charlotte needed her.

Didn't she?

They reached the Fletcher wagon as Samuel arrived with the Ravenwell buggy. Lilly felt herself blush as Mrs. Fletcher appraised him frankly. "Remember what I said about shriveled turnips, lass," she said quietly, then turned to Tom. "Help me up, lad. Charlotte's coming to dinner, so lend her a hand, too."

Sam put on the brake and jumped down. He'd spent an hour at the hive near the road, observing the worker bees that returned to the hive. He'd noted two different dances, but since he hadn't tracked the "dancing" bees prior to their arrival at the hive, he couldn't correlate their pollen collecting with their later movements.

Still, it was valuable information, and Sam had documented it in his notes.

He caught sight of Lilly bidding farewell to Charlotte and Tom, and a woman who must have been Tom's mother. Jumping down from the buggy, he went to them, avoiding Reverend Graham and his son.

"You're just on time," Lilly said.

She wore a trim, rose-colored walking dress along with white gloves and a hat. Sam did not offer his arm, but Lilly did not seem offended.

"Where did you go during services?"

"Bee hunting."

"Ah."

The crowd of people began to dissipate as the two

of them walked toward the buggy. "And did you find many?"

"On a fine day like this? Sure."

She did not wait for him to help her into the vehicle, but climbed up quickly, before there could be any awkwardness between them. She kept her distance, but she was close enough for Sam to catch her scent, a subtle floral fragrance that tickled his senses.

Soft tendrils of hair curled at the nape of her neck, and Sam felt a most amazing urge to press his lips to them.

"Where is your home?" she asked after Sam guided the horse onto the road. "You're American, but your address is London?"

"That address is my brother's house. I don't really have a place that I call home. Although—" he gritted his teeth "—that's going to change."

"What was it like, going from place to place? Never putting down roots?"

Sam had never really thought about any of it before—the canvas bag in which he packed his clothes, the crates that carried his camera and plates, the old leather portfolio that had traveled the world with him. He considered the foreign train stations and dockyards he'd seen, and the crush of people in flowing gowns and turbans. For the first time in months, he was not overcome by a cold, clammy dread at the thought of it.

"Your ears get tuned to different sounds," he finally said, answering her question. "The language— that's the first thing I notice."

"What then?"

"The smells. Different spices, the animals and humans… The places I've known each has its own distinct aromas.''

''Oh!'' She angled her body toward him, listening expectantly. ''What else?''

''Colors,'' Sam recalled. ''Not the staid and tasteful hues of civilization, but wild, vibrant colors, all pieced together in one ensemble. Turbans. Other headgear. Baskets. Noise.''

He heard her sigh. ''It must be wonderful.''

Yes, it was, Sam thought. The only life he'd ever wanted.

''If you'll turn off just here,'' Lilly said, ''I'll show you the most wonderful spot in the Lake District.''

Sam didn't think there could be any finer place than right where he was, beside Lilly Tearwater, but he turned the buggy onto a narrow track that made a gradual climb through a grassy meadow, until it petered out and they could go no farther.

Lilly took off her gloves. When she removed her hat, her hair fell out of its combs. Appearing not to give it a thought, she twisted it and somehow secured it again. ''We must walk from here.''

A suitor would have taken Lilly's hand as they hiked on the path that led to one of the high fells. But Sam was not Lilly's suitor.

The path became steeper, resulting in a much more strenuous climb. It did not deter Lilly even slightly. Sam followed her until the path changed again.

''It's a bit of a climb from here.''

''Lead on,'' Sam said.

She didn't make a fuss about the dust on her skirts or the heels of her shoes. She scrambled over craggy rocks, then skirted branches and brambles, continuing until they reached a peak that overlooked a magnificent vista. Four mountains converged over a deep green valley. A river meandered through the base of the valley and two waterfalls crashed over rocks in the distance, feeding the river.

It was spectacular. Sam experienced the sensation of standing at the top of the world and looking down. He glanced over at Lilly and saw by her expression that she felt the same.

"It's called Penny Top. I know it's not the Parthenon, but…"

She walked to the edge of the cliff, and Sam's heart stopped when she stepped off. "Christ!" He grabbed for her.

She'd only dropped down about three feet, and turned to look at him with an impish smile. "I didn't frighten you, did I?"

His heart started to beat again. "Just don't tell me I'm the only one ever to be taken in by your trick."

She laughed while he vaulted to the ledge beside her. It was a wide, rocky slab, covered with lichen and moss. Lilly sat down, drawing her knees up to her chin, and looked out at the scene before her.

"Charlotte and I explored every inch of these fells with Tom. There are trickling waterfalls and caves hidden in cliffs all over. Maude would have confined us for a week had she known we were climbing up here. And given us bread and water, besides!"

Lilly's cheeks were pink, her lips slightly parted as she gazed at the sky and the valley below. Sam wanted desperately to take her in his arms.

He'd nearly done it a moment before, when he thought she was falling. Perhaps he could do it again.

If it happened spontaneously, without thought, he might just be able to slip his hands around her shoulders and pull her close.

He cleared his throat. "So you just happened upon this place?"

She nodded.

He sat down nearby and eased back on the soft, green moss. When the whisper of a breeze touched his mouth, Sam closed his eyes. It was easy to imagine that it was Lilly's fingers stroking his lips, his face.

The sensation continued, tickling his ear, embracing his shoulders. He felt Lilly's lips on his own, soft kisses mixed with her warm breath. He pulled her close and pressed her soft curves to the hard planes of his body.

She caressed him, his shoulders and chest, his waist, his thighs. Sam felt so aroused, it was painful.

He needed desperately to be on top of her, inside her.

Sam heard himself groan. He pulled Lilly under him and opened the buttons of her gown. A soft, lacy fabric covered her breasts, but he pushed it aside and lowered his head, taking one pebbled nipple in his mouth. A moment later, her skirts were gone and he pressed his hand against her most exquisite heat.

He heard her sigh, felt her working the buttons of his trousers. Nearly ready to burst, Sam made a harsh sound of relief when she finally touched him.

He could not bear her stroking for long. He raised himself over her and plunged, feeling her tight heat envelope him.

Nothing else existed. Just the two of them, fitting together perfectly, as nothing in the world ever could. She moved with him, and made small sounds of pleasure, then suddenly contracted around him, triggering his own climax. It went on until Samuel thought his heart would burst.

But when it was over, and he lay on the soft moss with Lilly in his arms, he knew he'd never felt such contentment. He could lie coupled with her forever.

An ear-wrenching crack sounded, making Sam jump. He sat up abruptly, barely in time to see a nearby outcropping of rock rip away from the cliff and plummet to the valley below.

He suffered only a moment's disorientation when he realized that he was fully dressed, as was Lilly, who remained seated several feet away from where he'd been.

"Move, Lilly! We've got to get out of here!"

She turned and quickly climbed up the embankment to solid ground. Scrambling away from the ledge, they hurried down the hillside, sliding and stumbling on the rough path until they reached the buggy, certain that the rest of the mountain was about to fall into the abyss at any second.

"What the hell was that?" Sam asked when they finally reached safety. "There was no storm, and this area isn't known for earthquakes." Unless he counted the earth-shattering orgasm he'd just experienced.

It was just one more thing he couldn't understand. Had he fallen asleep and dreamed of making love with Lilly? *It had seemed so real.*

But she'd been sitting a decorous distance away when the crash had startled him to his feet. She certainly hadn't been wrapped cozily in his arms the way he'd imagined.

"I...don't recall anything like that ever happening before," she said, climbing up into the buggy. Her cheeks were pale and her voice strained, but Sam couldn't read her expression.

"Would there have been any people down below?" he asked.

She shook her head. "There aren't any houses on this side of the valley. And there are no footpaths down there. The terrain is too rugged."

Sam didn't know what to make of it. First, the erotic dream, then the cataclysmic rending of the cliff, not fifty feet from where he and Lilly had been sitting. It was absurd to think that the two events were related, but they were unquestionably connected in Sam's mind.

Just as each of the phantom caresses he'd experienced had been connected with a strange sudden wind, or shooting stars or an unexpected rainstorm.

He should be able to make sense of it. He was a scientist, damn it! Not some fool who was unable to collect data and draw logical conclusions.

He climbed onto the buggy. Picking up the reins and releasing the brake, Sam was absolutely no closer to understanding why these strange events were happening, or why Lilly sat so stiffly beside him. Was it the shock of seeing half the mountain crash down beside her?

Or had she experienced the same dream he had?

Lilly would not let on that she knew exactly what had happened when Samuel had closed his eyes. Or that she'd felt every fondling touch, every caress and the world-shattering conclusion to their lovemaking.

She closed her eyes as the buggy flew down the

hill, and tried to block out the vivid images of the two of them intertwined, sharing the most intimate of acts.

But the memory of their encounter would not leave her. Watching the mountainside shatter alongside Penny Top was nothing compared to what she'd shared with Samuel. Every detail was indelibly burned into her mind—something to remember and cherish once Samuel had left Ravenwell forever.

"Are you all right?" he asked once he'd stopped the buggy from its mad retreat.

She felt his eyes on her, and knew she must try to appear as if the only thing that had occurred was the sudden avalanche. She would never admit to seducing him without his knowledge or consent. Without his active participation. "I—I suppose so. That was…"

"A more unstable spot than you thought. You shouldn't go back up there…" His voice sounded harsh and strained. Risking a glance toward his face, she saw a raw hunger in his expression, and a passion that was barely leashed. "…unless you're with me."

Lilly could not respond. Samuel's body leaned toward hers, his head dipping close, until they were but a breath apart.

"If you don't mind, Lilly," he whispered, "I believe I'm going to kiss you."

Chapter Sixteen

The desire to taste her lips was as strong as Sam's need to breathe.

He moved closer, inhaling her scent, anticipating the touch of her soft lips against his. He could hear his blood pounding in his ears, feel the sweat beading on his forehead.

Christ! What was he doing?

He pulled back and dropped his head into his hands. Desire warred with the irrational dread that kept him separate from her—from everyone.

Sam's hands shook, and Lilly trembled beside him. He could feel her breathless expectation, sense the same ardor in her that drove him. But he could not bring himself to touch her. There was nothing he could do to overcome the barrier keeping him from making their experience on Penny Top a reality.

He swallowed thickly and took control of the overpowering arousal he felt. It was clear that the strange dream had addled his senses. Just because he'd made love to Lilly in some unreal fantasy did not mean he was capable of making it occur in reality.

He had to get back to Ravenwell and leave Lilly there. A bit of distance was what he needed. And work. He had the notes and drawings he'd made earlier, and he really ought to add them to his data. And there were photographs to be taken of the hive in the chestnut tree.

In short, the more he concentrated on his project, the less he would think about Lilly Tearwater and all the strange events on Penny Top.

Her eyes were full of questions when he glanced her way, but neither of them spoke as he flicked the reins and continued down the path.

Lilly's nerves were still shaky when Samuel left her at the door of the inn and drove off. He had planned to kiss her. But the obstacles in his mind kept him from going through with it.

A lady would have been piqued by the effrontery of his attempted kiss, and relieved when he retreated. Yet Lilly could feel nothing but a terrible emptiness, a loneliness clear through to her soul.

"The door to Mrs. Evanston's bedroom is stuck," Mrs. Bainbridge announced when Lilly entered the front door. "And the apricots that were delivered yesterday are all spoiled. Mr. Clive is in an absolute snit over it."

"Yes," Lilly said absently. "They were for a sauce that he'd planned…"

"Well, Davy is working on the door," Mrs. Bainbridge said. "And there's naught to be done about the apricots. Are you feeling well?"

"Oh." She must cease her ruminations and get to work. Mrs. Bainbridge never worked a full day on Sundays, and it was nearly time for her to leave.

''Yes, fine. Let me just change clothes and I'll take over.''

''What happened to your skirts? You look as if you've tramped the whole of Cumbria in them.''

''No, just up one of the paths. I'll be right out.'' She circled 'round the desk and entered her private rooms, eager to escape Mrs. Bainbridge's inquiries.

The experience on Penny Top raised a number of questions of her own that Lilly could not face. At least, not now. Not while her nerves still hummed with the awareness of what she'd shared with Samuel.

She now knew how it would feel to become his lover.

It was quiet in the apartment, and Lilly was struck with the thought that this must be how Charlotte's world must seem. Utterly silent.

Lilly wondered what would happen if she *changed* Charlotte. What if she fixed her ears so that she could hear? Would she would be able to speak, to converse about the day's events? To share the experiences that made up her day?

Would she still need Lilly?

The question was moot. Changing Charlotte would be wrong—besides, some unpredictable, terrible event would happen along with the cure.

But still, Lilly wished she had someone to talk to.

She was so lonely. And her loneliness and frustration grew with every month, with every passing year she was compelled to stay at Ravenwell.

But there were a hundred things to do before tea, and Lilly had no time to ruminate over her situation. She changed clothes and went to the kitchen, somehow managing to soothe Mr. Clive's frayed nerves.

They settled on a new menu for supper, and when Lilly left, the staff had already begun preparations for tea.

She saw Samuel return to the inn from the barn, but he did not stop on his way to his room.

Lilly could not blame him. After all that had happened on Penny Top, it was likely that the mere sight of her embarrassed him.

Or her actions had made him believe he was losing his mind.

Sam was sure he must be losing his mind.

He gritted his teeth. He could *not* have made love to Lilly. They hadn't even been physically close when the avalanche had startled him into reality. Their clothes were intact, and there was no sign that he had ever touched her.

Except for the unmistakable feeling of satisfaction that came from knowing her intimately, from spilling his seed inside her.

None of it made sense. Not from the moment he'd closed his eyes on Penny Top until the mountainside had come crashing down beside them.

The urge to kiss Lilly when they got to safer ground was the only understandable event of the morning. Whatever had happened on Penny Top, it had caused a driving desire to hold her.

That desire had not yet abated.

But what could he do about it? Storm the inn and take her in his arms? The dream that he'd had on Penny Top had changed nothing. It was folly to think that he could suddenly master his aversion to touch, just because an hallucination made him believe he could make love to Lilly.

He turned his attention to the bee he had marked. It would visit hundreds of blossoms before returning to the hive, and it was a mindless task to follow it as it made its path through the meadow. Unfortunately, that gave him too much time to ponder his present dilemma and his future as a professor at the Royal College.

Sam didn't know how he could face it.

There had to be a way to overcome his malady so that he could undertake the project in India with Mr. Phipson's group.

If only Sam could figure out how.

When the bee's pollen sacs were nearly full, Sam headed back to the chestnut tree and climbed onto his platform to focus his camera, ready to photograph the insect when it returned to the hive. He did not need photographic evidence to prove his theory, but it would add a modern dimension to the paper when it was published. Later, he would measure the distance and direction the bee had flown.

Even without accurate measurements, Sam could predict the movements the bee would make when it returned to the hive. He'd documented these movements hundreds of times before, and knew that this was the bee's way of communicating with the other workers in the hive.

He was certain the bee was telling the hive exactly where she'd been, what distance and direction, where to find food.

Sam was ready to study mammals again. The opportunity to do research on the chinkara population of Maharashtra would come about once in a lifetime. He would be a fool to turn it down.

"Turned warm today, eh, Mr. Temple?" called

Tom Fletcher, standing near the base of the tree. Sam hadn't even heard the man's approach.

"That just might be an understatement, Fletcher," Sam replied. He took his photograph, then covered his camera.

"Will you be in for a bit of swimming?"

Sam mopped his brow. He was hot and uncomfortable. A swim would feel great just about now. "Sure."

"Come on, then. Get your swimming costume and meet me at the beach."

Most of the guests were on the terrace having tea, anxious to catch any breeze that might cool them.

Mr. Dawson sat with his friend, George Hamlet, who had arrived on the noon train. The newcomer was not much taller than Lilly, but he was built like a bull. Thick about the shoulders and waist, the man appeared as solid as a brick. He was a good deal younger than Mr. Dawson, though his ruddy face would never be called handsome.

His nose was crooked and his lips were hardly visible, his mouth being a bare slit above a squat chin. The stylish muttonchops on his cheeks did nothing to improve his features, and Lilly felt a pang of sympathy for his homeliness.

She was surprised to see Miss Simpson again, sitting between the two gentlemen as the three of them took their tea. The old spinster beamed with delight to be in the company of the two Londoners, and Lilly wondered if the woman's brother knew she was spending time with a stranger.

Deciding it was not her concern, Lilly followed Charlotte into their apartment and changed into her

bathing costume. The weather had turned so hot and
close that she had allowed herself to be talked into
going for a swim. But there wasn't much time.

She'd put Davy in charge of the reception desk,
and Lilly did not anticipate any problems. But she
didn't like to leave him alone for too long. He was
young and needed direction.

However, anything that had to be done in the next
hour would have to wait.

After all that had happened, and the questions that
plagued her, Lilly welcomed even a brief interlude
at the lake. It wasn't often that she or Charlotte were
able to take an afternoon to do nothing but laze in
the water.

They followed the path down to the beach and saw
that quite a number of Ravenwell guests had had the
same idea. Greeting those they knew, Lilly and her
sister quickly made their escape and skirted 'round
to the far side of the rocks. They headed toward the
stretch of beach and the sheltered cove where they'd
done their swimming ever since they were children.

Charlotte indicated that Tom would meet them
there, and a moment later, Lilly caught sight of him
tromping out of the water, dressed in a striped swimming costume. He was covered from his neck to his
knees, but his arms were bare and pasty-white from
the elbows up.

He was smiling and playful, so different from the
staid and solid sheep farmer he'd grown up to be.

"Come on! Come on!" he shouted. "Put down
your things and jump in! We've been waiting hours
for you!"

Charlotte had already dropped her towel onto the
sand and was sloshing into the waves. Lilly placed

her canvas bag on a rock at the edge of the sand. She sat down beside it and unfastened her shoes, then debated whether to remove her stockings in the bright daylight.

Tom always mocked their bathing costumes, saying that all those clothes were more likely to drown them than protect their modesty. And Lilly had to agree. She leaned over and rolled down her stockings, then stood and unfastened the skirt of her swimming clothes. Wearing only bloomers and her blouse, she dashed toward the water and threw herself into it, feeling immediately refreshed.

Taking long strokes, Lilly swam out toward the "Rocky Isles," as she and Tom had called the natural formation of rocks where the three of them had climbed and played as children. Raising her head above the surface of the water, she pulled herself up onto a rock, only to come face-to-face with Samuel.

"You're a strong swimmer," he said, his eyes coursing over her wet bathing costume, then boldly appraising her bare arms and legs. Only once before had Lilly felt more naked—this morning on Penny Top, when they'd undressed each other.

But that hadn't been real.

"I'll race you to the island!" Lilly cried, and dived into the water. She felt him plunge in after her, but paid no attention as he kept pace with her. The island was only a few yards away, and when they reached its bank, Lilly remained in the water. She was not going to expose herself to his view again.

"I beat you!" she exclaimed.

"Ha!" He splashed her. "You most certainly did not, even though I gave you a head start!"

With a laugh, she sank below the surface and

kicked away from Samuel. He gave chase, but never managed to catch her, even though he was agile and his strokes much more powerful than her own.

He could easily have captured her if he'd wanted to do so.

"I've never seen a swimming dress like yours," he said, and Lilly felt herself blush. "Is it some new fashion for women?"

"Hardly." She swam away, unwilling to admit that she intentionally flaunted the boundaries of propriety.

He caught up to her. "Don't be offended. I like it," he said with a wink, then swam to the rocks, where he climbed up and sat looking toward the middle of the lake.

Lilly joined him on the edge and dangled her legs in the water, less concerned by her inadequate attire. She was much more interested in the play of muscles in Samuel's arms, and the thick, damp hair on his brawny legs. She was entranced watching his long, tapered feet kick at the clear water below them.

The same amazing tension Lilly had experienced on Penny Top started to coil in her belly as she sat near Samuel, and she yearned for the intimate touch that would release that tension in a torrent of pleasure. She wondered if he was thinking of the intimacies they'd shared while he believed he was dreaming.

Lilly should never have listened to Mrs. Fletcher's talk about shriveled turnips. It had made her act rashly again.

Samuel stood abruptly and jumped into the water, swimming toward shore. But then he stopped and rolled to the surface to lie on his back, gently kicking his feet to stay afloat. Lilly jumped in and swam up beside him, but he did not turn his head to look at her.

''I could float out here for hours,'' he said. ''The water is soothing. When you close your eyes, and your ears are below the surface of the water, it's as if you're alone in the world.''

''Is that how you'd prefer to be? Alone?''

''No.'' The sound was a hoarse rasp. He shifted his body so that he was upright in the deep water, facing her. ''I want you, Lilly. I want to take you in my arms and feel your skin, bare against mine. I would kiss you if I could. I would put my mouth on your breasts and suck them until you cried out for me to make love to you.''

His eyes, blue and intense, never left hers.

And if he could do all that, then he would be free to leave Ravenwell. To leave her.

Sam should have let Lilly go back with Charlotte and Fletcher, while he lingered behind, but he was loath to leave her company. She had an unprecedented effect on him, and the strange dreams and phantom touches were only part of it.

She was beautiful and lively, interested in hearing about his work and the places he'd been. Sam believed Lilly would have spent the rest of the day listening to stories of his travels over the years and his work on the Galapagos Islands, in Africa and Persia. She was truly interested—the perfect mate for a man who was free to travel to remote corners of the world.

Instead of walking down the beach, the foursome took a narrow footpath through the woods that lay on the far edge of Ravenwell property. They soon encountered a stocky young man wearing a summer suit and straw hat, who tripped as he stepped off the path ahead of them. The fellow's movements seemed furtive to Sam, as if he'd tried to get out of sight but lost his balance before he could manage it.

"Oh! Mr. Hamlet!" Lilly cried. "Are you all right?"

He brushed off his trousers and nodded.

"You're far from the beach," she said.

"I must have lost my bearings," he replied, removing his hat and bowing slightly to the ladies.

"Well, come along with us, and we'll show you the way back."

"I thank you, Miss Tearwater," Hamlet replied.

Sam didn't like the man's looks. He was built like a fighter. One of his ears was mashed, as if he'd been in one brawl too many. His manner was sheepish, his eyes darting nervously, as if looking for a means of escape.

"Feel free to go your own way if you prefer," Fletcher said. "The lake is just down the path, and if you turn to the east, you'll get to the Ravenwell beach. The trail to the inn is clear from there."

"Thank you, mate," Hamlet said. "I think I might do that."

When he was gone, Tom turned to Lilly. "I don't like the look of that one. Keep your eye on him, and I'll talk to Davy about him, too."

"I'm sure he's all right," Lilly said. "He's Mr. Dawson's friend, just come up from London today. It's no wonder he got lost—"

Charlotte stopped them for an explanation, which

Tom gave her. Sam thought that Tom was right. Caution was wise with regard to Mr. Hamlet.

Sam walked back to Ravenwell with the others, and encountered Alan Graham at the registration desk, talking to Lilly's handyman. The young vicar turned when he heard them.

"Miss Tearwater," Graham said, extending a large bouquet of flowers in her direction. "I came to— You're wet!"

All four of them were wet and wearing swimming attire. Lilly had put on her stockings and added more layers of clothes while the men's backs were turned. It had to be obvious what they'd been doing.

"Yes, so if you'll excuse me," Lilly said, accepting the flowers from Graham's outstretched hand, "I'll change and be right with you."

But Graham separated her from the group and took her arm before she could leave. Sam stepped forward as if he had the power to prevent their contact. But he did not. He had no control over who courted Miss Tearwater.

He wasn't her father, nor was he her suitor.

Since it was pointless, as well as awkward, to remain in the room while Graham paid suit to Lilly, Sam left Tom and Charlotte and went up to his room. The exhilaration of the afternoon had vanished, leaving him feeling empty.

The only cure for it was to get back to work.

He put on dry clothes, then took his leather portfolio and went down to the garden, with hopes of avoiding Lilly and Graham.

The tables were empty, but for an elderly couple who seemed never to venture far from the inn grounds, and the newly arrived Mr. Hamlet, sitting with Mr. Dawson. The two men took note of Sam's arrival, but continued to talk quietly while Sam made himself comfortable at his own table in the shade.

Sam's earlier dislike turned to mistrust now that he saw Dawson and Hamlet together. He hoped the two of them did not plan to stay at Ravenwell very long.

He spread out his notes and drawings and started to work, intentionally keeping his mind off Lilly and Reverend Graham, and the two London cronies who sat huddled nearby, as if they were secretly conferring with Lord Gladstone on the Home Rule question.

But keeping his mind off Lilly was impossible. She touched him in every way, except physically. When Sam was with her, he almost believed he could overcome the fears that haunted him. The prospect of joining Phipson's expedition no longer seemed impossible.

At least, not entirely.

"Mind if we join you?"

Sam had been too absorbed by his thoughts to notice Dawson and Hamlet coming his way. Their arrival startled him.

"Suit yourself," he said, though he did not move any of his books to accommodate them.

"You're a man of science," Dawson said as he and Hamlet took seats at Sam's table. "What do you make of these ghosts?"

Sam shrugged and continued to sketch. "I don't make anything of them."

"But surely you're curious. After all, the ghostly apparitions are not the only strange things going on here at Ravenwell."

Sam looked up. "What do you mean?"

"Think about it, Temple," he said. "Every time those ghosts appear, something strange happens."

"You're right," Sam retorted. "I can't think of many things stranger than seeing ghosts."

"No! No, that's not what I mean."

Sam leaned back and crossed his long legs at the ankle. "Why don't you enlighten me?"

"You must have noticed the strange storms that seem to affect only Ravenwell. And the shattered windows, the broken pots…"

Of course Sam had noticed those things. And more. He just didn't know what to make of them. "What is your opinion, then, Dawson? What do you think is happening around Ravenwell?"

Henry Dawson took a deep breath. "It's Miss Tearwater," he said. "Somehow—"

Sam laughed. "Of course," he said derisively. "Miss Tearwater breaks her own windows. And creates rain clouds over her inn. She is a scientific wonder."

Hamlet remained silent as Dawson ran his hand over his face. He clearly believed that Lilly was somehow responsible for every weird occurrence that took place on Ravenwell grounds.

Sam wasn't going to admit that he'd had the same suspicions. They sounded ridiculous when Dawson articulated them. It was absurd to think that a human being had the power to alter the forces of nature. There must certainly be some logical explanation for the changes in weather.

"What about the ghosts?" Dawson persisted. "Do you think they're real?"

"I haven't found any evidence to suggest they aren't," Sam said.

"Ah! So, you've looked for it!"

"Of course. I wouldn't be much of a scientist if I hadn't."

"But you've seen nothing to indicate fraud."

Sam shook his head as Dawson cast a glance at Hamlet, who had been listening attentively.

The ghosts were real.

It was the first time Sam had admitted as much to himself. He had found absolutely nothing to suggest that anyone at Ravenwell was causing the apparitions.

He knew there was nothing going on in Mr. Edison's laboratories that could produce such effects. Writing to his friend at Menlo Park would be a waste of time.

As to the other curious events at Ravenwell…why wouldn't the appearance of ghosts alter the atmosphere? Cause pressure changes that could produce rain? Or break glass? If he accepted the existence of ghosts, then all the other bizarre events at Ravenwell must be acceptable, too, if not explainable.

The odd sensations and the dream that Sam had experienced were entirely different. They had to have resulted from some aberration in his brain. The events in Sudan had probably had a greater effect than he knew. Why else would he have these vivid hallucinations when he was with Lilly?

The only solution was to avoid her. If he stayed away from Lilly, he had no doubt that these impossible illusions would cease.

Chapter Seventeen

The hair on the back of Lilly's neck prickled with awareness. Dropping the clump of weeds she'd just pulled, she turned to see who was there. The garden was empty. No one was in sight, other than a few Ravenwell guests milling about near the door of the inn.

It wasn't the first time in the past week that Lilly had felt someone watching her, only to discover no one was there. It was an eerie feeling.

She picked up the two baskets she'd used while gardening, and walked toward the inn, anxious to escape the unsettling sense that she was someone's quarry.

It was all foolishness, anyway, brought on by the suspicion that someone had invaded her private rooms the previous week. Of course no one had been inside while she and Charlotte had been gone! And no one was stalking her now.

For some reason, she'd been on edge all week, and it hadn't helped that Samuel had been avoiding her. She'd seen him only at mealtimes, and it seemed that every time she had a spare moment and thought of joining him at his table, he disappeared.

He'd barely said two words to her since their outing at the lake with Tom and Charlotte the previous Sunday.

It wasn't that she didn't know where to find him. Charlotte spent an hour or two with Samuel every afternoon down by the chestnut tree, collecting the information he sought, taking photographs and making drawings. Charlotte had already learned a great deal from Samuel, and Lilly was grateful to him for his patience.

And she didn't blame him for wanting to avoid her.

He had stopped asking questions about the ghosts, and no longer made insinuations about their veracity. Lilly didn't know precisely what that meant.

The afternoon had turned cool, and rain threatened. It would be a perfect setting for Sir Emmett and Lady Alice to appear, especially since Lilly had only conjured them once in the past week. That was partly due to Alan's frequent visits.

Lilly didn't know if his purpose was to court her or to keep watch for sprits to exorcise. Either way, she did not particularly welcome the vicar's attentions, but he seemed oblivious to her polite hints that she was uninterested.

She had barely gotten through the door to the reception area when Mr. Hinkley approached her. Accompanied by two of the merchants from Asbury, the mayor carried a new leather satchel and two long rolls of parchment.

"Miss Tearwater," he said. "If we could have a word."

Once again, he caught her unprepared, wearing her gardening clothes, with dirt on her hands, caked under her nails. Eyeing the official-looking papers, Lilly knew at once that he and the others had come in force to convince her to expand the inn. "Of course, Mr. Hinkley," she said. "If you'll be so good as to wait for me in the sun parlor while I make myself presentable. Shall I send tea?"

She made a quick exit, retreating to her private rooms after arranging for tea to be sent to the gentlemen.

Wasting no time, Lilly washed her face and hands, pinned up her hair and changed into a sensible blouse and skirt. Her intention was to appear older, and as a more experienced businesswoman than she could ever hope to be.

But when she returned to the sun parlor, she knew she seemed no more than a green lass to them. One who'd managed to bring a good deal of business to Asbury, but who was tremendously inexperienced and easily manipulated.

"Now then, gentlemen," she said, as if she had control of the situation. "What brings you to Ravenwell?"

Mr. Beecher, the storekeeper, set his teacup aside and unrolled the first scroll on the table before him. "I took the liberty of having some drawings made. At no cost, mind you…my wife's brother dabbles in this sort of thing."

"I see."

It was a rendering of her inn, done in ink. But it wasn't the Ravenwell Lilly knew. In place of the attic were two additional floors, and an extra wing jutted out from each side of the building.

The changes were hideous.

"Here is a view from the back." Beecher unrolled the second scroll, and Lilly found herself staring at it, speechless. Gone were her gardens and the wonderful canopy of trees that shaded the back of the inn. The tea terrace was swallowed up by a crass, brick-paved *restaurant*. Dining tables filled the space.

Mr. Hinkley opened his satchel and took out a sheaf of papers. "And here are the estimates for a stage line running from the train station up here to Ravenwell," he said. "The Royal Cumbria Bank is prepared to offer you a very nominal interest rate for whatever loans are necessary to undertake such a venture."

Lilly's eyes crossed as she stared at the long list of figures on the page. There were projections of the number of guests Ravenwell would accommodate after it was enlarged, the income from their rooms at the inn and their transportation costs.

"Seems to me," said a voice behind her, "that the town of Asbury ought to put in its own stage line."

"Gentlemen, this is Mr. Temple," Lilly stated. She wore a very proper ensemble, and her hair was carefully arranged. But there was a small smudge of dirt on the edge of her jaw, just under her ear. Sam felt a compelling urge to touch his lips to the spot. He took a deep breath and turned his attention to her introductions. "You remember Mr. Hinkley, and here are Mr. Beecher and Mr. Crofton."

The three men sat gaping at him, obviously surprised by his intrusion, his American rudeness. After a moment's delay, they stood and stretched out their hands. Sam looked down at his own and wiped it on his vest. "You'll have to pardon me, I seem to have gotten tree sap on my palm…"

"Mr. Temple is working on a scientific experiment in our meadow, down near the lake," Lilly explained.

Sam had no idea why he'd intruded upon this meeting. He'd managed to avoid Lilly for the better part of a week, though he'd missed the shudder of awareness that shot through him whenever she was near. He yearned to hear her easy laughter, to breathe her alluring scent.

In the week since Penny Top, he had not once felt phantom hands caressing him. He hadn't experienced the extraordinary sense of making love to Lilly.

But instead of feeling better, he'd felt a different kind of madness—one that came from missing her.

"It seems rather risky," Sam said, "for an individual entrepreneur to bear the entire financial burden of this kind of venture."

"See here, Mr. Temple," said Crofton. "I don't know that it's any of your concern."

"Oh, but Mr. Temple and I have discussed the mayor's proposition," Lilly said, clearly grateful for Sam's intervention.

She sat down and the men followed suit, while Sam declined to take a seat.

The mayor spoke up. "Then you must have advised Miss Tearwater that upon enlarging the inn, she stands to gain a far better profit, since a greater number of guests will be paying for bedrooms and requesting services."

"I believe Miss Tearwater is considering those factors." Sam stood just outside the circle of chairs, in front of the fireplace.

"And a stage line to service an operation such as Ravenwell—"

"That would, no doubt, readily transport visitors into Asbury for the purpose of trade," Sam said.

"Why, of course," agreed the mayor.

"Which is why a stage line ought to be a joint venture, since Asbury stands to gain significantly from having Ravenwell guests visiting your town."

"But Ravenwell itself would be the driving force behind such an undertaking. Therefore, it only makes sense for the inn to bear the expense," said Hinkley.

Sam leaned one arm against the mantel over the fireplace. "To restate your proposal, then…you believe Miss Tearwater should borrow funds to establish a form of transportation so that her guests can travel frequently between Ravenwell and Asbury."

"It's a sound plan," said Crofton.

"For the merchants of Asbury," Sam retorted.

Clearly annoyed by Sam's interference, the men turned to Lilly. "Miss Tearwater." Beecher picked up the sheaf of papers and held them out to her. "Look over Mr. Hinkley's figures. They will convince you that you cannot err in this enterprise. There is profit to be made by all."

Lilly took the documents and laid them on top of the drawings. She appeared to study them for a moment, then looked up at her guests. "Gentlemen, I've decided to consult with a business advisor before making any decisions in this matter."

The Asbury men all sat forward and began speaking at once, though Crofton's voice overpowered the rest.

"But this is a very straightforward proposal. Add fifty rooms to Ravenwell," he said, "and put in a stage line. What harm could possibly—"

"No harm, Mr. Crofton," Sam said, joining the group. They just meant for Lilly to turn Ravenwell into something she wouldn't recognize. And for her to take all the financial risk.

There were a great number of variables to consider. What if the ghosts stopped appearing? What if the tourist trade dropped off for some other, unforeseen reason? Lilly and Ravenwell would be bearing the burden of the debt.

"Miss Tearwater is wise to seek advice before making any decisions," Sam added.

Crofton stood abruptly. His face and neck were red with frustration. "Mr. Temple, since Ravenwell is not your concern—"

"Now, now, Mr. Crofton," said Mayor Hinkley in a conciliatory tone. "No need to excite yourself." Then he also stood and turned to Lilly. "Miss Tearwater, these drawings speak for themselves. And the income projections are quite accurate, if I do say so myself…"

Crofton grumbled something under his breath and walked toward the door. Beecher picked up his hat and followed.

"Please give due consideration to these proposals, Miss Tearwater," Hinkley said, following the others. "We can certainly make revisions to the plan…hire another set of drawings if these are not satisfactory."

"Mr. Hinkley," Lilly said. "I feel I must tell you that I am not inclined to change Ravenwell in any way. Since your bank holds our mortgage, you must be fully aware of our current debt. And I am certainly reticent to add further to the burden we already bear.''

''But Miss Tearwater—''

''I'll consider your plan, Mr. Hinkley,'' she said. ''But that is all I can promise you.''

The mayor opened his mouth to respond, but reconsidered. He gave Lilly a curt bow, then turned and left the room.

Sam should have gone out, too, but when the townsmen departed, Lilly went to the parlor doors and closed them. Then she turned to him.

''Thank you.''

He gave a casual shrug, even though his heart began to pound the moment they were alone. She was so beautiful at close quarters. ''That's all right. They were trying to swamp you.''

''Swamp me?''

''Sink your ship. Overcome your objections by a show of force.''

''I see.'' She leaned against the thick mahogany doors. ''I don't know of any business advisors. *Is* there such a thing?''

''I imagine,'' he replied, quirking his mouth in a smile. ''I don't see that it matters. Ravenwell is yours. You decide what you want to do.''

''Did you see those drawings?''

Sam should have slipped past her and gone up to his room as he'd planned. Instead, he found himself picking up one of the drawings and taking a seat. ''Pretty damned awful,'' he said, looking up at her. ''You haven't changed your mind, then?''

Lilly joined him, standing behind him, looking

over his shoulder. "Can you imagine, putting this monstrosity over my gardens? And look at this." Reaching across him, she moved the second drawing into view.

Sam barely saw the document. Instead, he closed his eyes and felt her presence. They were not quite touching, but her nearness flooded his senses with pleasure.

All he needed to do was shift his body slightly. Or take her hand in his, then pull her onto his lap.

She gave a quick laugh, the husky sound washing through him like a monsoon. "Who would ever think of turning Ravenwell into this? Or chopping up the front with doors here and here?"

He forced his attention on the drawings and agreed that they were absurd. Ravenwell was a stately old building that needed no renovation. "A number of ancient structures in Greece and Italy have been changed this way, the modern trying to improve upon the ancient."

"It does not work well, does it?"

"It might, every now and then."

She came around and knelt between Sam and the table. "And these numbers," she said. "How can Mr. Hinkley possibly know all this? Shillings and pounds, all lined up in nice, neat columns." When she turned to show him, her eyes glittered with mirth.

"I could almost hear his brain tallying loan payments and interest rates while he sat here," Sam said with amusement. "If all went according to their plan, a larger Ravenwell would be a boon to the Asbury merchants. And they've already decided that it will happen. Especially Crofton. Now, he's a sour chap."

Lilly laughed softly, the sound sensual and husky,

full of dark promise. "He's always been that way. But did you see how angry he became when you entered the room? I'll never forget the fire in his eyes when…"

Sam barely heard her words. His eyes were fixed on the smudge below her ear. Slowly, he moved his hand toward her face and touched his thumb to the spot.

A rush of sensation shot through him, but it was not pain or disgust. There was no frenzied dread, no horror, no terrible repugnance when he made contact.

Her skin was smooth and soft. A shiny curl of her hair dropped onto his fingers, and he did not recoil in dismay. On the contrary, he leaned toward her, his head dipping lower until their lips were a mere inch apart.

He felt as if his life depended upon kissing her.

Lilly's eyes fluttered closed and she whispered one word. "Yes."

Sam touched his mouth to her lips.

All manner of sensations pulsed through him. He was instantly aroused, beyond anything he'd experienced when the phantom hands had caressed him. This was much more intense than the fierce arousal that had exploded through him on Penny Top.

This was Lilly, and she was real.

But Sam could do no more than brush his lips against hers. Their contact was a paltry sip to a thirsting man, yet he could not make himself delve any deeper.

Lilly pulled away slightly. "Samuel…"

He trembled at the sound of his name on her lips, the touch of her breath on his mouth.

"Are you…" He saw her throat move as she

swallowed thickly, then whispered, "Perhaps we should…go slowly."

Like a man starved for too long, Sam could think of nothing but putting his tongue on the throbbing pulse in Lilly's neck, of tearing the delicate blouse away from her shoulders and burying his face between her breasts.

He wanted her fast and hard.

Yet the familiar feelings of aversion had not abated entirely.

He trembled from the conflict pounding at his heart and mind. He felt his hands go damp, his mouth go dry, and heard the blood rush through his head as he reached for Lilly.

The soft heat of her body shocked him as he cupped her shoulders. Gently he touched her, his fingers savoring the sensation of warm feminine flesh. She made a small sound when he slid his hands down her back, barely touching her, and encircled her waist.

It was sheer heaven, but agony, too.

Lilly kept her hands bunched in her skirts. She was afraid to move, afraid to touch Samuel for fear that he would stop what he was doing. A fierce expression burned in his eyes, and Lilly had no doubt that he desired her. But it was a struggle for him to touch her.

She heard her last words echoing in her mind, sensed that any move she made would send him away. But she longed to thread her fingers through his hair, to press her lips to his in a much more ardent kiss than he'd given her. She wanted to feel his body against hers, to make all that had happened on Penny Top a reality.

It was mad, she knew. No decent woman would intentionally seduce a man.

But Samuel was not just any man. He was the man she had fallen in love with, the only one with whom she would ever experience intimacy. Once he was gone from Ravenwell, she would go on as she had before, making ghosts appear, and taking care of her guests.

But there would be a hole in her heart that no magic could fill.

Chapter Eighteen

Sam didn't like to think he'd run away from Lilly, but that was the truth of it. Feeling inept and agitated, he'd left her in the sun parlor and sought refuge at the hive.

The desire to touch Lilly had been equal to the desire to be touched. Sam could not bear it. Passion and apprehension warred within him, but his fears prevailed. He'd left the most beautiful woman alone and wanting.

He took the field glasses from Charlotte, who'd joined him, and raised them to his eyes, but could only gaze blindly into the meadow. He saw Lilly wherever he looked—the bewilderment in her exquisite eyes when he'd left her, the slump of disappointment in her shoulders.

He'd made not only himself miserable, but Lilly, too. If only he could take her to his room and make love to her the way he'd dreamed...

It was pointless. She was tied to Charlotte and Ravenwell, and if Sam had been able to touch her, to make a life with her here, then he'd be able to leave England and return to the work he'd always meant to do.

Charlotte tapped his arm, and he looked up from the binoculars. When she pointed to the southern edge of the field, he raised the glasses to his eyes again and saw what had made her curious. A large swarm of bees appeared to be making a nest there, in the ground.

"They're swarming," he said, but he knew she wouldn't understand. He searched for a way to demonstrate the process by which an old queen took part of the hive away to make a new nest, and after a number of elaborate hand signals, he finally seemed to make Charlotte understand.

"Stay clear of the area," he said, miming what he said. "The new hive is on the ground somewhere, but it won't be easily seen. You could get stung."

One sting was not usually a problem, but if an entire cadre of guard bees was threatened, the intruder could suffer multiple stings. Sam didn't want that to happen to Charlotte.

Dusk began to fall and Sam realized that she would be needed back at Ravenwell. He pointed to his pocket watch and indicated that she should return to the inn. She nodded and asked him if he was coming along.

Sam shook his head. He could not face Lilly so soon after their encounter in the parlor. He'd behaved like a coward, unable to overcome his irrational fears even for the woman he loved.

The realization that he loved Lilly hit him like a blow. It stole his breath and made him slightly lightheaded. He was hardly aware of Charlotte turning away, until she tripped over a rock and nearly fell.

Sam's hand shot out and caught her arm before she hit the ground.

Bewildered, Charlotte looked up at him, while Sam gaped at the hand that had hold of her arm. Sure enough, his own fingers were biting into her flesh, his knuckles white with tension.

Sam let her go as if her arm had turned to nettles. He expected a sting of pain, the stab of nausea, the familiar, penetrating panic to incapacitate him. But none of those things occurred. There was no reaction at all.

He looked down at his hand. "You touched me. Earlier, when you handed me the field glasses, you touched my arm," he said, more to himself than to Charlotte. He did not understand how it had happened, but his horror of physical contact had receded. Charlotte had tapped his arm, but somehow, his abhorrence to touch was gone.

It was because of Lilly. Sam was sure of it. He'd imagined her touch so often that he'd actually become accustomed to it. And this afternoon when he'd kissed her, she had allowed him the distance he needed. He'd been able to outstrip the inhibitions resulting from his months in captivity.

Sam stood unmoving and watched Charlotte disappear up the path to Ravenwell. He swallowed, then shoved his fingers through his hair.

Everything had changed.

If he could touch Charlotte, what else might he do? Walk through a crowd of people without feeling the crush of bodies closing in on him? Tolerate the odors of a foreign marketplace? Leave the civilized shores of England?

Join Phipson's expedition in Bombay?

He ought to walk up to Ravenwell and see if it was true—if he could shake hands with Darius Payton and the rest of his company…if he could take beautiful Lilly by the hand and lead her into the dark garden, where they could watch the sky and perhaps conjure a shower of shooting stars.

Turning on his heel, he headed toward the lake instead.

He was not ready to face the possibility that it was all a mistake, that somehow he'd managed to keep Charlotte from falling, but might never be able to touch someone again.

Charlotte had something she wanted to tell Lilly, but the supper hour had been so chaotic, there hadn't been time for Lilly to stop and pay attention to her.

Lilly had taken the place of one of the serving girls, who was ill, and had managed to thwart one of Mr. Clive's full-blown tantrums. The Ravenwell chef was truly gifted in the kitchen, but if he kept up his temperamental behavior, Lilly would have no choice but to replace him.

By the time Mrs. Bainbridge left the inn for the night, Lilly was left to deal with questions about the ghosts, and guests who had come to Ravenwell for the primary purpose of seeing them.

It had been several days since there had been an apparition, but she was too preoccupied to deal with one now. None of her guests were scheduled to leave Ravenwell tomorrow, or even the next day. So she had at least two nights to provide what they'd come to see.

She kept watch for Samuel, but he never came in for supper, and she didn't see him enter the inn to go to his room. It was possible that he was still at work in the meadow, but more likely, he was down at the beach.

He had to be just as puzzled as she was by what had happened between them in the sun parlor. She couldn't have been mistaken about Samuel's reticence to be touched. And she wondered if his desire for her had overcome it.

That was a stirring thought.

Lilly wandered through the rooms on the main floor, hoping to find him, yet sure that he wouldn't be anywhere inside. Instead, she suffered that odd sensation of being watched by someone in the shadows, even though no one was there.

Agitated now, she removed her apron, folded it and stored it under the reception desk, then entered the apartment, where she found Charlotte playing trumps with Tom, just as the three of them had done as children.

"You two look quite comfortable," Lilly said irritably.

Charlotte put the playing cards aside and started to tell Lilly about an incident that had occurred earlier in the meadow.

"I thought she might have been mistaken," Tom said when she'd finished. "But she's adamant. Mr. Temple took hold of her arm to keep her from falling. And when Charlotte forgot herself and touched his sleeve, he didn't draw back from her."

The walls of the sitting room seemed to close around Lilly. If what Charlotte had said was true...

Lilly knew that if she didn't get outdoors, she would not be able to catch her breath. She heard

Tom calling her name as she reeled out through the office, and stopped to face him.

"I'm just going out for some air," she said.

"Lilly—"

"I'm all right, Tom. I'll be in soon."

She turned away and kept moving until she reached a door that led to the back gardens.

Samuel would be free to leave now. His need to stay in Cumbria was past. Lilly should be pleased for him, but all she could feel was a sharp sense of loss.

"Miss Tearwater, are you all right?"

She whirled at the sound of a voice and saw Alan Graham approaching her from the side of the building.

"Yes, of course," she said, pressing one hand to her breast, as if that would help contain her pounding heart.

"You seem to be... Well." He cleared his throat and handed her a package. "I've, er, come to call."

Blindly, Lilly accepted it. She felt her eyes fill with tears of misery. She did not want a gift from Alan.

"Perhaps we could sit out here," he said. "It's a pleasant evening."

Lilly swallowed back her tears and followed him to one of the tables, but did not take the seat he offered. "Alan, I—"

"Open it...the gift I brought."

Lilly bit her lip and did as he asked, pulling pink silk ribbon from a box wrapped in flowered paper. She barely noticed that it was pretty and feminine. It held no appeal for her.

"They're chocolates," Alan said. "And other sweets. My mother said that ladies like sweets."

Lilly gave a short nod. She should have felt flattered by the attentions of this man. Handsome and well-bred, Alan Graham was the perfect suitor. Had Lilly cared for him, she would have sat right down and enjoyed a sample of his extravagant gift. But she could not. Unmindful of her rudeness, she muttered some excuse and slipped away, taking the path that would lead through the woods and down to the lake.

She heard Alan following, calling her name, but he gave up before long, and she was soon alone.

It was late and the beach was deserted. Lilly sat down on the rock she'd once shared with Samuel, and looked up at the sky. She supposed it was possible that Charlotte was mistaken about him, that he hadn't actually grabbed her friend's arm. But she knew that wasn't true, not after what had transpired in the sun parlor that very afternoon.

She'd had hopes…

What hopes she'd had were utterly foolish. Lilly's responsibility was to Charlotte. She had no business falling in love with Samuel and dreaming of what might have been had he not been hobbled by the fears resulting from his imprisonment.

Lilly wondered if Samuel had already started packing. He would need daylight to gather the equipment stored in the meadow, but it would not take long to pack up the crates he'd brought. He could be on the afternoon train to London tomorrow.

She took a deep, shuddering breath and thought of Alan. The vicar had likely returned to the inn, puzzled at her strange behavior. He'd made it clear over the past week that he was looking for a wife, and that he favored Lilly.

Alan had met Charlotte, and seemed to understand that she was Lilly's responsibility. But Lilly didn't know how he would feel about taking on the considerable debt that Maude had incurred in the few years before her death. He'd made it clear that he thought Ravenwell should be closed, but how would they pay off the loans with the income from the vicarage?

And how would she manage to live with the intimacy he would be sure to expect of a wife?

Stricken with dread, Lilly stood.

She paced across the sand, wringing her hands together. There was no law that required her to marry, just because a man had expressed his interest. Lilly was content at Ravenwell. She and Charlotte fared much better than most women who lived without a man's protection, especially now that Lilly's ghosts appeared regularly.

There was no reason for her to submit to marriage—and to an unwelcome intimacy—with Alan.

Lilly knew she could never share a marriage bed with the young vicar. He might possess the comeliest face in all of England, but there was only one man Lilly would ever love.

And if she were ever to know intimacy with a man, it would be with Samuel.

Lilly stopped in her tracks and gazed up at the sliver of moon that hung in the sky, directly over the lake. A few early stars glittered nearby, and the barn owls that nested at Mrs. Webster's farm hooted in the distance. The peaceful night could not have been a greater contrast to the turmoil going on inside her.

Samuel would be leaving tomorrow, which meant she had one chance to share all that she could give to him.

She was certainly no lady for even contemplating what she was about to do, but if she had only this one opportunity to experience all that Samuel could give, she would take it.

Squaring her shoulders, she returned to Ravenwell. Fortunately, Alan was nowhere to be seen. The reception area was quiet and it was dark in her apartment. Tom was gone, and Charlotte was in her room, presumably asleep.

Without hesitation, Lilly went into her small kitchen and gathered a plateful of food, then covered it with a linen cloth. She left again through the office, making her way to the staircase, where she climbed to the second floor. Davy had already turned down the gaslights and locked up for the night, so Lilly encountered no one as she went down the hall to Samuel's room.

Then it struck her. She wasn't quite sure what she would say, or do, once she arrived.

Taking a deep breath, she tapped lightly on his door.

When she heard the sound of his chair scraping the floor, Lilly experienced her first doubts. She should have changed into fresh clothes. Combed her hair. Pinched her cheeks.

It wasn't too late. It would take only a few minutes to put on something pretty and—

His door opened. "Lilly?"

She turned to face him, then swallowed and forced the words to come. "I—I brought your supper."

He didn't even look at the plate in her hands. "Come in."

His shirt was partially open, and he'd pushed the sleeves up to his elbows, leaving his strong, muscular forearms bare. He'd pulled off his suspenders and they hung at his sides, bracketing his hips. In one hand was a pen and a blot of black ink stained one finger.

Lilly wondered if he would touch her.

She set the plate on his desk and noticed the letter he'd apparently been writing—to a Mr. Phipson in Bombay. *India!* A quick glance at the letter made his intentions clear to her, and Lilly strengthened her resolve not to let this moment pass.

"Everything's changed," she said.

He nodded. A lock of hair fell over his forehead, and Lilly's fingers ached to smooth it back.

She forced her voice to remain steady. "When will you leave?"

"Soon. Tomorrow."

Lilly bit her lip to keep it from trembling. She raised one hand and lightly touched the lock of hair that so tempted her. He did not recoil.

Leaning closer, she slid her hand to the back of his neck, and was encouraged when he closed his eyes and made a low, feral sound.

They would have only this night. A few short hours for Lilly to experience a true physical bond with the man she loved, and not just the passionate imaginings of a lonely spinster. "Samuel…"

He took hold of her free hand and brought it to his lips. "I've wanted nothing more these last few weeks than to touch you, Lilly."

He pulled her close, fitting her soft curves against

his hard, muscular planes. He caressed her back, sliding his hands low, cupping her bottom. Lilly took a shuddering breath and felt his palms climb to her shoulders, then to her neck. He threaded his fingers through her hair, pulling it from its ever-precarious mooring. It was as if he were testing his newly recovered abilities while he learned every inch of her.

"Your hair is so wild, so beautiful."

Lilly trembled and closed her eyes, savoring each caress, each stroke. She breathed in his scent as he lowered his head and kissed her, felt the sharp stubble of the day's whiskers.

Heat stabbed through her as his mouth devoured hers slowly and deeply. He nibbled at her lips, and when she opened to him, he sucked and sipped of her until she felt dizzy with desire.

His hands moved possessively, surely. Cupping her breasts, he teased her nipples with his thumbs. His hot breath singed the sensitive flesh of her ear, while his lower body tantalized her with the promise of breathtaking pleasure.

Aching with anticipation, Lilly pushed aside the thought that he was leaving. Perhaps as early as tomorrow, he would be on his way to London…and *India.*

She looked into his eyes and concentrated on the here and now, savoring the sensation of his fingers on her skin as he touched her.

Lilly took a step back. With trembling hands, she began to unfasten the buttons of her bodice. His eyes were hooded and dark as he watched her fumble with the fastenings, and he moved her hands aside to finish the task himself.

The blouse fell away, leaving her barely covered

by her thin chemise. With great care, he unhooked her corset and lowered the delicate straps of the chemise. "I've wanted to touch you," he murmured, pressing his lips to her shoulders, "to kiss you…"

A moment later, he freed her from her skirt, which slid off her hips to the floor.

And she stood nearly naked before him, trembling as much from nerves as from arousal.

"Lilly." He took her mouth in a searing kiss that consumed her.

Her hands ached to touch him, to caress the hard planes of his back, to slide over the muscles of his chest and arms, but she was unsure whether he could bear more than a soft caress.

Samuel alleviated that worry when he took her hands in his and placed them on his shoulders. Then he reached down, lifted her in his arms and carried her to the bed. He lay her down gently and stood gazing at her for a moment before joining her.

Rising up over her, he grabbed the back of his shirt and yanked it over his head, tearing buttons and seams in his haste to become as naked as she.

Then he came back to her and feathered soft kisses over her jaw and throat. Lilly arched into him, savoring the tantalizing rub of his crisp hair against her nipples.

"Touch me," he rasped.

She shivered with pleasure and stroked the hard nubs that lay nested in the hair of his chest.

When he groaned, she pulled back.

"Yes," he growled. "More, Lilly."

More?

Soon he would have all she had to give.

Chapter Nineteen

Nothing had ever felt so right to Sam.

Lilly pressed her lips to his chest, pulling one nipple into her mouth as she fondled the other. He took hold of her hand and placed it on the placket of his trousers, shocking them both with his brash move.

"I need you, Lilly," he breathed, taking possession of her lips. Her tongue slipped into his mouth and Sam nearly crawled out of his skin when he felt her working the buttons of his trousers.

His heart did not beat again until her hand was closed around him.

"Oh, my…" she whispered. "I never imagined…"

Sam let out a shuddering breath and moved his hands over hers, showing her how to please him.

"I didn't expect it to be so…"

"Yes?"

Her eyes darkened with embarrassment in the flickering light. "I can't believe I'm talking to you about your—"

"Don't stop!" he rasped, as she ran one finger over the tip.

After so many months of physical isolation, raw male need spurred him to plow into her ripe, feminine body. He was driven to possess her in an elemental way.

But she was untried and innocent. And Sam didn't want to frighten or hurt her. Struggling to move slowly, he pushed her petticoat away and slid one leg between hers. Exploring with one hand, he drew his fingers across the delicate skin behind her knee, then caressed his way to the soft sensitive flesh between her legs.

"Please," she whispered.

She was moist and ready for him.

He slid one finger inside her while he teased the tender nub that was most receptive to his touch. She whimpered in pleasure and moved against his hand.

Sam looked into Lilly's beautiful eyes and knew that there could be no other woman for him. She was more vibrant, more alive than anyone he'd ever known. "Take me inside you."

"Yes!"

Melding their mouths together, Sam settled into position. Perspiration beaded his forehead and the center of his back as he moved carefully, taking possession of his sweet Lilly.

"I don't want to hurt you."

"You won't, Samuel," she said. "Please!"

She was very tight, but Sam pushed through, breaching the barrier of her innocence. He braced himself over her and held perfectly still.

A solitary tear slid out of the corner of her eye, and Sam immediately started to withdraw.

"Don't go!"

"But you're—"

"I'm all right…" She slid her hand down the taut ridge of his back, pulling him closer.

The most primitive of needs kept Sam in place. He shuddered and moved inadvertently, and when Lilly wrapped her legs around him, taking him deep inside, he lost all control.

The months of isolation, the agonies he'd suffered, all culminated in the release of the pent-up passion he felt for Lilly. He plunged, burying his face in the curve of her shoulder. He nuzzled her neck and felt her quicken around him.

Braced above her, Sam angled his body to increase her pleasure, and when he felt her contract around him, he surrendered to his own release.

The shuddering climax racked his body, wrenching a tortured sound from his lips as a liquid rush of exhilaration overtook him.

It was several long minutes before he rolled to his side, pulling her with him, and they lay together in the flickering light, facing each other, naked. Sam ran one finger up Lilly's side, from her hip to her breast. He teased the dusky nipple, then leaned in to kiss it softly. There were no dark memories to haunt him now. The anguish of his imprisonment receded when Lilly was in his arms.

All he felt was contentment.

Lilly lay with her head pillowed on Samuel's chest as she toyed with the dense hair that grew there. She heard every beat of his heart, felt every breath he took.

And she could never have imagined how this moment would feel.

She closed her eyes and pressed a kiss to his chest,

snuggling even closer. She knew what all this meant. As soon as he had felt comfortable touching her, he'd become free. To leave. To travel to India and any other place he wanted to go.

"Lilly?" he asked, his deep voice rumbling through her. "Are you…"

"Umm." She didn't trust her voice to remain steady. She was going to lose him, and it would be soon.

They lay together in silence for a few moments, with Samuel's hand tracing petal-soft circles on her hip, and Lilly savoring the short time she would have in his arms. It seemed that he was accustoming himself to her touch, to touching her.

She felt certain that her phantom touches had eased the way for him to be comfortable with human contact again, but she could never tell him that. Maude's admonitions to keep her talent secret held especially true now. If Samuel ever learned that she had used *magic* to cure him of the malady that kept him from the work he loved, Lilly didn't think he— Well, she had no idea what he would think.

Her unusual abilities would contradict everything Samuel believed about the universe, about his science. To him, the world functioned in a particular manner, and he esteemed those very orderly patterns. Lilly and her talents would be anathema.

Samuel shifted, pushing himself up on one elbow to look at her. "I don't know what it is about you, Lilly Tearwater… Somehow you made me come to life once more. After what happened in Sudan, I never thought…couldn't believe I'd ever touch a woman again. Never shake hands with a man without feeling like retching my guts out."

"Samuel…"

"The things I saw when I was in that pit of a prison, the things that were done to me…"

"Don't think of it now, Samuel."

"That's just it. You make it so that I *don't* think of it. At least not all the time, and not as if I'm still there. With you, it's a remote memory, almost unreal."

"If I've helped you—"

He bent down and caught her lips with his. "You can't possibly imagine."

He slid back and pulled her on top of him, so that she straddled his waist. She started to lean over but he kept her upright. "You're so very lovely."

Lilly knew it was untrue. Her hair was a tangled mess, and she doubted her body was anything special, or she'd have received the same attentions Charlotte always had.

Sam filled his hands with her breasts, and she shivered, letting her head fall back. Her hair grazed her hips, and trailed across Samuel's thighs.

He made an inarticulate sound, and Lilly felt her blood thicken in her veins. She felt feminine and powerful. Leaning over him, she braced herself on her hands and let his mouth wander where it would, sucking a nipple, then nibbling her collarbone. Her breath caught in her throat when his tongue flicked her neck, then her ear.

Lilly's muscles tensed and she tilted her head to kiss him, savoring the exquisite taste and texture of him. He took over the kiss, plundering her mouth as if he could never get enough. He shifted suddenly, reversing their positions so that he lay poised over her.

"The world seems right when I'm with you," he said, his expression intense, aroused.

Lilly ran her hands up his chest, stopping to fondle his tightly beaded nipples.

"Yes," he rasped.

She drew her fingers through the dense hair, then up to his shoulders. When he entered her this time, she dug her nails into his back, unmindful of the scars that marred his skin. Her heart pounded wildly as he surged within her, every movement drawing her closer to the amazing peak she'd experienced before.

"Your legs, Lilly—pull them around me. Tighter!"

The moment she did, she burst into flame.

"Did Maude ever take you anywhere other than London?" Sam asked.

Lilly lay close, sharing the pillow, facing him. He could see that she was sleepy, and she snuggled into his body.

Sam swallowed hard and pulled her nearer. He should never have bedded her, although he could not make himself regret it. He loved her, and somehow he was going to find a way to sort out a life together.

"No." She stifled a yawn. "And because Charlotte was so distressed, we cut our trip short. The train ride was quite a nightmare."

Sam wondered how he could get Lilly to leave Ravenwell with him if Charlotte would not go.

He wrapped one of her curls around his finger. She'd been magnificent, rising over him as he filled her—a mythical siren milking him of his masculine power.

"Was she born deaf?"

"I imagine so. I don't remember when she came to the orphanage. But she's been deaf ever since I've known her."

Lilly had mentioned that the inn was mortgaged. Sam wondered how bad the debt was, and whether Lilly could sell the place without taking a loss.

He'd be willing to take on the note, but they still had to figure out a solution to Charlotte. If she wouldn't come with them... "What about Tom?"

"Hmm?" Lilly tilted her head back and looked up at him with puzzled eyes, and no wonder. His questions must seem disjointed, though they made perfect sense to him.

"Charlotte seems quite close to Tom and his mother."

"Oh. We three were childhood playmates. Tom takes special care of Charlotte because...well, she needs it more than me."

Sam wondered if that was the reason Fletcher paid such close attention to Charlotte. He had an inkling that there might be more to it, but tomorrow was soon enough to ask the rest of his questions.

He gathered Lilly close and held her as she fell asleep.

Reluctantly, Lilly left Samuel asleep in his room before dawn, and went down to her apartment to bathe and dress for the day. Charlotte's door was still closed, but it was quite early. She would likely sleep another hour before her busy day began.

It was laundry day at Ravenwell. There were meals to prepare and maids to oversee. And guests who needed direction for their day's activities. Since

Mrs. Bainbridge would not be in, there was much to do, and it would all keep Lilly from dwelling on Samuel's departure. She had barely restrained herself from admitting how she felt about him, aware that last night's interlude was all she would have. Neither of them had wanted to face, or discuss, his departure.

Activity had already begun in the kitchen when Lilly arrived. The oven was hot and the first loaves of bread had just been removed. She had little appetite for food, but accepted the slice of fresh bread that Mr. Clive insisted she take and went outside. Instead of thinking about Samuel and his imminent departure, she focused on the expansion of the inn that the Asbury townsmen wanted. But even then, thoughts of Samuel edged in.

They had made quite a pair against the townsmen's badgering, and Samuel's point was well taken. If Ravenwell incurred the additional costs of expansion, then the town of Asbury ought to finance and manage their own coach line.

Lilly put her teacup on a table and pressed one hand to her breast, as if she could contain the ache there. She did not want Samuel to go.

Yet everything she'd done—befriending him, allowing their attraction to increase, caressing him without touching him, going to his bed—had only helped to heal him. To make it possible for him to leave.

Would she have done anything differently had she realized what would happen? Lilly didn't think so. Not even going to his room last night. If she had nothing else of him, at least she could cherish the memories of their one night together.

She heaved a deep, melancholy breath and faced

the truth—that he would soon be on his way to India, while she remained tied to Ravenwell.

The back of Lilly's neck suddenly prickled with awareness and she turned, certain she would see someone approaching. But no one was there. She glanced up at the guest bedroom windows, but the curtains were all drawn. No one was looking out from the kitchen, either.

Feeling exposed and vulnerable for no earthly reason, she returned to the kitchen, leaving her teacup and the unfinished bread on the table.

Her sense of loss was misplaced. The night she'd spent in Samuel's arms had been bliss, but he'd made no promises. He'd taken no more than she'd been willing to give.

And Lilly was not going to make his exit difficult. Though it seemed cowardly, she was going to make herself scarce until he left. It was the only way she would be able to stick to her resolve.

The morning's tasks kept her occupied, though her mind frequently strayed toward her night with Samuel. Intentionally, she kept herself busy and out of sight until after luncheon, assuming Samuel would look for her in a few familiar places and then give up.

He'd said he planned to leave sometime today, and Lilly knew she could not face saying goodbye.

When the train whistle sounded in the distance, she was no longer able to hold back her tears of loss. Blindly, she left the inn and took the path down to the woods. She needed a half hour beside Samuel's chestnut tree to compose herself and face the rest of the day.

Once again, she experienced the disturbing sense

of being watched, but forgot it when the chestnut tree came into sight and she saw Samuel carefully focusing his camera. Lilly thought her heart would burst when he turned toward her and smiled.

Chapter Twenty

Leaving his camera, Sam dropped down to a lower branch, then jumped to the ground. "Lilly!" He took her hands and pulled her close. "I missed you this morning. Where did you go?"

She could only hold him, press her face into his chest and breathe deeply of his scent. "You're still here."

He laughed. "Of course I'm here. Where *would* I be?"

"B-but you…you're going to India."

He lowered his head and captured her lips in a soul-melting kiss. Lilly's knees buckled, but he held her upright.

"I'm not ready to go to India, Lilly," he said when he finally released her. "I'm not nearly finished with you."

Oh, but he had to be, Lilly thought. He could no more stay with her at Ravenwell than she could leave the inn to travel with him.

He ran one finger down the side of her face and cupped her chin. "Have supper with me tonight. In my room."

"Samuel, I shouldn't," she whispered. Not only was it something no respectable woman would do, Lilly needed to guard her heart. The past few hours had been nearly unbearable, but she'd gotten through them.

She didn't know if she could manage it again.

"But you will." He took her hand and pulled her to the ladder hanging from the tree. "Come and look at my work."

She took hold of the rope ladder, but he slid his hands around her waist before she could climb. Standing behind her, he nuzzled her hair, then her ear. "Did I tell you that I'm wild about you, Lilly Tearwater?"

Lilly swallowed. She had to resist his seductive words. He may not be gone yet, but he'd told her himself that his departure would be soon. "Samuel, I—"

He cupped her breasts through her cotton blouse and she forgot what she wanted to say. She felt him press against her buttocks—the long, hard length of him so exquisitely arousing.

She let her head fall back, and Samuel nibbled at her ear, then moved his lips down the side of her neck while he teased her nipples into hard peaks. It was all she could do to pull away and face him.

No one had ever aroused Sam so. Lilly stood just inches away, with her breasts heaving, her pulse visibly pounding in her throat and her hair curling in charming disarray.

"Samuel, it's daylight. Anyone could come upon us."

He moved toward her, feeling predatory and more

than slightly aroused. ''Then climb up with me to my lair, sweet Lilly!''

''Samuel...''

He touched her cheek and let his thumb drift over the fullness of her lips. Her eyes darkened, then drifted closed with his touch. He knew he should not push her beyond the bounds of propriety, but he could not help himself. ''I thought I'd never be able to touch you.'' He cupped her jaw and stroked her ear.

His work was essentially finished here. He'd planned to pack up his equipment that afternoon and travel to London on the evening train. But his world had changed last night. He had Lilly.

He bent to kiss her, but she shifted away from him, her body tense and distraught.

''No one will come,'' he said.

Her back was turned to him and she seemed small, deflated. Something was wrong.

She moved a few steps farther away before taking a deep breath and turning to face him. When she took a deep, shuddering breath, Sam was certain some disaster had occurred. ''I'll s-send Davy out here to help you load your equipment into the wagon. You'll be able to make the six o'clock train to London.''

Sam stared blankly for a minute before he realized that she thought he still planned to leave her. Just like that—take her to bed, then abandon her.

''Good Christ, Lilly!'' He took a few steps toward her. ''Do you seriously believe I'd make love to you, then walk away at the first opportunity?''

Some emotion flashed in her eyes, but it was gone in the next second as she stepped back. Sam did not relent. He stalked her until he'd backed her against the tree. He bracketed her shoulders with his hands, dipped his head and lightly touched her lips with his own.

"You must not think very highly of me, Lilly."

"Oh, but I—"

He kissed her hard. "When I leave Ravenwell," he growled, "you will go with me."

She ducked under his arm and took a few steps away. "That's just the problem, Samuel," she said, oblivious to a single shimmering tear that slid down her cheek. "I cannot leave."

"Lilly..." He closed the distance between them and blotted away her tear with one finger. "Travel with me. I want to show you all the places you've ever dreamed of."

He heard her shuddering breath. "I have a responsibility here," she said. "Without me, the inn would fail and Charlotte would have no living."

Sam had been thinking about that, trying to figure out some way to deal with the inn and all its debts. There had to be some solution to the problem, as well as the question of what to do about Charlotte.

Lilly wouldn't desert her, nor should she. Sam was counting on Tom to have the perfect solution, but Sam hadn't seen him this morning. He'd been planning to go in search of Fletcher when Lilly arrived.

His beautiful Lilly, who didn't have a selfish bone in her body. She'd given herself so guilelessly, without any expectations of him, but he was going to give her the world.

"We'll work something out," he declared, scooping her into his arms. "I want you in my life.

She trembled, and he stroked her back. He loved

her. Taking her to bed had only been part of that—a thoroughly astounding part, something he promised himself never to take for granted.

Lilly should have felt joy at Samuel's words. Tucked into his embrace, she could almost believe they had a chance together. But reality quickly intruded.

She couldn't just abandon Charlotte.

But all her thoughts and worries fled when Samuel gathered her close and touched his lips to hers. Lilly's eyes slid closed and she gave in to the kiss, her bones melting when their tongues met. She tasted him, reveled in the heat of his body, the strength of his arms around her.

Lilly's heart thundered in her ears and a deep ache centered in her lower body. She leaned into Samuel and he shifted, lifting her in his arms. He started to carry her toward the deep woods, but a frantic cry from behind stopped him.

It was Charlotte, rushing to the chestnut tree. Bees swarmed around her, and she whimpered in distress, batting at her face with her hat.

''She's been stung!'' Samuel said, lowering Lilly to the ground. He took several long strides, quickly reaching Charlotte to brush away the remaining bees from her exposed face and neck.

Lilly was horrified and helpless. The sting marks were fiercely red and beginning to swell. Charlotte had had a terrible reaction the last time she'd been stung, when they were children, but it had been nothing like this.

''Damn it, she must have stepped on the new hive down near the beach,'' Sam said.

"We must get her back to the inn!" Lilly cried. "Maude's ointment will—"

Charlotte made a choking sound and dropped to her knees in the dirt. Sam caught her before she fell, and lowered her gently to the ground.

"She is swelling," he said, loosening the buttons at Charlotte's neck. Her eyes rolled back and her face turned ghostly pale. "She's going into shock, Lilly."

Panic filled Lilly's heart. She couldn't let Charlotte die. "I'll run up to Ravenwell and get Maude's remedy. That will surely—"

"There's no time," he said, his expression grave. "She's deathly allergic. If I'd known…"

They were just bee stings. No one died of a bee sting!

Charlotte made another horrible choking sound, and Lilly could see that her tongue was already swollen to twice its size. Her friend couldn't breathe.

"Samuel!"

Tears streamed down Lilly's face, unnoticed. She watched Sam lift Charlotte's head up to optimize her breathing, but it was no use. Charlotte's color was turning dusky.

She was dying.

"Lilly, there's nothing that can be done. I've seen this reaction before…"

But Lilly hardly heard him. She was not going to allow this. Charlotte was her closest friend, her sister. She was young and vibrant, and Lilly had always taken care of her.

She would not stop doing so now.

"I won't let you die, Charlotte," she said. She

closed her eyes tightly and used her talent for the most important intervention of her life.

Sam blinked once, then again.

It could not be. At one moment, Charlotte was in a headlong rush toward death. A second later, her color was normal and her eyes opened.

And Lilly's expression was not one of joy, of relief. If anything, she looked guilty.

It made no sense. Charlotte had clearly suffered anaphylaxis—a severe allergic reaction to the bee stings that should have killed her. Yet she bore no sign of distress now, nor was there any trace of the multiple stings *he knew* she had suffered.

"I—I couldn't let her die," Lilly whispered.

Sam couldn't possibly have heard her correctly. Her words made no sense. "Lilly, what—"

A small pellet fell from the tree and bounced off his shoulder. Sam picked it up and held it in his hand.

It was a chestnut…a fresh, mature nut.

"Impossible," he muttered, then looked up at the long-dead tree where he'd built his platform. Where he'd worked among the dry and brittle branches day after day. "What the…?"

The chestnut tree had blossomed. Its leaves were fresh and green, with candles of white flowers creating an elegant, fragrant canopy over them.

Lilly made a low sound of dismay, then jumped to her feet. Confused beyond reason, Sam looked at her with questioning eyes, then turned to Charlotte. Before he managed to gather his wits to compose a logical question, Lilly picked up her skirts and ran away, leaving Sam and Charlotte behind.

Charlotte appeared as puzzled as Sam felt, but normal. No swelling was visible, not one sign of a sting.

It was uncanny. And Sam had no idea what to make of it. Charlotte seemed to have recovered fully, so Sam left her where she stood, and went after Lilly.

He had questions.

But he had no idea where to begin.

He caught up with her at the lake, past the tall black rocks by the cove where he'd gone swimming with Lilly, Charlotte and Tom. Her shoes and stockings had been abandoned in the sand, and she stood almost knee-deep in the water. Sam was afraid she intended to put even more distance between them, and would try to swim, weighted down by her skirts.

"Lilly!"

A look of utter devastation marred her perfect features when she turned to him, her eyes bright with tears, her nose red from weeping. Sam couldn't understand what had upset her so, any more than he was able to comprehend what had happened to Charlotte and the chestnut tree.

"It was me," she said as if reading his thoughts. "I never asked for it, and I've never harmed anyone with it…but somehow—" A muted sob racked her body, and she hugged herself and turned away.

"What are you saying, Lilly?"

"This talent, or power—it's something inside me," she cried. "The ability to make things happen. *I kept Charlotte from dying.* It's my fault the chestnut tree came into bloom again, although I didn't intend that."

Sam's gaze remained locked on her, though his eyes wavered and went out of focus. It was not like

Lilly to be irrational, but this was illogical. She could not have saved Charlotte.

Nothing could have saved Charlotte.

But the girl was back in the woods, as healthy as if she'd never been attacked by the swarm of bees. And the long-dead chestnut tree had new blossoms on it.

Sam shoved his fingers through his hair. "Lilly," he said as calmly as he could manage. He'd been right about Ravenwell. The entire district was haunted, just as he'd thought on his first day at the inn, when he'd heard a tree fall for no apparent reason. But sorcery?

He'd finally accepted that the ghosts at Ravenwell were real. Now he had to confront witches?

"Come out and talk to me."

With downcast eyes she slogged to the shore, her demeanor betraying absolute misery.

"I want to understand."

"You'll never understand it," she said quietly. "Even I don't know what to make of this talent of mine."

"Tell me, Lilly."

She looked up at him then, her eyes so full of anguish that he wanted to pull her close and pretend that nothing had happened. But he could not. If what he had just seen was true, then Sam's entire world of theories and his beloved scientific process was invalid.

"As long as I can remember, I've been able to make things happen—with just a thought," she said in a low, quiet voice. "I used to think everyone could do it… But when Maude brought me to Ravenwell and realized that it was me making the garden

grow, stopping the rain when I wanted to play outside, laying out a meal when none had been prepared, she made me stop. Said it was unnatural.''

"You *make* things happen." His voice was nothing but a raw croak.

Lilly nodded. "But there's a drawback. Every
time I intervene—use my talent—something strange
happens. Something unpredictable and unplanned."

"What are you saying?"

"A broken window in the attic...a sudden gust of
wind..."

Sam thought of some of the other strange things
that had occurred since his arrival. The odd weather,
the old widow's amazing vegetable garden, the phantom lovemaking on Penny Top...

He took a step back.

It wasn't possible. None of this was true.

"The ghosts?" Lilly remarked in an offhand way,
although her lower lip quivered and she spoke in an
unsteady voice. "They're not real. But they're not
fraudulent in any conventional way."

Sam's head started to throb. "It's you? You make
the ghosts appear...with just a thought?"

"I did it on a whim one night. Everyone was enthralled and I knew—"

"You made it all up so that Ravenwell would at-
tract paying guests."

"We never have empty rooms anymore," she said
in a small voice.

"The night they showed up in the dining room,"
he said, not ready to question her about Penny Top.
"What was that?"

"I don't know," Lilly replied, her color deepening. "Somehow the apparition shifted out of my control."

Sam tried, but he couldn't wrap his mind around this strange ability of Lilly's. There was no known data to support the existence of such a talent. It could not be.

But he'd seen Charlotte on the verge of death, then impossibly rescued. Nothing could have accomplished that feat, other than the talent Lilly described.

"What of the hands...touching me?"

She looked down at the sand. "I didn't know I was doing it at first."

Sam tried to swallow, but his throat had gone dry. "And what I feel for you?" He could barely choke out the words. "What I *thought* I felt?"

He rubbed at the hammering behind his forehead, but it didn't feel any better. If Lilly hadn't been aware that her thoughts were touching him, then perhaps she didn't know that she'd made him fall in love with her.

"I never made you..." she began. "I didn't intend..." She turned away from him.

How could Sam believe her? Everything about Ravenwell was a fraud. The ghosts, the gardens, the woman.

The afternoon sun shone brightly, and birds chirped nearby. The world seemed just the same, although Sam now knew differently. Unbelievably, Lilly was some kind of witch, a sorceress who could cast spells to attain her every desire.

Sam wondered if that was why she was so beautiful, so impossible to resist.

He couldn't breathe. After all he'd seen, after all she'd said, he had to get away.

Chapter Twenty-One

Lilly didn't know where Samuel had gone. Only that he'd stalked angrily away from her.

There was nothing more to say. He was clearly disturbed by what she'd already told him, and unwilling to trust that she hadn't used her talent to manipulate him.

She sat down hard on one of the rocks where she'd left her shoes and tried not to cry. But it was no use. Bitter emotion welled in her chest and throat, threatening to choke her. She covered her face with her hands and let the tears come.

There was no point in weeping—she'd lost Samuel well before he'd seen her use her power. She had already faced the fact that he was leaving for India while she remained here.

But it hurt nonetheless. Maude had called her talent witchcraft, although Lilly had never practiced any craft. She didn't call upon any dark powers to help her, nor did she practice some occult ritual. Her talent just *was*. It existed in spite of anything Lilly did about it.

And Maude had been right about keeping her talent to herself, never using it, never telling anyone about it. Samuel had been horrified by her, possibly more than Charlotte or Tom might have been, had they known. After all, Sam had slept with her, and she was an aberrance. A monstrosity. *A witch.*

Another useless tear slid down Lilly's cheek and she wiped it away. It was pointless. Whatever Samuel had said before Charlotte's crisis was meaningless. She couldn't have gone away with him in any event.

But knowing he had a poor opinion of her was like having a knife twist in her heart.

She leaned over and brushed the sand from her feet, then donned her shoes. Carefully avoiding the dead chestnut tree that was now fully in bloom, Lilly took the path back to the inn. Her clothes were a mess and she suspected her face was little better, so she went 'round to one of the side entrances in the hope of avoiding an encounter with any of the guests. Unfortunately, Mr. Payton was there, seemingly waiting for her.

"Oh, there you are, Miss Tearwater," he said. "I wonder if you could tell us the best way to get to Grasmere— Uh-oh, what's happened to your clothes?"

"Oh, I just took a bit of a—"

"Are you all right, Miss Tearwater? You seem…"

"Yes, quite," she said, straightening her shoulders and drawing herself up to her full height. It was time to take charge again. To resume as though her heart were not lying in shreds. "I'll have Davy hitch the buggy for you. Will you need a guide?"

"Not today, Miss Tearwater. It looks like rain. But

I would appreciate it if you could arrange the trip for tomorrow.''

She concluded her business with Mr. Payton and walked away with as much composure as she could muster. Davy was not behind the desk in the reception area, but the office door was ajar, so Lilly assumed he—or possibly Charlotte—was there. She skirted the desk and stopped cold when she caught sight of the mess in the office.

Drawers hung open. Papers and files were strewn about the floor. The ink pot had tipped and a huge blot stained her ledger.

The door to her private apartment was open, and Lilly stepped carefully over the clutter to get to it. A feeling of dread clutched at her as she entered the sitting room and saw that all the cushions had been pulled from the furniture. The lampshades were askew and her precious books had been torn from the shelves. One of the windows was broken.

In shock, Lilly gaped at the damage to her home. Who had done this? And why?

And, more to the point, *where was Charlotte?*

Lilly scrambled through the rooms, over discarded clothing and broken pottery, looking for her sister. But there was no sign of Charlotte anywhere in the apartment.

Lilly forced herself to stay calm. Just because the day had gone badly so far, it was no reason for her to jump to the worst possible conclusions. It was entirely possible that Charlotte had not returned home after her misadventure in the meadow. Or perhaps she'd gone upstairs to help the day maids with all the bed-making that was required on laundry day.

Tamping down her panic, Lilly hurried out of the

apartment and ran up the service staircase at the back of the inn. Two of the young maids came toward her, each carrying a bundle of clean linen.

"Clara, Meg—is Charlotte up here with you?"

"No, miss," they replied in unison.

"Have you seen Davy?" Lilly asked.

"A while ago," said Meg. "He was talking to Mr. Temple. And then Mr. Temple left."

"Left?" Lilly's heart sank as she pushed open the door to Samuel's room.

"Packed up and left," said Clara. "Davy is going to send the rest of his things to London."

She shouldn't feel so crushed, Lilly knew. There'd never been any question that Samuel would return to London.

"Maybe Miss Charlotte is in the kitchen. It's nearly time for tea and she usually—"

But Lilly heard no more. She quickly retraced her steps and took the back hall to the kitchen. "I'm looking for Charlotte," she announced.

"Miss Tearwater, your sister has not been in the kitchen since breakfast. I know, because she left in a snit over the soufflé," Mr. Clive announced.

"Soufflé?" Lilly muttered the word. Mr. Clive was talking about soufflés when Charlotte was missing and her private rooms had been ransacked.

And Samuel was gone.

She turned away and went in search of Davy.

He stood behind the reception desk, gaping into the vandalized office.

"What in hell?"

"Davy, have you seen Charlotte?"

He shook his head. "Not today, Miss Lilly—or at

least, not since early this morning. I think she was
going off to the beach. What happened here?''

''Someone came in here looking for something,''
she replied. ''And when they didn't find it, they tore
through our apartment, too.''

Davy swore under his breath. ''I had to leave the
desk for an hour while I unplugged the drain in the
second-floor bath,'' he said, then nodded toward the
office. ''I was only gone a short time, Miss Lilly.''

''It's not your fault, Davy,'' she said, reining in
her panic. ''You can't be everywhere.''

''What do you think they were looking for?''

''I don't know,'' Lilly replied, suddenly remembering the other time she'd thought their apartment
had been disturbed. ''Davy, we've got to find Charlotte. Whoever did this—''

''Right. You stay here and check the inn, Miss,''
he said. ''I'll run down to the beach and—''

''I just came from the beach,'' Lilly replied.
''She's not there.''

''The field, then. Or Mrs. Webster's.''

''All right. Go.''

Lilly considered asking Mr. Clive to come to the
desk and keep watch until they found Charlotte, but
she was loath to let the guests know anything was
amiss, and the chef would soon be serving tea. Besides, the damage had already been done.

Starting with the attic, Lilly began her search.
When she discovered no trace of Charlotte, she went
downstairs to the guest bedrooms and knocked on
every door. Most everyone was already in the dining
room for tea, so she used her master key to enter the
unoccupied rooms.

It wasn't something Lilly would ordinarily have

done, but this was anything but a commonplace situation. Charlotte might be in any one of the rooms…even the one Samuel had vacated.

Lilly pushed open his door. It was empty of all his belongings now, but she remembered every detail: his battered valise, the folded maps, the unfinished letter on the desk, his boots. She closed her eyes and stood still, remembering.

His scent was still there. It was subtle, like the smells of the meadow and the lake, and Lilly breathed deeply.

He'd undressed her gently, made love to her so carefully, seeing to her pleasure, as well as his own.

She snapped her eyes open. Samuel was gone, and dwelling on the memories she'd made with him only caused her pain. Pulling the door closed, she brushed away tears and resumed her search of the guest rooms, finding nothing unexpected until she let herself into Mr. Dawson's room.

It was empty, too.

He had cleared out. Every personal item he must have had was gone.

Within minutes, Lilly had ascertained that Mr. Hamlet had also gone, leaving no trace. There could be no doubt that the two men were somehow involved in the burglary and possibly with Charlotte's disappearance, though Lilly could not fathom why Henry Dawson and George Hamlet would break in to her rooms or take Charlotte.

Lilly's head began to spin. Her simple life at Ravenwell Cottage had become unreasonably complicated. The moment Davy returned, she would send him to Asbury for the magistrate. Lilly had the feeling that time was of the essence.

She took a deep breath and returned to the main floor. Still, no one was about, so she went outside. It seemed impossible that anything could have happened to Charlotte. It was more likely that she was in the barn, checking on Duncan's kittens.

Hoping that was the case, Lilly ran to the far side of the inn and headed toward the outbuilding. She desperately hoped she would find Charlotte inside, blissfully unaware of the turmoil she'd caused.

"Miss Tearwater!"

The voice took Lilly by surprise. It was Henry Dawson, beckoning to her from the far side of the barn.

"Come quickly!"

Lilly's heart leaped into her throat. "Is it Charlotte?"

"Yes! There's been an accident!"

He hurried away from her, down the path toward the road. Lilly began to imagine all sorts of horrors as she followed him. She could not imagine what had happened, and in her haste, caught her skirt on a sharp twig and tore it. Since that was the least of her worries, she hurried after Mr. Dawson while a multitude of questions besieged her.

"Where is she?" Lilly called.

"Not much farther!" Mr. Dawson answered. "She needs you!"

Lilly must have misjudged Mr. Dawson and Mr. Hamlet. Surely he wouldn't be leading her to Charlotte if they were somehow involved.

They moved out of sight of the inn, heading in the direction opposite Asbury, toward the trail to Penny Top. The terrain changed and they started to climb uphill. Suddenly, without warning, Lilly's feet flew out from under her and she crashed to the ground, face first.

"Grab her hands!"

She tried to push herself up, but someone shoved her head down, pushing her into the dirt.

"Hurry up! She'll *do* something to us!"

It was George Hamlet's voice.

"Where's Charlotte?" Lilly cried. "What have you done with—"

Mr. Dawson thrust a heavy cloth permeated with a strange, sweet-smelling odor across her nose and mouth. Lilly struggled to get away, but Mr. Hamlet held her fast. She felt nauseated and started to choke, but then everything went dark.

The train station was deserted, except for Sam and the ticket agent, who was a good deal more talkative than Sam would have liked.

"Not too many ever come for the six o'clock to York," he said, smoothing down his thick gray muttonchops. "In a hurry, are ye?"

Sam's reply was little more than a rude shrug.

He was angry. Hell, he was furious!

He had never been so manipulated, so taken in. At least now he knew he wasn't losing his mind with hallucinations of Lilly's touch. And he knew how she'd managed the ghosts. He glanced up at the misty slopes of the fells in the distance and thought about magic, and realized he was no better off than before.

It was all scientifically impossible. Nature followed set patterns. Rules. Laws. No one could do what Lilly had done for Charlotte that morning.

Except that Sam had seen it with his own eyes.

He dropped his valise on the wooden planks of the railroad platform and began to pace. Everything she'd told him went against the very discipline he regarded so highly.

Science versus magic.

The universe would be pure chaos if people had the kind of power Lilly displayed. And if they suffered random repercussions from using that power the way Lilly described. It was inconceivable.

It was astounding.

"Looks like rain clouds gathering," said the agent, glancing in the direction Sam was looking.

Sam nodded. He bet Lilly could make them disappear.

"We'll likely catch it before your train arrives. It's going to be quite a storm. Might as well go along for tea, since your six o'clock's going to be delayed. Crofton's Tea Shop is as good as any down London way." He placed a Closed sign in his window.

"No, thanks," Sam said, curtly.

The agent locked the door. He pulled out his watch and checked the time. "Be a good chap, will you, as long as you're staying, and tell anyone else who comes that I'll be back soon."

"Sure," Sam said, barely managing not to snap at the man. Ghosts. Well, at least he'd won the wager with Jack. Ravenwell wasn't haunted.

It was merely inhabited by a sorceress who could manipulate nature as she pleased. She'd beguiled and bewitched him from the very first, until he'd started believing he'd lost his mind.

He stood still as the first drops of rain hit his shoulders. It felt good. And real. Unlike the phantom touches that Lilly had used to get past his defenses.

Sam couldn't believe how well she'd exploited his weakness, touching him, caressing him…hell, *making love to him*—the poor, pathetic wreck of a man who'd lost his reason for living. Sam admitted it. He'd only been going through the motions of life when Jack had challenged him to travel up here and investigate Ravenwell's ghosts.

Jack had said that there were things that couldn't be explained by science, but Sam hadn't believed it. He wasn't sure he believed it now.

But could he ignore the evidence he'd seen?

Charlotte had been moments from death when Lilly had pulled her back from the brink. It did not appear as if Charlotte understood what had happened to her, although that might be due to her deafness, and not because of anything Lilly did.

The clouds opened and Sam sought refuge from the downpour. With the office closed, there wasn't much shelter, just a small overhang beside the building. He moved under it and absently gazed at his old valise, being soaked by the rain while he wondered if he would ever have overcome his aversion to touch had Lilly not started the process with her magic.

Because of Lilly, he was free of his phobia, and able to return to the life he loved, a life that only this morning he could not have imagined without her.

He'd wanted to see the sights of India with Lilly, to set up housekeeping in a big, open tent. To ride an elephant with his arms around her, to scavenge the markets and find exotic treasures for her.

And they would spend hours in their bed, the fine

mesh of mosquito netting cocooning them together, night after night. Lilly would have loved it.

Knowing something of the power she possessed, Sam wondered why she hadn't visited any of the places she was so keen to experience. Why she hadn't *transported* herself somehow to Egypt. Or to ancient Rome. She had so many books. He'd seen her poring over the pictures of Rome and Athens. Why didn't she just go where she wanted?

Sam's hair was slick with rainwater, and he jabbed his fingers through it. *Lilly hadn't gone anywhere.*

She had the power to do anything she liked, to go anywhere, be anything. Yet she stayed at Ravenwell and looked after Charlotte. Made a life for the two of them at the inn.

Why hadn't she restored Charlotte's hearing if that was such a problem?

He shoved his hands into his pockets and began to pace again, oblivious of the rain. Why did she work so hard to keep Ravenwell Cottage solvent, when she could very likely conjure up as much money as she needed to cover her debts?

Hell, she could make herself and Charlotte rich.

Lilly had no servants, other than Davy and the help she brought in from town. She owned no elegant clothes or jewelry, but wore just the serviceable gowns she needed for business every day. She did her gardening on her hands and knees, and hosted the supper hour every evening. She used no magic for any of that. It seemed that she used it only rarely, when there was absolutely no other way.

When they'd come together at the chestnut tree, she'd been trying to tell him that she couldn't leave Ravenwell with him, but he hadn't listened. He'd been so full of love for her, full of plans and schemes for their future, that he hadn't paid attention.

And he hadn't listened to her when she'd run down to the beach to escape the questions she knew he would have.

He thought of her standing in the water, her skirts sodden, her arms hugging her waist. Her face had been a picture of absolute misery. Sam didn't think it was because she'd lied to him.

It was because she'd never wanted anyone to know what she could do. She hadn't made him fall in love with her. There would have been no point, since she couldn't leave Ravenwell, anyway.

His belly churned. Of course she hadn't told him of her talents. If he had believed her, which was doubtful, there was a good chance that he would think she was an oddity. A perversion.

But she wasn't. She was sweet and generous. She was strong and intelligent. And he had doubted her.

Absently Sam picked up his bag and started walking away from the station, with no destination in mind. It was wrong of him to leave Lilly this way. She might be a sorceress, but she'd become his lover last night. And her reactions to their joining had been naive, ingenuous. Sam couldn't believe there'd been any magic involved, other than what they'd created together.

He walked up the main street of Asbury and thought of the way she'd tried to tell him she hadn't bewitched him. Sam hadn't given her a chance. He'd been shocked, bombarded by disbelief in the miracle he'd seen with his own eyes. Charlotte's distress had been no illusion.

And Lilly had cured her with a thought.

Sam couldn't imagine what a burden it must be, having to guard her thoughts at all times. If she didn't, strange things would be happening all around her, with every whim.

Or perhaps that wasn't how it worked.

People hurried past Sam carrying umbrellas, but he walked dazedly through town, past the tea shop, beyond Mr. Beecher's store. He could see Saint Jerome's steeple above the trees at the end of town, where Alan Graham was probably planning his next visit to Ravenwell.

Hell.

Sam started backtracking to Beecher's Store when a young woman suddenly burst from the chemist's shop. It was Charlotte Gray, and she was running toward the road that led to Ravenwell. An extremely thin woman with graying hair and a pinched expression followed her, calling, "Wait! Stop!"

Chapter Twenty-Two

Charlotte, of course, did not hear the woman's calls. Clearly distressed, she lifted her skirts and sprinted as though her life depended upon it.

Sam dropped his valise and ran after her. He didn't know why she was in town, or where Lilly was, but something was definitely wrong.

Charlotte wasn't aware of him, but kept running until he took hold of her arm and stopped her. She made a soft sound and grabbed his soggy sleeve.

"What is it, Charlotte?" he asked. "What's the matter?"

"Foolish child," said a stern woman's voice. "She's a ninny. Doesn't understand a thing."

Sam turned on her, pushing Charlotte behind him. "Ma'am, if there's any ninny here on the street, I can assure you it isn't Charlotte. It's not me, either."

"Why, I—"

"You can stop blustering and tell me why Charlotte's running from you, before I find a constable...or whatever kind of civil authority you've got here."

"Well, I have no idea why she would run." The

woman puffed up her scrawny chest and had the gall to use an indignant tone. "Mr. Dawson asked me to bring this…this *young lady* to town and give her tea in my home. All I ever did was—"

"Mr. Dawson? From Ravenwell?"

"The very same," the woman said, cringing in the rain. "He said it was important that I keep her here until precisely six o'clock. And since he is such a kind gentleman, I thought it only fair to do him this small favor."

Charlotte clung to the back of Sam's jacket as if her life depended upon it, and she was soaked and shivering with cold.

The woman started to walk away. "Lady!" Sam called to her. "Why did Dawson want Charlotte away from the inn?"

She turned and looked at him over her shoulder, then spoke in an overly dignified tone that was barely loud enough for Sam to hear. "I am not privy to all that goes on at Ravenwell, sir. But I've done what was asked of me. I do not care if you take her back now—it will be well past six when you arrive."

Sam narrowed his eyes and gritted his teeth. "What did Dawson say?"

"No more than I've told you," she retorted, then resumed walking.

Sam swore under his breath. Dawson was up to something and Sam was certain it wasn't anything good. He had to get back to Ravenwell and see that Lilly was all right, but what was he going to do with Charlotte in the meantime?

He pulled off his sodden coat and draped it around her shoulders, then led her back to the street where he'd left his bag.

''Where can we rent a buggy?'' he asked, making signals so that she would understand.

Charlotte indicated that he should follow her and she would show him.

Staying clear of the chemist's shop, they went down a side lane, away from the center of town. Several large barns lined the road, and Charlotte took him to the farthest one, a blacksmith's shop.

The door was open and it was warm inside, owing to the fire in a stone hearth near the far wall. A young man in a leather apron was hanging tools on a rack nearby. He turned when Sam called out a hello.

''I'm just about to close up for the night,'' he said, but when his eyes alighted on Charlotte, his gaze softened.

''You know Miss Charlotte from Ravenwell?'' Sam asked, willing to use any ploy to expedite matters. He couldn't get back to Ravenwell quickly enough to suit him.

The blacksmith blushed and gave a curt nod.

''We got caught in the rain and she's chilled. Have you got a covered buggy I can rent to take us out to Ravenwell?''

''I do.'' Wiping his hands on a cloth, he named his price and Sam paid him, agreeing to have the rig back the following day.

Sam and the blacksmith hitched a horse to the buggy, then Sam gave Charlotte a lift up. He drove out of the barn, and when they passed the chemist's shop, Charlotte tapped his arm to tell him something, but Sam couldn't give her his attention now. He had to get them out of town without further incident.

The rain continued to pour as they drove through the muddy ruts, and Sam could only hope they could make it home before the road became impassable. He had to get to Lilly. He loved her.

Lilly was the other half of his soul. And incredibly, she was a sorceress. Sam would just have to trust that she hadn't used her magic on him.

Perhaps that was what Jack had meant when he'd told Sam that it wasn't possible to fully explain the world in scientific terms. That he'd have to take some things on faith.

He'd been an idiot to leave Lilly. She hadn't bewitched him—at least, no more than any ordinary woman might have done. She was beautiful and caring, patient with Charlotte and the Ravenwell staff. Her friendliness was what made Ravenwell successful, more than her ghosts. He loved her smile and her touch, and if all those things added up to some sort of witchery, he cherished it.

Sam pulled the buggy to the side of the road when he saw a man on horseback speeding toward them. The fellow had to be a lunatic, kicking up mud and riding so recklessly in this weather.

Charlotte stood up and grabbed Sam's arm. She made a sound and pointed at the rider. Sam looked closer and realized it was Tom Fletcher.

Sam stood up, too, and shouted.

A moment later, Tom brought the Ravenwell gelding to a halt and dismounted. He tore off his hat, jumped up on the buggy and took Charlotte in his arms. "I'm never letting you out of my sight again," he muttered. Then he kissed her, and Sam noticed that it was not the chaste peck of a brother, or a childhood friend.

As he'd suspected, there was more to Fletcher's relationship with Charlotte than Lilly knew.

What perfect irony. If Lilly had known about Tom and Charlotte, she might have felt free to leave Ravenwell.

Tom released her and they spoke together for a moment in their silent language. Then Tom turned to Sam. "Lilly's gone missing. First Charlotte, now Lilly."

Sam took hold of Fletcher's arm. "What are you talking about?"

"Davy was the last one to see her. He went down to the meadow and to Webster's farm, while Lilly searched the inn for Charlotte. When it started to rain, he headed back, thinking Charlotte would look for shelter. He checked the barn first, but saw some tracks before the rain ruined them, and thought maybe Charlotte had gone up to Penny Top. Now I'm thinking it must have been Lilly."

"*Christ!* I'm taking your horse, Fletcher!"

Sam tossed the buggy reins to the other man and jumped down into the mud.

"We won't be far behind!"

Sam barely heard Fletcher's words as he headed off in the driving rain toward Ravenwell. He understood why Dawson had wanted Lilly. *The man knew.*

He'd either seen Lilly in the act, or figured out that she had the ability to make the ghosts appear. And then he'd enlisted his pal, Hamlet, to help him take her.

What did Dawson think he could do with her? With just a mere thought, she could probably turn him into a walnut.

Unless they rendered her unconscious.

He kicked his heels into the gelding's sides and rode every bit as recklessly as Tom had done. There were dangerous ledges all the way up to Penny Top. One wrong step in this rain and… He couldn't think about what might happen.

He finally reached Ravenwell's yard and went around to the back. He slid off the gelding, taking its reins in hand, then circled the barn looking for some trace of Lilly…or even of Davy.

When he found nothing to follow, he mounted the horse again and headed up the trail in the direction of Penny Top. He didn't know if that's where Lilly had been taken, but it seemed a likely destination. There were all sorts of craggy overhangs and Sam remembered seeing a few caves when Lilly had taken him up there.

It seemed so long ago.

But the lovemaking was something he would never forget. Sam didn't think the rest of the valley would forget, either, since half the cliff had gone crashing down when it was over. He'd bet his last shilling that that had been the unplanned event she'd spoken of.

Bending low, he saw signs that the path had recently been used, but he couldn't tell how long ago. The rain was quickly washing away what evidence there might have been, although the occasional broken branch at the side of the trail kept him going.

When the path began to climb, Sam dismounted and left the gelding tied to a tree. He scrambled for footholds in the slippery mud, amazed that he and Lilly had managed to climb this trail with such little difficulty when it was dry. He hadn't noticed how perilously close the path was to the edge until he came upon an area that had washed out. When he looked for a way to get around it, Sam discovered

Davy Becker on a dangerous ledge just below the path. He lay unmoving in the rain, and Sam was afraid the young man might be dead.

Sam maneuvered his way down to Davy and touched his shoulder. The lad stirred. "Davy."

There was a deep gash on his forehead that Sam was sure would have run red had the rain not continuously washed it clean. Sam ran his hands down Davy's arms and legs to check for other injuries, and discovered a broken arm at the very least. He didn't know about other scratches or sprains.

"Davy?"

The young man groaned and blinked his eyes against the rain. Sam shielded him with his body.

"What happened?"

"Davy, you've got a broken arm."

"Hurts," he said groggily.

"Can you yell?"

"I'll try," he croaked.

"Good. Because Tom Fletcher—and maybe a few others—will be coming. Where's Lilly?"

He swallowed. "I don't know."

"Did you see anything?"

He groaned. "One of them hit me with a rock. Then he shoved me off the path." He looked around. "Guess I was lucky I fell here."

"Davy." Sam realized the lad was injured and possibly disoriented. But Sam was quickly losing what patience he had. "Where would they have taken her?"

"I don't know...maybe to the cave." Davy swallowed thickly and knitted his brow as if trying to think more clearly. "It's on the other side of Penny Top. We call it Underwood because you have to climb through some brush to get down to it. Can't get to it any other way.''

"I just keep on this path?"

"Aye. There's a way to go down. Get to the far side and look for a thicket of greens. Slip through near the center and you'll find a path. It's tricky, so watch yourself when you go."

"Are you sure it's all still there after the avalanche?"

"Aye. I was up here just yesterday. You'd better leave now. I don't know how long it's been since they knocked me out here."

"I'll help you up," Sam said. "You'll be sheltered if you stay under this tree."

"I'll be all right," Davy said. "Go on. Find Miss Lilly."

Lilly's head felt as if a very large hammer was pounding it. She was nauseated and afraid to move for fear of retching all over herself. She did not even dare open her eyes.

And then she heard a voice.

"How long's it going to last? She's been out for a while."

Henry Dawson!

Lilly still felt muzzy-headed, but she recognized his voice. He'd tricked her into going with him, then he and someone else had knocked her down and... She didn't remember what had happened next. But here she was.

Wherever that might be.

It didn't smell like Ravenwell. It was cool and dry, and the odors were familiar, but she knew she was not at the inn. And she also knew it behooved her to let them believe she was still unconscious.

"You sure this is going to work?"

"I tell you, I know what I saw. That girl was going to die this morning. From bee stings. But Lilly Tearwater fixed it so that—"

"No, I mean, if she can do all that you say, what's to keep her from—I don't know—from striking us with lightning?"

What indeed? Lilly thought.

"As long as the deaf one is missing, we're in control."

"You mean she needs us to tell her where the girl is?"

"Exactly. But we won't need her for long," said Dawson. "I only want one thing from Miss Tearwater, and then we can drop her off the cliff. No more worries."

"Only one thing? But I thought—"

"Money, dear Hamlet," said Dawson. "Everything else will follow, as long as we have a sufficient amount. In my line of work, I've seen all sorts of riffraff treated like kings. And why? Because of the gold that lines their pockets."

"Right."

"All we need is some of that gold and we'll be in good stead. Power, property, women…everything we could ever want."

"But she's got to wake up first."

Lilly didn't move a muscle. She didn't know the limits of her power; her first real test had been just hours ago, when Charlotte lay dying beneath the chestnut tree. And Lilly hadn't given any consideration to what she was doing—she'd only known that she couldn't let Charlotte die.

But what if these men had already killed her friend?

It was all Lilly could do to remain still. But she dared not move until she had a plan. If only her two captors would keep talking, she might learn what they'd done with Charlotte, and how best to handle the situation.

''What are you going to tell her to do when she wakes up?'' Hamlet asked.

''I'm just trying to decide how best to fill my coffers. Gold? Or perhaps a large deposit into my account in London.''

''That would be easiest, right?''

Lilly was disgusted by their greed. She would never use her talent to bring riches to these two. They'd be lucky if she didn't just fling *them* off a cliff.

That's what it smelled like—the cliffs. Or rather, the caves in the fells. She and Charlotte and Tom had explored all the caves as children, and still climbed when they had free time. Especially Charlotte and Tom.

Now that she knew where she was, Lilly felt more confident. It didn't matter how long Mr. Dawson had been a guest at Ravenwell, he couldn't possibly know the terrain as well as she did. She definitely had the advantage.

Lilly let out a deep breath and moved her legs.

''Look! She's coming 'round.''

She let her eyes flutter open. ''What happened? Where am I?''

Mr. Dawson coughed into his hand. "You, er, had a little mishap and we, uh…"

"Where's Charlotte?" Lilly allowed some of her apprehension into her voice. "You said she's had an accident."

"Well, about that accident, Miss Tearwater…"

"We need your help," said Hamlet in his gruff voice.

Lilly sat up and discovered that her hands were bound together. So were her feet. "Why am I tied up?"

She recognized the cave. In the flickering candlelight Lilly could see the place where Tom had climbed up and carved all their initials into one wall when they were young. It was Underwood, just below Penny Top.

There were dangerous ledges outside the cave, and Lilly did not relish the prospect of having to climb down in the dark. With the rain, the path could easily become dangerous and inaccessible, but if she used her magic, she might unleash some cataclysmic effect.

"Miss Tearwater, I have a proposition for you."

"What proposition?"

"We have your sister," said Hamlet.

"Where? Where is Charlotte? Is she all right?"

"As soon as you do us one small favor, we'll tell you where she is, and let you go to her. Isn't that right, George?"

Hamlet nodded.

Lilly knew they intended to ask for riches of some sort, but the predatory gleam in their eyes frightened her.

"You have a special talent," Hamlet said.

"I saw you," said Dawson. "I know what you can do. I want ten million pounds—no, make that fifty million pounds. Make *fifty million pounds* appear on the balance sheets of my accounts in the Bank of England."

"And how do you expect me to do that, Mr. Dawson?" She decided to go along with him for the moment. "The money is no problem, but your accounts... How am I to know which accounts are yours?"

Dawson frowned and Lilly looked past him, to the entrance of the cave. It was raining hard. If she could get out of Underwood, she had a chance of getting away from them. There were other caves and paths Lilly was certain they would not be able to find in this weather.

"I can produce the numbers of each account."

"All right. And you'll have to release me. I cannot work trussed in this manner. I must have my hands free. And my feet."

"I don't know..."

"You heard her," Hamlet whispered. "If we want the money, we've got to let her go. She won't try anything as long as she doesn't know what we've done with her friend."

Dawson looked dubious, but after a short delay, Hamlet reached into his pocket for a knife and slit the ropes that held her hands together. Then he freed her feet.

"I have a gun, too," Dawson said. "So don't try anything." He picked it up off a rock ledge and pointed it in Lilly's direction, although he did not appear quite comfortable holding it. Lilly wondered if it was loaded and whether to risk the consequence of disarming him. If Penny Top cracked off the mountainside...

She pushed herself up to a sitting position. Dizzy and nauseated, she ignored how she felt and focused her attention on getting out of this insane situation. "First, where is Charlotte?"

"I'm sorry, Miss Tearwater, but that is not how we intend—"

"You need me—my talents," she retorted. "Tell me where my friend is, and then you shall have whatever you want."

As soon as she knew Charlotte was safe, she would enclose these two in an unbreakable cage and dangle it over the edge of the highest cliff in Cumbria. Lilly was so angry, she had to guard her thoughts so their punishment did not occur prematurely.

"Well?"

Hamlet pushed Dawson aside. "She's in town taking tea with the chemist's sister."

"With Ada Simpson?"

"Now do it!" growled Hamlet. "Put the money in... Wait just a minute. Why does it all go to *your* accounts?" he demanded, turning to face his cohort.

Dawson poked Hamlet's chest with his finger while he held the gun in his other hand. "Don't start making things more complicated than they need to—"

The candle suddenly went out and the cavern was shrouded in shadows. It was Lilly's chance to make her move, and she turned quickly toward the cave wall. It would take them a moment to realize where she'd gone.

But someone else came into the cave, bounding past her to confront Dawson and Hamlet.

Samuel!

Chapter Twenty-Three

Lilly was shocked to see that he'd come back, but there he stood, facing her captors. He struck the first blow, quickly knocking Dawson to the cave's floor. The gun slid out of the man's hand, and Lilly reached for it while Samuel grabbed Hamlet and threw him to the ground, too.

"Lilly?" he asked. "Are you all right?"

"Yes! But Charlotte—"

"I brought her home. Or, rather, Fletcher did."

"She's unharmed?"

He nodded. "Hold the gun on these two. We need to restrain them so they can't do any more damage. Is that a rope over there?"

Samuel tied the two together while Lilly watched and tried not to hope. He had come back for some reason, but it seemed unlikely that she was it. He had been so appalled a few hours ago that he'd left her…

She bit her lip and waited for him to finish with Dawson and Hamlet.

"These two can stay here and rot," Sam said, taking Lilly's arm and escorting her out of the cave.

The rain had stopped, but it was nearly dark now. "We'll need to hurry," he cautioned.

It was disorienting to follow the path now, when she had no memory of coming this way under her own power. Samuel stayed close behind, his hand outstretched and ready to assist her if needed.

"Let me go first," he said, when they got to the point where they would have to climb through the brush. He made his way through and turned, reaching for her. Lilly took his hand and he pulled her up, but did not let her go.

Her heart thrummed in her chest when he tugged her close and pressed his lips to her hair.

"Lilly." She felt him swallow. Felt the beat of his heart against her, his warm breath on her forehead. "Can you forgive me? I was—"

"Samuel!" she cried, wrapping her arms around his waist. "You came back!"

"I was a fool," he said. "I should never have left you."

Sam couldn't bring himself to let her go. "I want to stand here and hold you all night," he said. "But I've soaked you through already."

She seemed to notice for the first time that he was dripping wet. "I don't care. Kiss me."

He dipped his head and touched his lips to hers, gently, reverently. Her lips were cool and moist, and she opened to him as she slipped her arms around his neck to pull him closer. Instantly, the kiss turned fiery. Sam invaded her with his tongue and thought of laying her down in the moss and making love to her here...

But reality intruded. The ground was sodden and

there were other, more immediate details to deal with, up here and down at the inn. Reluctantly, he broke away. "Lilly," he rasped. "I want you. Now. Desperately. Always."

Amazement shone in her eyes, and Samuel could not blame her for being dazed. He'd walked out mere hours ago, like a coward, without a word of explanation. "You are so much more than I deserve, sweet Lilly," he said. "Marry me."

"Samuel." Her voice was but a whisper, one that held an edge of despair.

"It will work out, Lilly," he said. If he wasn't mistaken, the problem of what to do about Charlotte was already solved. But Sam would not say anything—not until Tom and Charlotte made their own declaration. "We'll make it work."

"I want to believe you, Samuel," she replied. "I love you."

He touched his forehead to hers. "I'm sorry for hurting you. For jumping to the wrong conclusions…"

She kissed him then, and he felt all the love and passion she had to give. It was pure magic.

"Come on," he said, when he was able to breathe again. "We've got to see if Davy's been found." Sam elaborated briefly on how he'd discovered him.

Lilly started to ask questions, but Sam took her hand and pulled her along. "Fletcher has probably already found him, but we should get down there before it grows any darker."

Making their way over the wet ground, they stumbled along. Sam led the way down the path, helping Lilly over slippery areas and sections that had washed over the edge. The descent seemed more arduous to Sam than his climb to find Lilly, but he'd been focused on rescuing her, not caring so much about the condition of the path.

"Is that Tom down there?"

Sam nodded. "Looks like it. That's where I left Davy."

"You're sure Davy will be all right?"

Sam stopped and turned to face her. "I'm certain," he said, and tipped up her chin for his kiss. She tasted sweet and pure. And he was the luckiest man on earth.

They arrived at Davy's location in time to help Tom lift him from the ledge where he'd landed. The young man had sprained his ankle, as well as broken his arm, and it was necessary for the two men to carry him down the hill to the place where Sam had tethered the horse. With a good deal of difficulty, they seated Davy on the gelding, and Tom led the horse back to Ravenwell, with Lilly and Sam following.

Charlotte was the first person they saw, pacing nervously in the yard with all her kittens around her—nipping at her skirts.

As soon as she saw the party approaching, she ran toward them.

Sam put his arm around Lilly's waist and restrained her when she called out and waved to Charlotte. "Lilly, there's something you should know," he said.

"Charlotte!" Lilly started to go to her, but stopped short when Charlotte propelled herself into Tom's arms.

"Charlotte?"

"Lilly, wait," Sam said. "Let them tell you."

Speechless, she watched them, her eyes blinking once, slowly, and then again, as if to clear them.

"They're…" She looked up at Sam.

He nodded. And when Tom put one arm around Charlotte and began to lead the horse to the inn, Sam felt Lilly's head drop against him. "I wonder how long… Why didn't they tell me?"

"I guess you'll have to ask them."

"I must have been blind to have missed it. Tom loves her."

Sam did not reply, but pulled her closer and slowed their pace.

"She's…do you suppose they were afraid to tell me?"

"I think it's fairly certain they didn't want you to know," Sam replied.

Lilly came to a sudden standstill. "Charlotte wouldn't leave me. She felt responsible for me!" A sudden sob wrenched free of her. "Did Maude make Charlotte promise, too? Did Charlotte feel bound to Ravenwell the way I did?"

Sam hugged her close. "Your promise kept you here, Lilly, until I could find you."

"I've been wanting to get you alone like this all evening," Samuel said, pulling Lilly into his arms. The tension finally left her body and she melted into him, giving herself up to his kiss. "I love to touch you."

Charlotte and Tom were staying in the sun parlor with Davy, waiting for the doctor to arrive. Most of Ravenwell's guests had retired for the night, unaware of all that had transpired.

Lilly slid her arms up Samuel's chest. They stood

against the gate leading to the rose garden, and though Lilly would have chosen a more secluded spot, Samuel had led them out here blindly.

"Tell me again, Lilly," he whispered, nuzzling her ear. "Tell me you love me."

"I do," she said. "I love you, Samuel."

"If only I'd been here with you! Dawson and Hamlet would never—"

"Oh!" She lifted her head. "I've got to do something about those two. They know about me, about what I can do."

"You're right. They'll talk…"

"I'll make them forget what they saw," she replied. "But something will happen. Something I don't intend…"

"You'll have to risk it, Lilly. You have no choice."

"One of them has been following me. For weeks I've felt someone watching at odd times."

Samuel took her hand and they walked into the garden, where the rain droplets sparkled in the moonlight. Lilly couldn't have conjured a more beautiful sight.

"Dawson must have been the one who sneaked into the kitchen that night when I bashed my head."

"I thought you'd just bumped your head in the dark."

"No. I saw someone skulking around and followed him. I thought it was your cohort—whoever was making the ghosts appear. But it must have been Dawson who bashed my skull when I got too close." She touched the spot she had healed.

"I fixed it. I couldn't bear to see you hurt."

He hugged her close and she felt his quiet laugh.

"You couldn't keep your hands off me…real or phantom."

She turned serious. "I want those two to go to jail. They're evil and greedy."

"Then, instead of making them forget, can you just change the scenario? Make them think they stole from you. Your rooms were ransacked. Put some of your money, or your valuables with them in the cave."

"Samuel Temple, you have a devious mind."

"But you love me."

"I do."

And she did what he suggested. When Dawson and Hamlet were found, they would be in possession of a few pieces of her jewelry and the week's receipts.

"And you'll come to India with me?"

"I will," she said. "Anywhere."

"Funny, I don't remember your roses ever looking so well," said Tom.

"Must have been last night's rain," Lilly replied, although there was no doubt that the blossoms were due solely to the magic she'd performed when she'd settled up with Dawson and Hamlet.

The magistrate and his men had come from town earlier and climbed Penny Top to collect the two felons and their booty. Breakfast at Ravenwell had gone on as usual, and the inn's guests were enjoying the beautiful landscape.

"Those two were a cagey lot," Tom remarked. "Getting that old prune Simpson to take Charlotte to town so that Lilly would go off searching for her."

"It worked."

Charlotte touched Lilly's sleeve and began to speak in her own way as Lilly interpreted. "I'm sorry I did not tell you about Tom sooner. I was afraid…"

"You didn't want to leave me alone. I understand." Even without her promise to Maude, Lilly could never have left Charlotte, either, though Sam had told her he was prepared to stay at Ravenwell if his suspicions about Tom and Charlotte had proved unfounded.

"I've been putting some pressure on Charlotte to choose, Lilly," Tom remarked. He took Charlotte's arm and placed it possessively in the crook of his own. "I love her. We want to stop sneaking around you and marry."

Samuel ducked under the garden gate and joined them. He stuck his hand out to Tom for a congratulatory shake. "When is the wedding?"

"I might ask the same."

Samuel smiled and slipped his arm around Lilly's waist. "As soon as we can arrange it."

"Will you close down the inn?"

Lilly nodded. "We're going to India."

"What about Ravenwell Cottage? Will the ghosts be haunting a vacant building?"

"Miss Tearwater!" Mr. Hinkley and Mr. Beecher came through the parlor door, carrying the same folders and documents they'd brought before. "A word, Miss Tearwater."

Since there wasn't a dry seat outside, they returned to the parlor, where Mr. Hinkley set down his papers.

"Lilly," said Tom, "I think you should know that I rode down to Asbury this morning and mentioned to the mayor that you were likely to close Ravenwell Cottage in the near future.''

''The town wants to buy it!'' cried Mr. Hinkley.

''But Mr. Hinkley,'' said Lilly, ''as you know, there is a sizable balance on the mortgage.

Beecher cleared his throat. ''Miss Tearwater, the offer is a generous one. Mr. Hinkley has assured our consortium that you and Miss Gray will profit quite nicely once the debt is paid.''

Lilly took the document from the mayor's hand and looked at the figures. The mortgage could be paid, as well as Maude's other debts, and she and Charlotte would each have a small sum left over. It wasn't what Lilly could truthfully call a generous offer, although it was adequate.

''I'm not so sure, Lilly,'' said Sam, glancing over her shoulder. ''I thought it might be nice to stay on here, run the inn as it is.''

''Another five thousand pounds,'' Hinkley quietly said.

Tom took the document from Lilly and perused it. ''It might be nice to move my mother up here, too. With the maids to do the work, her arthritis would—''

''All right, ten thousand more, but that's all I'm authorized to offer.''

''Lilly?''

She loved Samuel Temple so much right then, she could hardly answer. He had suggested that she sign Ravenwell over to Charlotte and Tom, so that they would always be secure. He'd told her he would take care of her, that he would cherish her forever.

And then he'd promised to give her the world.

Epilogue

The Sahyadri Mountain Range, central India,
February 1887

A spectacular waterfall crashed down from a distant
mountain peak, cascading into a chasm of rocks and
water, while birds with broad wingspans and strange
names floated on the breeze overhead.

Lilly's body still hummed with awareness after
spending hours in the nearby caves with Samuel,
viewing the ancient, erotic depictions that were
carved into the walls. Lilly knew Sam felt it, too,
and would have made love to her right there had they
not been accompanied by six other members of their
expedition.

A light mist shrouded the ground, but the elephants they rode were surefooted. Lilly could hardly
wait to get home.

Sam slid his hands around Lilly's waist and pulled
her back to his chest, and she let her body sway with
the rhythm of the rocking elephant. The mahouts on
the ground chattered among themselves and Sam

shouted something to them in a language that Lilly did not understand. The men laughed and called their answers up to him.

"What are they saying?"

"You don't want to know," he whispered in her ear.

Sam's warm breath sent a shiver of promise down Lilly's spine, and she slid her hands down his muscular thighs that bracketed her hips. He made a low sound, deep in his throat.

She tipped her head back, and Sam touched his lips to her neck and ear, unmindful of his colleagues who rode ahead of them in their small caravan. Over the past few weeks she'd heard their quiet remarks about them—the newlyweds—and knew that most of them would keep a discreet distance ahead.

The sun was a bright ball of orange hovering over the horizon as they neared their camp. Before long, Lilly smelled the cook fires that had already been started, and heard the sounds of foreign instruments playing native music. When they entered the camp, their half-naked mahouts slid to the ground and commanded the elephants to kneel.

"I'm not hungry for supper, Mrs. Temple," Sam murmured in Lilly's ear just before helping her dismount, his hands lingering at her waist longer than was strictly necessary. His eyes darkened. "What do you say we leave the others to their meal and—"

"A word, Temple?" asked George Freemont, who skirted around the massive elephant to speak to Sam.

Lilly extricated her hand from Sam's and turned to smile at the professor. Then she backed away from her husband and his colleague, keeping her eyes on Sam's. A few minutes alone to prepare for their evening was just what she wanted. She had important news to tell him tonight, and she wanted everything perfect.

Slipping away to their billowing white tent, Lilly pulled open the flap. It was richly appointed, suitable for a Turkish pasha, with thick, plush carpets covering the ground, silken pillows to sit on and a feather bed near the center of it all, draped with mosquito netting. Sam's desk, covered with books and papers, was at the far end, along with two Western-style chairs and several trunks covered by colorful silk cloths.

It was nearly dark, so Lilly lit a few of the oil lamps that hung from the wooden supports. Then she arranged the pillows into a sensual bower on the brightly patterned carpets.

Finally she knelt in front of the trunk where her clothes were stored. Hidden inside were a small vial of oil, a pot of kohl and a carefully wrapped bundle of silk. Lilly lifted everything out, untied the bundle and removed the delicate sari she'd purchased in Bombay.

The voices continued outside, along with the sounds of the tabla drums, but Lilly knew she had little time to prepare. In a few minutes Samuel would come in, and she wanted to be ready.

She unhooked her shoes and removed them, then took off her stockings, followed by her gown and petticoat and the rest of her underthings. When she was completely naked, she poured a bit of the scented oil into her hands and rubbed it over her skin, sliding her hands around her breasts, over her belly and down her pelvis and legs.

She pulled out the combs that held her hair in

place and let it fall in loose curls down her back. Next she put on the long, dangling earrings that Samuel had given her when they were in Rome, and the jangling bracelets he'd bought her in Bombay. She added a band of tiny, tinkling bells to each ankle, then shadowed her eyes with kohl.

When Lilly looked in the mirror she hardly recognized herself. Her breasts were fuller, but the child that now grew deep inside was not yet evident. Her belly remained as flat as ever, but she looked like some exotic temptress, intent upon seduction.

She certainly did not appear a proper English lady.

Not quite sure whether to be emboldened or embarrassed, Lilly picked up the sari. The diaphanous silk was the color of ancient pearls, trimmed in gold thread. Pulling on the bodice, a tiny, short-sleeve blouse that covered her breasts but left her midsection bare, Lilly laced it loosely in front. She wrapped the skirt around her waist and draped the remaining length of fabric over one shoulder in the Indian style.

She was ready by the time the musicians started a new song. When she heard the resonant strains of the stringed esraj and bansuri pipe, accompanied by the rapid beating of tabla drums, Lilly began to sway to the music. She raised her arms and moved her feet, patterning her movements after the Indian dancers she'd seen in the towns and villages they'd passed on their journey to this remote valley in Maharashtra.

The door of the tent opened. ''I thought I'd never—''

Lilly turned toward the sound of Sam's voice and suppressed a smile at his astonished expression. The bells on her ankles jingled as she continued her dance, moving closer to Sam as he tossed off his hat and removed his linen waistcoast.

The exotic scent of the oil mixed with the heat of Lilly's body and she was drawn by the subtle flaring of Sam's nostrils and the intensity of his gaze. He opened a few buttons of his shirt, then bent to remove his boots, never taking his eyes off her.

Lilly did not stop moving to the sound of the music, even as Sam came to her with eyes glittering with desire. He feathered his hand down the side of her face, capturing a curling lock of her hair and twisting it lightly around one finger. He followed her movements, touching her waist, but keeping an arm's length between them.

The better to watch her.

Lilly felt her nipples grow tight with his light touch, but continued to move with the music, turning away from him, tipping her head back to let her hair fall to her knees behind her.

''Lilly…'' He uttered her name on the whisper of a breath, and when she turned back to face him, he took hold of the swath of silk over her shoulder and slipped it off, letting it fall to the floor at her feet.

He touched her belly then, sliding the tips of his fingers into the waist of the sari, teasing her sensitive skin with his touch. Lilly danced closer, raising her hands to Sam's shoulders and lowering his suspenders. She unbuttoned his shirt and pulled the tails from his trousers, then pushed the shirt down his arms and off his body. When he was half-naked, she drew a shuddering breath and ran her hands over the dense muscles in his shoulders and arms.

The tabla drums sounded louder in Lilly's ears and she spun away from Sam, jingling her bracelets and bells. But Sam did not let her escape. He closed the distance between them and came up behind her, encircling her waist with his arms.

He pressed his body against her back, moving with her, cradling her, just as he'd done when they'd ridden together on the elephant's back. "Do you feel what you do to me?" he whispered in her ear.

He slipped his hands down her belly, deep into the waist of the sari. When he pressed his fingers against her, Lilly arched her back, welcoming his touch.

"Mmm." He nuzzled her neck. "You taste like the lotus blossoms growing down by the river."

Lilly barely heard his words as his fingers played and teased and inflamed her. They were magic.

She pulled away and turned to face him. As she began to move to the music again, she allowed the sari to unwind from her body, and soon she was naked but for the thin bodice that loosely covered her breasts.

Sam's throat moved visibly as he swallowed. A thin sheen of perspiration covered his brow as his eyes followed her dance. She lifted the short bodice slightly, aware of the effect it would have on him, then let it drop again. He reached for her, but she moved away, deliberately enticing him, drawing out their pleasure.

He followed her, and Lilly took mercy, drawing him into her dance. She skimmed her hands up his chest, stopping to linger over his nipples, then to his shoulders and around his neck, to toy with the hair at his nape.

He made a tortured sound and let her have her way, though she knew it cost him.

"I love you, Sam," she whispered when her

mouth was merely a breath away from his. She reached down and unfastened his trousers, slowly, provocatively, then pushed them off his hips, kneeling to pull them from his legs.

When she leaned her cheek into his groin, he groaned aloud. The music faded from her consciousness and she pressed her mouth against him, licking, savoring, tasting him. His hands cupped her head and she shuddered with her own arousal.

Sam felt close to exploding. He shifted positions and laid Lilly back against the pillows, then slipped the last scrap of filmy silk from her body. Her breath came in quick pants when he took one of her dusky nipples into his mouth and teased the other with one fingertip.

"You are pure magic, Lilly Temple."

The tiny bells on Lilly's ankles jangled in response. Sam took hold of her foot and kissed the arch. He pressed his mouth against the sensitive skin of her ankle, then trailed kisses to her knee.

He felt an exquisite tenderness for her, his beautiful, magical wife. "I'm entirely under your spell."

"Sam! Please!" She tried to put her legs around him, but he continued his torturous seduction, laving attention on her thigh, and then the very heart of her.

"Now, Sam!"

He changed position and let her have her way. Plunging slowly, he entered her with the intent of loving her gently. But Lilly pulled him against her, crying out as she moved her hips in an abandoned frenzy. Any restraint he might have had disappeared when he saw the raw desire in her eyes.

He bracketed her head with his hands, and as the

pleasure sharpened, quickened his pace. Quiet, fierce sounds escaped Lilly's throat and Sam felt her legs and arms tighten around him. He felt her fingers in his hair.

Sam kissed her then, and with every potent thrust of his hips, annulled the boundaries that separated them. They were joined as one.

Lilly cried out, pulling him tighter, deeper, as her body tensed around him in the spasms of climax. Sam shuddered and drove into her, his body feverish, his mind intense. His heart pounded, his breathing stopped and Sam buried his face against Lilly's shoulder as his own climax tore through him.

Small aftershocks of pleasure continued to pulse through them, even after Sam rolled to his back, pulling Lilly onto him, cradling her against his chest. He kissed her forehead, then her cheek, while his fingers explored her back.

"You are my life, Lilly. My heart and my soul."

"Sam—"

"I love you, sweet Lilly."

The little bells jingled as she bent her knees and crossed her ankles in the air. "I have something to tell you...."

* * * * *

Savor these stirring tales of romance with Harlequin Historicals

On sale May 2004

THE LAST CHAMPION by Deborah Hale

Once betrothed, then torn apart by civil war, will Dominie de Montford put aside her pride and seek out Armand Flambard's help to save her estate from a vicious outlaw baron?

THE DUKE'S MISTRESS by Ann Elizabeth Cree

Years ago Lady Isabelle Milborne had participated in her late husband's wager, which had ruined Justin, the Duke of Westmore. And now the duke will stop at nothing to see justice served.

On sale June 2004

THE COUNTESS BRIDE by Terri Brisbin

A young count must marry a highborn lady in order to inherit his lands. But a poor young woman with a mysterious past is the only one he truly desires....

A POOR RELATION by Joanna Maitland

Desperate to avoid fortune hunters, Miss Isabella Winstanley poses as a penniless chaperone. But will she allow herself to be ensnared by the dashing Baron Amburley?

TAKE A TRIP TO THE OLD WEST WITH FOUR HANDSOME HEROES FROM HARLEQUIN HISTORICALS

On sale March 2004

ROCKY MOUNTAIN MARRIAGE
by Debra Lee Brown

*Chance Wellesley
Rogue and gambler*

MAGGIE AND THE LAW
by Judith Stacy

*Spence Harding
Town sheriff*

On sale April 2004

THE MARRIAGE AGREEMENT
by Carolyn Davidson

*Gage Morgan
Undercover government agent*

BELOVED ENEMY
by Mary Schaller

*Major Robert Montgomery
U.S. Army major, spy*

Visit us at www.eHarlequin.com

HARLEQUIN HISTORICALS®

FALL IN LOVE WITH
FOUR HANDSOME HEROES
FROM HARLEQUIN HISTORICALS.

On sale May 2004

THE ENGAGEMENT
by Kate Bridges

Inspector Zack Bullock
North-West Mounted Police officer

HIGH COUNTRY HERO
by Lynna Banning

Cordell Lawson
Bounty hunter, loner

On sale June 2004

THE UNEXPECTED WIFE
by Mary Burton

Matthias Barrington
Widowed ranch owner

THE COURTING OF WIDOW SHAW
by Charlene Sands

Steven Harding
Nevada rancher

Visit us at www.eHarlequin.com

HARLEQUIN HISTORICALS®

In the moonlight, anything can happen…

APRIL MOON

MERLINE LOVELACE
SUSAN KING
MIRANDA JARRETT

Join these three award-winning historical authors for one magical night, one silvery moon…and three unforgettable love stories.

Available everywhere books are sold, April 2004.

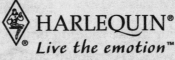

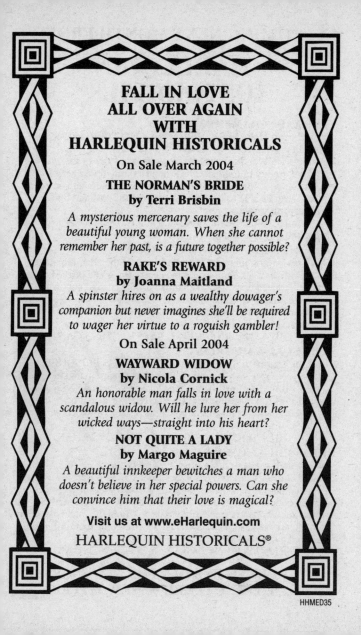

COMING NEXT MONTH FROM

HARLEQUIN HISTORICALS®

- **THE LAST CHAMPION**
  by **Deborah Hale,** author of BEAUTY AND THE BARON
  Though once betrothed, Armand Flambard and
  Dominie De Montford were now on opposite sides of the
  civil war raging in England. But when Dominie found herself
  in dire straits, Armand was the only man who could help her.
  Would they be able to put aside the pain of the past and find
  a love worth waiting for?
  HH #703 ISBN# 29303-8 $5.25 U.S./$6.25 CAN.

- **THE ENGAGEMENT**
  by **Kate Bridges,** author of THE SURGEON
  After his brother jilted Dr. Virginia Waters at the altar, mounted
  police officer Zack Bullock did the decent thing and offered a marriage of convenience…but then broke off the engagement when vil-
  lains threatened Virginia's life. And to make matters worse, Zack's
  commanding officer ordered him to act as the tempestuous beauty's
  bodyguard.…
  HH #704 ISBN# 29304-6 $5.25 U.S./$6.25 CAN.

- **THE DUKE'S MISTRESS**
  by **Ann Elizabeth Cree,** author of MY LADY'S PRISONER
  Three years ago Lady Isabelle Milborne had participated in
  a wager that had ruined Justin, the Duke of Westmore. Now Justin
  would stop at nothing to see justice served, but would he be content
  to have Belle as his mistress for just the Season, or would he need
  her in his life forever?
  HH #705 ISBN# 29305-4 $5.25 U.S./$6.25 CAN.

- **HIGH COUNTRY HERO**
  by **Lynna Banning,** author of THE SCOUT
  Bounty hunter Cordell Lawson needed a doctor to treat a wounded
  person stranded in an isolated cabin, and Sage Martin West was
  his only hope. As Sage and Cordell traveled to the victim, their
  attraction was nearly impossible to deny. Could the impulsive bounty
  hunter and the sensible, cautious doctor overcome their differences
  and find a lasting love?
  HH #706 ISBN# 29306-2 $5.25 U.S./$6.25 CAN.

KEEP AN EYE OUT FOR ALL FOUR
OF THESE TERRIFIC NEW TITLES

HHCNM0404